CARRIER

CARRIER . . . The smash debut thriller about the ultimate military nightmare: the takeover of a U.S. Intelligence ship.

VIPER STRIKE . . . A renegade Chinese fighter group penetrates Thai airspace—and launches a full-scale invasion.

ARMAGEDDON MODE . . . With India and Pakistan on the verge of nuclear destruction, the Carrier Battle Group Fourteen must prevent a final showdown.

FLAME-OUT . . . The Soviet Union is reborn in a military takeover—and their strike force shows no mercy.

MAELSTROM . . . The Soviet occupation of Scandinavia leads the Carrier Battle Group Fourteen into conventional weapons combat—and possible all-out war.

COUNTDOWN . . . Carrier Battle Group Fourteen must prevent the deployment of Russian submarines. The problem is: They have nukes.

AFTERBURN . . . Carrier Battle Group Fourteen receives orders to enter the Black Sea—in the middle of a Russian Civil War.

ALPHA STRIKE . . . When American and Chinese interests collide in the South China Sea, the superpowers risk waging a Third World War.

continued on next page . . .

ARCTIC FIRE ... A Russian splinter group has occupied the Aleutian Islands off the coast of Alaska—in the ultimate invasion of U.S. soil.

ARSENAL ... Magruder and his crew are trapped between Cuban revolutionaries ... and a U.S. power play that's spun wildly out of control.

NUKE ZONE ... When a nuclear missile is launched against the U.S. Sixth fleet, Magruder must face a frightening question: In an age of computer warfare, how do you tell friends from enemies?

CHAIN OF COMMAND ... Magruder enters the jungles of Vietnam, looking for answers about his missing father. Little does he know that another bloody war is about to be unleashed—with his fleet caught in the crosshairs!

BRINK OF WAR ... Friendly war games with the Russians take a deadly turn, and Carrier Battle Group Fourteen must prevent war from erupting in the skies. Little do they know— that's just what someone wants!

TYPHOON SEASON ... An American yacht is attacked by a Chinese helicopter in international waters, and the Carrier Team is called to the front lines of what may be the start of a war between the superpowers ...

ENEMIES ... A Greek pilot unwittingly downs a news chopper, and Magruder must keep the peace between Greece and the breakaway republic of Macedonia. But what no one knows is that it wasn't an accident at all ...

book sixteen

CARRIER
Joint Operations

KEITH DOUGLASS

JOVE BOOKS, NEW YORK

This is a work of fiction. Names, characters, places, and incidents are
either the product of the author's imagination or are used fictitiously,
and any resemblance to actual persons, living or dead, business
establishments, events, or locales is entirely coincidental.

CARRIER: JOINT OPERATIONS

A Jove Book / published by arrangement with
the author

PRINTING HISTORY
Jove edition / December 2000

All rights reserved.
Copyright © 2000 by Penguin Putnam Inc.
This book, or parts thereof, may not be reproduced in any form
without permission.
For information address: The Berkley Publishing Group,
a division of Penguin Putnam Inc.,
375 Hudson Street, New York, New York 10014.

The Penguin Putnam Inc. World Wide Web site address is
http://www.penguinputnam.com

ISBN: 0-515-12975-5

A JOVE BOOK®
Jove Books are published by The Berkley Publishing Group,
a division of Penguin Putnam Inc.,
375 Hudson Street, New York, New York 10014.
JOVE and the "J" design
are trademarks belonging to Penguin Putnam Inc.

PRINTED IN THE UNITED STATES OF AMERICA

10 9 8 7 6 5 4 3 2 1

ONE

Flight Deck
Chinese vessel **Rising Sun**
0600 local (GMT-10)

The stars had already faded by the time Ishi Zhaolong started his morning routine. He trotted across the flight deck, heading for the starboard torpedo tubes, his maintenance instructions in his hand.

The cargo area, he reminded himself. Not a flight deck—not on this ship. At least not yet. Soon enough.

The eighty-four-thousand-ton ship had spent the last four weeks at sea, transiting the Pacific Ocean from her home port in Guaydong Harbor to this point two hundred miles due west of Hawaii. So far, other than the warmer weather and the afternoon rains that were becoming predictable, one piece of ocean looked pretty much like the next.

Still, the warmer weather was a relief. It was hard enough to maintain the illusion of being a merchant ship, doing maintenance on the aircraft hidden beneath the massive metal shrouds, keeping the rest of the flight deck in decent condition, conducting the covert weapons drills and emergency drills that were part of life at sea—and all while pretending to be a normal merchant ship.

Granted, all of them had had more experience on merchant ships than on aircraft carriers. The *Rising Sun* was the first—perhaps the first of many—but the first nonetheless. The massive ship had been built originally as one of the Soviet Union's first aircraft carriers. When international money problems made the Russians eager for hard currency, China had been able to pick up the rusting hulk for a pittance, albeit a pittance paid in American dollars funneled back through China's lucrative traffic in heroin.

No steam catapults, limited repair facilities, and a main propulsion system that was far more comfortable at ten knots than combat speeds, the *Rising Sun* was home to eighty Harrier VSTOL fighter/attack aircraft as well as a vertical launch missile system installed just aft the island. Silkworms, anti-air batteries, and armament for the aircraft completed her weapons loadout.

And the crew. Most of them were from the Chinese Navy, although their experience had been limited to smaller combatants and amphibious warfare ships. A relatively large contingent from the Air Force brought their experience in flight operations to the ship, along with a measure of Army personnel just for good measure. All in all, there wasn't a branch of the military inside China that was willing to miss out on the first deployment of this particular Trojan Horse.

Especially the Army. For decades, they'd set their sights on an amphibious landing on Pearl Harbor. This time, they'd have their chance.

Ishi pulled back a tarpaulin to reveal a steel tube three meters long and one meter in diameter. He knelt down next to it and checked the high-pressure air hose leading into it. During this combination shakedown cruise and first deployment, they'd discovered that the hoses that had been installed had a tendency to crack in cold weather, and the first half of the deployment they'd lost around half of their exterior fittings. Ishi held out no hope that the hoses would fare any better in the warmer waters off Hawaii.

The high-pressure air system was an essential part of this combat system. It was one of the most unsophisticated systems onboard, and yet well might prove to be the most critical of all. Ishi bled off air into the system, then fired an air slug out of it. He saw the surface of the ocean ripple in response.

Russia had been grateful for the hard currency—grateful, yet uneasy. Her own relationship with China was fraught with turmoil, and she had no desire to have her neighbor too heavily armed. Yet the Chinese had been insistent that the aircraft carrier must be delivered with complete and operable weapons systems.

There'd been a compromise, and the ancient cracking air hoses were just one part of it. Russia had substituted a number of older, less-efficient combat systems for the more modern ones on her own ships, particularly in the area of antisubmarine warfare. The tube that Ishi was servicing was a surface-launched torpedo tube that expelled its warhead with a mass of compressed air, with the initial guidance provided by a relatively deaf but generally reliable sonar system. ASW had been Russia's particular concern, since she maintained the largest diesel and nuclear submarine fleets in the world.

Ishi's nimble fingers probed the edges of the joint between the rubber tube and the torpedo launch tube. It felt solid, secure, with no evidence of corrosion or leaking. He reached up to the housing of the surface launch torpedo tube and cracked the air valve open. He could hear it hissing into the tube, pressurizing it, but not a trace escaped from the joint.

Satisfied, he turned the compressed air off and pulled out the maintenance form from the front pocket of his coveralls. He noted the date, the time, and then checked off the box that indicated the system was functioning optimally. He scrawled his initials in the signature box, then neatly folded the form and tucked it back inside his pocket.

Submarines. His blood ran cold at the thought. The American submarines were particularly hard to locate and track, or so he'd been told by the more senior technicians. What exactly it was that made them such difficult targets, he didn't know, but they'd repeatedly told him about the masses of submarines that circled like hawks around the outer perimeter of the largest islands in the chain. They'd have one chance, and only one, to get a weapon in the water and on target before themselves coming under devastating attack from the American submarines. One chance.

Well, as far as Ishi was concerned, one chance would be enough. He stood up and leaned against the torpedo tube for a moment. He hoped when the time came, that he'd kill many American submarines. He'd be standing here, fueling torpedoes and loading them into the tube as fast as he could when the time came. And despite the cautionary words from the others, he was pretty sure the American submarines weren't all that invulnerable to twenty pounds of high-explosive warhead detonating against their hulls.

He could see the other Chinese merchant ships barely visible on the horizon. While his own ship was outfitted to carry jump jets, the others had different roles. One, for instance, supposedly carried liquid natural gas or oil. But she actually had a series of vertical launch tubes for missile shots built into her deck. Most of the rest of the ship was loaded with sand in order to make her ride low in the water, as though she were loaded with cargo.

Even further to the south, a third ship that appeared to be a roll-on roll-off, a RO-RO, actually carried two divisions of Chinese troops. The ship itself was a shallow draft vessel built to come in close to the beach, drop down a well deck door, and discharge a small armada of troop transport vessels.

The carrier's disguise was elegant and would take only minutes to remove. Outwardly, she appeared to be a simple merchant vessel.

"My aircraft—is it ready?" The cold tones immediately told Ishi who the speaker was.

Commander Chan Li had approached so softly that Ishi hadn't heard him. Ishi swung around in terror.

The commander was a tall man, sleek with muscles bulging under the smooth green fabric of his flight suit. He usually looked as though someone was about to commit a grievous sin that would, unfortunately, require him to take direct and personal action to correct the wrongdoer. It was the eagerness that particularly bothered Ishi, a sense that if severe, even brutal punishment were required, Chan would enjoy it far too much. He shivered at the possibility of ever giving Chan reason to reprove him.

Had life been fair, Chan would never have been asking Ishi the question. Torpedoes, sonar gear, those matters encompassed Ishi's training, knowledge and responsibility. He knew a bit about the aircraft, as did everyone on the ship, mostly from whispered conversations in the berthing areas from those who did work on them. And what he heard was not entirely good.

But Chan would expect him to have an answer. Demand it, even. To the commander, the enlisted men were interchangeable cogs onboard the ship, each one having no other purpose than to ensure that Chan's life went smoothly and his expectations were met. Ishi did not exist for Chan apart from that.

Such arrogance. Such power. Were the American pilots the same? Ishi wondered. Demanding more from their enlisted people than they'd ever expect from themselves, hardly working while the enlisted people slaved away on brutal hours and insufficient food?

They must be, Ishi concluded. There was something about flying jets that simply inculcated that air of superiority into any man. Perhaps it was a natural consequence of leaving the earth, soaring in realms that man had never been designed to challenge. Flying created brutal monsters, as far as Ishi was concerned, and he had done his best thus far to stay out of the pilots' paths.

"Yes, sir. All is ready," Ishi answered, aware that any other answer would be followed by more questions. He didn't know the status of Chan's aircraft, but he was willing to bet that his fellow sailors were too terrified to let anything go untouched on it. "All is ready."

Chan studied him for a moment, and Ishi felt a flash of fear. Surely the man could read through his subterfuge and knew that Ishi was faking it.

"Very well," Chan said finally. "I shall hold you responsible if it is not." Chan studied him for a long moment, as though committing his features to memory, and Ishi felt true terror. If all was not in readiness, Chan would indeed hunt him down on the ship and make him pay for the discrepancies.

USS Centurion
0605 local (GMT-10)

Sonar Technician Second Class Renny Jacobs glanced up at the digital clock for the fourth time in as many minutes. Enticing odors were wafting around the ship from the galley, and with each fresh spurt of air from the ventilation system, his stomach complained anew. It was surf 'n turf night, and one deck down and fifty feet aft, the cooks were forking over tender fillets and fishing fresh lobster tails out of the steaming caldrons. Once it looked like everyone was fed, they'd start handing out seconds. And if his relief didn't show up pretty damned soon, Renny was going to be shit out of luck for those as well.

And just where the hell was Otter Pencehavan? And why the hell couldn't he ever be on time for watch relief?

It wasn't like Renny expected Otter to skip chow— hell, no one did that. No, the routine was well established. Otter was supposed to go to early chow, show up in line the moment the chow line opened. Get his food, eat at a reasonable pace, then get his ass up to the Control Room to relieve so that the rest of them could go eat. It wasn't like they could leave Sonar unmanned simply so all the sonarmen could go to chow at the same time.

Sure, they were just off the coast of Hawaii, and they'd just finished REFTRA, the refresher training that was the final evolution before their next deployment. It'd been four long days of drills, emergencies, simulated targets and evasions, the entire crew worn down to a thin nub by the continual clamor of the general quarters alarm. REFTRA was always more intense than an actual deployment ever was.

The skipper hadn't said yet, but Renny knew they'd passed. Passed, and passed with flying colors. It was just something you could tell after a while, watching the inspectors. They'd been impressed, you could see it in their eyes. Sure, they'd find some little shit to gripe about— they had to, didn't they? But it didn't mean much. In the areas that matters, the sub's crew had well and truly nailed the inspectors' collective asses to the bulkhead.

Not that that mattered all that much when you were on the verge of starving to death.

He heard footsteps padding quietly down the passageway, and turned to look up at the hatch. Otter's cheerful, beaming face appeared, followed quickly by the rest of his lanky body. A small smear of melted butter graced one corner of his mouth.

"Good chow," Otter said cheerfully. He slid into the chair bolted to the deck next to Renny. "Primo lobster tails."

"I wouldn't know, asshole." Renny started to embark on another tirade about Otter's timeliness, then thought better of it. It'd just eat up time, and right now there was only one thing Renny wanted to eat up. "I had it, you got it," he continued, in the traditional sailor's shorthand turnover brief.

Otter nodded and slipped on the headphones. "Anything going on?"

Renny pointed out a couple of commercial contacts tracking their ways across his passive acoustics screen, then updated Otter on their latest positions. "Nothing out of the usual," Renny concluded, then slipped his own headphones off in preparation for leaving. "Except one thing."

"What?"

Renny paused for a moment, trying to sort out his thoughts. "Weird noise, like torpedo tubes opening or something. Compressed air, I guess. A mass of bubbles—you could hear them breaking up—then nothing."

Otter shrugged. "Surface pukes venting something, probably."

Renny nodded. "That's what I called it. But I was expecting it to come back. You know how the commercial ships are—they get on a cycle. And it seems to correlate

with that main propulsion system." Renny traced out the
acoustic signature with one finger. "Turbine, not a diesel.
I couldn't correlate it to any of the known merchant traffic."

"Which means exactly zip," Otter concluded. "Big
boy's off schedule, that's all."

"Yeah." Renny could hear the lobster and steak calling
to him. "That's probably all it is. Some asshole navigator's whose got no better time sense than you do."

Flight Deck
USS **Jefferson**
0610 local (GMT-10)

Lieutenant Commander James "Bam-Bam" Flint leaned
back in his chair and sighed. The TAO, or tactical action
officer, was a big corn-fed blond from Iowa who often
found the long hours of sitting in a chair and staring at
the screen, waiting for something to go wrong, almost
intolerably tame. He'd spent many hours wishing for a
longer cord for his headset, or a speaker, or any way that
he could pass the watch standing up, pacing, some form
of movement that would relieve the kinks and knots that
settled into his muscles whenever he held still too long.

Today had been no exception, a relatively quiet day
despite the intensive refresher training schedule. The S-
3B Viking squadron has just finished a mock torpedo run
against an adversary sub played by the USS *Centurion*,
the Navy's lead ship in a new class of attack submarines.
The *Centurion* had been winning until the admiral had
finally ordered her to turn on her acoustic augmentation
gear to give the Vikings a fighting chance.

Bam-Bam mentally ran through the remainder of the

training schedule for the rest of his watch. Nothing major, nothing even very interesting. The only wild card in the deck was the SEAL team ashore in the mountains of Hawaii, conducting joint training with other service special forces. The carrier was supposed to be standing by to provide support services for the team, but from what he'd seen so far, the SEALs preferred to stay down and dirty on the ground with their own gear.

As the last of the S-3B Vikings pounded down the flight deck, Admiral Everette "Batman" Wayne leaned back in his chair and sighed. Bam-Bam, a Hornet pilot, turned around with a questioning look on his face. "Sir?"

Batman waved one hand idly in the air. "Nothing. Just thinking." He levered himself up from the chair and stretched. "They've done a good job so far. I'll be in the Flag Mess. Call me if anything interesting happens."

"Will do, Admiral." Bam-Bam turned back to the screen. The last S-3B was now showing up as a friendly air symbol on the large blue screen that dominated the port bulkhead.

"What does he mean by interesting?" the watch officer sitting to Bam-Bam's right asked.

"It depends on who the admiral is," the pilot answered. "For some of them, they mean anything that hasn't been choreographed down to the last second of flight cycle time. Micromanagers, you know."

"Like on the *Vincennes*," the Watch Officer said.

"Exactly. But with Admiral Wayne, it's a little different. He figures if you've passed your TAO test and oral board, you ought to have enough sense to figure it out. It depends on where you are, what's going on in the world, whether we're in the middle of a potentially explosive situation or whether we're cruising off the coast of Hawaii during REFTRA."

"So how do you know when to call him?" the watch

officer asked. "Some of it's an easy call, I guess. You lose an aircraft, have a collision at sea, someone starts shooting at you—that I'd be able to figure out. But how do you decide about the rest of it?"

Movement on the screen caught Bam-Bam's attention, and he leaned forward in his chair, suddenly not particularly interested in carrying on a theoretical watchstanding discussion with the junior officer. Adrenaline trickled through his muscles, sweeping away some of the discomfort.

The watch officer, sensing he'd lost the TAO's attention, turned back to the screen and asked, "What?"

At first glance, the more junior could see no reason for Bam-Bam's preoccupation with the tactical display. The Viking was headed straight out to the last datum they'd had on the submarine. The overhead speaker was monitoring the conversation between the aircraft and the operations specialist located in the USW module in the next compartment, a small section of the carrier's combat direction center, or CDC. While normally the Destroyer Squadron Commodore's staff, or DESRON, would have directed the prosecution, this exercise was intended to flex the alternate command structure in place within every battle group. The carrier's USW module was simulating the loss of the DESRON and had assumed full coordination and reporting responsibilities.

Slightly to the east, two F-14D Tomcats were orbiting, waiting for their turn at the airborne tanker. An F-18 Hornet was snugged up to the KS-3, sucking down a few thousand pounds of fuel before making its first run-in on the deck. Its wingman was already clear of the tanker's path and headed for the starboard marshal pattern.

"What?" the watch officer asked again, bewildered.

Instead of answering, Bam-Bam ran his screen cursor out and let it rest lightly on a symbol that represented a

Chinese merchant ship. He right-clicked, and a host of track information and data on the vessel sprang up on both the main tactical display and on the small data screen to his left.

"This is too weird," Bam-Bam muttered. His hand snaked out and came to rest on the white telephone centered in the console between the TAO and the watch officer. "I don't like this one bit."

The watch officer slid back slightly in his seat and craned his neck to look at the other man's data screen. Course, speed, last visual identification, final destination, origination port, all were displayed in an orderly fashion. The merchant had been overflown daily by both shore-based P-3C assets as well as the carrier's own aircraft, rigged repeatedly, and photos were available in the carrier's intelligence center, or CVIC, showing every detail of the ship's superstructure.

"She's making fifteen knots—correction, eighteen knots," Bam-Bam said as he watched the speed leader protruding out from the merchant ship grow slightly longer. "Every other time we've seen her, she's been at ten knots."

"Some liberty turns," the watch officer suggested, referring to the classic Navy maneuver of pouring on a few extra revolutions per minute above ordered speed when nearing home port. "Just ready to get in and dump that cargo, probably."

"Maybe. But maybe not. *Crap*," Bam-Bam said, and closed his fingers around the telephone. He continued swearing quietly as he punched in the number for the Flag Mess. His voice skidded to a halt suddenly. "Admiral, this is the TAO. I hold *Rising Sun* at twenty knots, inbound on Pearl Harbor, and turning into the wind now, sir." Bam-Bam listened for a moment, then nodded and said, "Aye-aye, Admiral." He replaced the telephone and snapped, "Get two more S-3's in the air *now*. Harpoons. Tell the handler and the air boss the admiral wants a new ship record set."

Questions crowded the watch officer's mind, but he was too busy complying with the TAO's orders to ask them. Seconds after his first phone call, the 1MC general announcing system on the ship crackled into life. "Flight quarters, flight quarters. Now launch the Alert Thirty S-3s." The watch officer could hear feet pounding down the passageway, noises overhead as the crew sprang into action.

Finally, after a last phone call to the handler assured him that two Vikings were spotted on the deck and turning, the watch officer turned back to Bam-Bam to find Admiral Wayne standing immediately behind him. Both were staring with growing anger at the tactical display. The TAO turned to the watch officer. "General Quarters."

The habit of obedience was too deeply ingrained for the watch officer to even ask his first question. His hand was closing on the alarm lever and sliding it into position even as the TAO finished speaking.

"There," Admiral Wayne said, hard anger in his voice. "Christ, I hope we're not too late."

Then the watch officer saw it. He felt the blood drain out of his face as the meaning sunk in. "Dear God," he said, more of a prayer than an oath.

The merchant ship was at twenty-five knots now, but the truly horrifying details weren't on the tactical display. Instead, they were on the small television screen mounted high in the left corner of the room. It served a variety of purposes, but at this moment it was relaying video back from the airborne Viking's photo recon pod slung under its belly.

"Those bastards," Admiral Wayne said. His face was a mask of cold fury. "This time they'll learn a lesson."

The rusty, bedraggled merchant looked as though it were caught in the middle of a tornado. Sheets of metal peeled back from its superstructure, cut ungainly arcs through the thick tropical air before shattering the smooth progression of swells into founts of white foam and water. Massive metal transport containers were incongruently fluttering in the wind as though they'd been robbed of every atom of structural integrity. Cargo cranes and handling gears slid smoothly to the sides of the ship, then sunk down out of sight as wide areas of deck peeled back to reveal elevators. The ancient metal tracks that served as a mini-railroad for the transport containers sunk down into the deck and diamond-glittering covers of nonskid snapped into place over them.

"Those are Harriers," the admiral said wonderingly. "Not exactly—but something like it." He reached for the Navy Red circuit handset located on the bulkhead next to him. "Sweet God, this can't be."

"A Trojan Horse," the watch officer said, stunned. "It's impossible."

"It's not only possible, it's happening right now," Bam-Bam snapped. "So get your head out of your ass and get me some aircraft in the air. I need Tomcats and Vikings loaded out with harpoons, torpedoes, anything they've got that will kill an aircraft carrier. Have the USW module get hold of the submarine on Gertrude—vector her in for the kill." Bam-Bam himself was already feeding data to Admiral Wayne as he held a hurried conversation with the duty officer for Commander, Pacific Fleet.

The watch officer had the air boss on one line held up to his right ear, the handler on the phone at his left, and the airborne aircraft howling over tactical about the scene unfolding beneath them. He made his first command decision: He broke the Hornet off tanking and vectored him to bingo at Hickum along with the Tomcats. With as much air power as they were about to be launching, he had no time for taking onboard empty, winchester aircraft. The tanker reported in that he had enough fuel to stay airborne for another cycle, as well as enough in stores to support at least the first wave of fighters.

As they watched, a cloud of dust and fury rose up from the deck of the transformed aircraft carrier. Two of the Harriers, one on each end of the ship, shuddered, tilted in an ungainly fashion, then heaved themselves up into the air. As they fought off gravity, they started sliding forward, quickly gaining speed and altitude as they transitioned from take-off configuration into full flight mode.

"No, no," Batman said, then toggled the mike to Navy Red on. He cleared his throat, then said, his voice husky, "CinCPac, this is *Jefferson*. Be advised that you have enemy aircraft inbound." CinCPac's reply was muffled by the noise inside TFCC, but everyone could see the horror on the admiral's face. "Wings dirty, sir. From here, it looks like they're carrying a full loadout of land attack missiles. I've got fighters inbound on them, but they're in a bad tail chase."

"The Air Force—" the watch officer heard, then had to turn his attention back to the tasks at hand.

"If they're not airborne now, they'll be too late," the TAO said quietly. "They'll catch them on the ground, just like—" he broke off, clearly unwilling to give voice to the words that were in everyone's mind.

Just like last time.

"Those SEALs, sir—they're still on the ground," the watch officer said. "Do you want me to try to raise them?"

Admiral Wayne shook his head. "Stay focused on getting my airwing loaded out and in the air. If anybody's got a chance out there, it's Murdoch and his men. And as for knowing what's going on—well, I think they're about to find out. The hard way."

TWO

Along the waterfront, the piers were crowded with ships making stopovers enroute deployments, ships returning from the Middle East, ships on Pineapple Cruises, the slang name for a cruise to Hawaii. Not all were combatants—each battle group traveled with at least one, and sometimes more, underway replenishment ships. While there'd been some propositions to tether the unrep ships to theaters and treat them as theater resources rather than as part of a battle group, nothing substantive had changed yet in the way they deployed.

Onboard the combatants, in-port officers of the day were just now hearing the horrifying news being spread over the secure Navy Red battle circuit. For many of them, the first notice they had of trouble was air raid sirens groaning to life then lifting up their voices in an eerie wail. At first, most of them thought that it was a routine test of some sort, although a few older veterans immediately turned pale and raced to combat stations.

Each ship had no more than a third of its crew aboard, and in some cases, only one fifth of its crew. In theory, at least, each duty section held enough varieties of ratings and officers to get the ship under way in an emergency.

In theory. The reality was far harsher.

Still, to their credit, the majority of the officers of the day took only a few moments to understand what was happening. They immediately dispatched their operations specialists to Combat, hauled out the keys that would activate the automatic, self-contained close-in-weapons systems, and started bringing up the massive complex of computer systems and firing equipment that would enable them to launch anti-air missiles. Two ships, realizing that neither had sufficient personnel onboard to light off either one, transferred all their engineering personnel to one ship along with their operations specialists, leaving the damage-control ratings onboard.

For the most part, the ships were drawing shore power and their engineering plants were in standby. All were either gas turbine or diesel engine driven, steam plants having long given way to more efficient means of propulsion. The gas turbine ships required only five minutes to light off, while the diesels took slightly longer. Both types of engineers skipped at least eighty percent of the safety measures contained in their light-off instructions.

As the engineering plants came online, each ship was simultaneously lighting off combat systems, drawing on the shore power supplied by massive cables running from a main patch panel to the pier and commercial power. The electrical load quadrupled within the first two minutes, then doubled again. Within the base, the generators screamed in protest. One dumped offline, and the others followed shortly.

But the base power crew was just as motivated as the ships crews themselves. Pearl Harbor itself had no anti-air missiles, no Patriot batteries, no way of defending itself other than the power and might of the ships nestled

up to her piers. The shore engineers slammed in battle
shorts, ran their generators at 150 percent of rated ca-
pacity, and somehow managed to restore the vital flow
of electrons to the ships. The break in power lasted only
twenty seconds, but it was enough to trip all the ships'
combat systems offline. The light-off procedure had to
be started all over.

Four minutes after the air raid siren shattered their
world, the first ship, the fast frigate USS *Louis B. Puller*,
pulled away from the pier. The lines were severed by
axes by the boatswains mates when they realized that
there was no one left on the pier to cast them off. The
first fast frigate moved smartly away from the pier, twisting on her bow thrusters as she ran missiles out on her
launch rails. Although more nimble than the larger cruisers and destroyers, the FFG carried a much shorter-range
missile than the later weapons' blocks on her larger
sisters. Still, twenty-five miles of missile was enough to
make a difference.

Lieutenant Brett Carter stood in the center of *Puller's*
Combat Direction Center, wondering if he'd just made
the greatest mistake of his life. As the command duty
officer, he certainly had the authority to get the ship under way in an emergency without the captain or the executive officer, but he was quite certain that neither of
them had even conceived that it would be required.

He'd had only seconds to decide what to do as the
news came blasting over the secure circuits, and in the
first few moments the terrifying photos he'd seen of Pearl
Harbor after the Japanese attack were all that he could
think of. The Navy had learned the hard way that ships
in port might as well be counted dead in the event of
attack.

Carter had taken almost twenty seconds to make his
decision, enough time to hear the first rumble of explo-

sions and see fire on the horizon. Then in a calm voice that did not reflect the panic in his gut, the young lieutenant had gotten his ship under way, declared weapons free, designated the first hostile target, and authorized the launch. Even though his fingers trembled, he turned the key that energized the weapons-release circuits.

Looking behind the ship now, he could see smoke billowing up from the pier at which they'd been moored. He felt a flush of relief—whatever consequences he would face on his return to port, he knew in that second that he'd made the right decision. Had he waited for any of the ship's senior officers or for permission from another source, his ship would right now be fighting fires onboard—or sinking—rather than powering up to launch weapons in anger.

His crew in Combat was inexperienced, aside from a senior weapons technician chief petty officer. Men and women were filling two positions each, and the bridge crew was similarly shorthanded. Yet even operating at a dead run with a pick-up crew composed only of the on-duty watch section, the officers and crew operated as they were trained to do. Six minutes after the air raid siren, the first missiles leaped off her rails headed for the air radar contact that the USS *Jefferson* had designated as hostile in the LINK.

The missile arced out across the bay, searching for the target designated by the computers, talking with the ship in a quick rattle of digital positions and vectors, corrected its course slightly and bore in on the lead aircraft. It was virtually a head-to-head shot, and the targeting required the utmost in precision. The young third-class petty officer who'd actually fired the missile from the ship had never done so alone, apart from a few training simulators. He watched his screen, saw his missile—*his missile*—acquire the target on its own seeker head and streak across the video terminal. His foot danced out a nervous rhythm on the deck, and he never even realized that it seemed much more like the video games he'd been playing just two nights ago than actual combat.

In the two minutes it'd taken to get the missile off the rails, the lieutenant OOD had had time to get scared. As luck would have it, he was the junior-most OOD among the ships in port, and already the more senior OOD's were howling over tactical, each trying to clear his ship of the traffic and avoid a collision while still launching missiles. Fortunately for the FFG, she was well clear of the channel, and her OOD had made the wise decision to run like hell while firing and get the hell out of the way of the cruisers.

Commercial shipping and fishing vessels crowded the port and channels, and except for those who'd heard the air raid sirens, they were mostly unaware of what was happening. From their viewpoint, the Navy had simply gone insane, trying to get that many ships under way at once without warning the other natural denizens of the waterways that they were conducting some sort of drill. Most of the civilian masters were howling to the Coast Guard and Port Control authorities, demanding explanations, protesting the interference with their rights of way. By the time the first missile was launched, however, the Coast Guard, which monitored Navy Red, knew what was happening. The civilian ships were told to clear the channel. Immediately. Ground their vessels if necessary, but under no circumstances would the Navy yield the right of way to any other vessel.

Two Aegis cruisers were the next ones to work their way out of the pierside tangle, and they entered the main channel with missiles already gouting out of their decks. The vertical launch system, combined with a computer system capable of targeting almost three hundred enemy aircraft simultaneously, was the most potent anti-air system ever developed for a military service. Under normal circumstances, the two cruisers alone should have been able to eliminate every enemy aircraft onboard the disguised Chinese aircraft carrier.

Under normal circumstances.

Unfortunately, recent decisions within the Navy had put into place stringent protections to prevent U.S. Navy ships from firing on friendly units. These included certain geographic block-out areas that were programmed to not accept firing solutions within those geographic boundaries, as well as increased minimum firing ranges for the missiles each ship carried. By the time the cruisers rippled off the first wave of missiles, the Chinese aircraft were already within minimums. One missile rammed into an aircraft, but the others would not detonate.

Twenty-nine of the thirty Chinese jump jets survived. Another was picked off by the frigate. Twenty-eight arrived overhead in Pearl Harbor.

Chinese vessel **Rising Sun**
0620 local (GMT-10)

As soon as the last aircraft lifted off the deck, the Chinese carrier cut hard to the north, headed straight in for the coastline. Behind her, the amphibious assault vessel was launching its own contingent of aircraft, as well as a tanker. They remained overhead, loaded out with air-to-air missiles, as protection against the fighters from the aircraft carrier.

They need not have worried, at least not right away. The *Jefferson*'s assets were concentrated on the enemy aircraft heading for the coast. The battle group had seen the aircraft carrier empty her decks.

Well below the waterline, Chinese sonar technicians had heard the ghostly, drawn-out voices over Gertrude, and had managed to triangulate the transmissions from the submarine. A linguist was perched on a high stool next to the console, holding on to the metal desk beside him to keep from slipping across the steeply canted deck as the aircraft carrier turned. He listened to the transmissions, then quickly translated the words that came over the unclassified circuit.

The final firing solution was not particularly refined. The submarine knew the danger of using Gertrude, and had transmitted only the briefest acknowledgement of her new orders. Still, that blip of sound was enough to narrow down the sonarman's search, and he selected the higher frequency active transmissions that would let him pinpoint the submarine's location.

Of course, going active was a risk as well. The American submarine would be able to hear the sonar pings at a greater range than the carrier would be able to hear the returns from her hull. Additionally, the high speed of the carrier was producing a massive amount of noise, further degrading the Chinese ASW ability. But the carrier was counting on being able to find and attack the submarine with a barrage of weapons and at least hold her at bay until the ship popped out its final surprise.

On the weatherdecks, Ishi Zhaolong struggled across the deck, moving as quickly as he could to the port SVTT tube. The first return from the active sonar had just squeaked across the sonarman's headphones, providing enough data for a bearing-only launch. Ishi had been sure that the submarine would be to their right, and he was slightly alarmed to find that he'd guessed wrong. Still, the other team would be loading up the port SVTT. He wasn't critically needed there, but as the senior torpedoman onboard, he wanted to watch the evolution. With the deck now clear of both aircraft and disguises, darting back and forth between the four sets of launchers, two to the port, two on starboards, was much less of a problem than routine maintenance had been.

He arrived at the port launcher just as the tube reached one thousand pounds of pressure. The other torpedomen had hearing protectors clamped down over their ears and were stepping back from the pressurized tube. If anything went wrong now, the men would be peppered with shrapnel.

Ishi stepped forward and double-checked the settings himself. The torpedo was set to run shallow for a surface target. Its seeker head combined advanced wakehoming technology along with a relatively rudimentary acoustic discriminator. It also housed a command destruct secondary charge that could be used if the torpedo insisted on acquiring its own aircraft carrier as a target.

He nodded to the man crouched down beside the SVTT tube, then stepped back into the doubtful protection of a stanchion. He couldn't resist peering around the metal support to watch the actual firing.

There was a surprisingly smooth blast of noise, only slightly louder than the test firings they'd practiced back in the Yellow Sea and then enroute Hawaii. A metal cylinder four feet long and a foot in diameter shot out of the tube, remained airborne for thirty feet, then slid smoothly into the ocean with only a small splash and some expanding ripples that the ocean swells quickly smoothed out. Before the last ripples had faded away, the crew was manhandling another torpedo into the tube.

"Torpedo inbound," a voice snapped over Ishi's headset. He shouted at the crew to move faster, now desperate to get as many torpedoes in the water as he possibly could. What had seemed so thrilling, so very daring when it involved disrobing the carrier and launching aircraft now seemed all too deadly and personal.

A snapshot, that was all it had been, he thought frantically, scanning the water around him for any trace of the incoming torpedo. A desperate shot back down the bearing the submarine had seen the torpedo on, intended to shake up the carrier and force her to react as much as to actually target her. It'd be the first—but it wouldn't be the last. As soon as the American submarine was relatively certain she'd shaken off Ishi's first torpedo, she'd let off a barrage of torpedoes more carefully targeted, each one individually guided in on the carrier by an experienced crew.

For a moment, Ishi felt a moment of hopelessness. The deck that had seemed so spacious and safe now seemed ominously empty.

USS Centurion
0621 local (GMT-10)

"Only two, sir," Otter was saying into the bitch box as Renny slid back into his seat next to him. "We're carrying dummy loads for REFTRA, sir, not a full loadout. We're in *REFTRA*."

"And we're damned well not supposed to be shooting war shots," Captain Tran answered. "I know that—I know. You get me a firing solution. Make it right, Otter. We can't afford to miss."

Otter turned to Renny, desperation in his eyes. "We're in REFTRA," he said, as though that made some sort of sense.

The chief sonarman was standing behind them now, his presence a calming and steadying influence. "That's all this is, son. REFTRA for real. You just do it like we've been doing it for the last five days, smooth and easy. I'm going to be watching the solution—we'll nail that bastard."

"What the hell is it?" Renny asked, all the while plugging in the bearings and readings he needed for a more accurate firing solution. Looking at it now, knowing that they had only been carrying three live torpedoes, getting off the snapshot might not have been that good an idea. Under normal circumstances, yeah, you'd want that. But not now.

"Bearing separation looks good," the chief noted. He toggled on the mike in his hand. "Conn, Sonar, we have a firing solution."

"Is it the one you want, Chief?" Tran asked, speaking to him as an equal. "Let me know."

"I'll take this one, sir," the chief answered. "Single shot. We're working up the second solution right now."

"Very well. Weapons free, Chief."

"Weapons free, aye." The chief's eyes were still fixed on the sonar screen. "Weapons, Sonar—you have—*hold it*. She's turning. Captain, give me fifteen seconds, sir. I want a better solution."

"Advise me when you have a solution."

Renny swore quietly but passionately as he watched the odd surface contact's acoustic signature waver across the bearings. "Zig-zag?" he asked.

"Yeah, the asshole," the chief muttered. "S'okay. As long as we know about it, we can compensate for it. Look, he's already starting to fall into a pattern. Get ready, Renny, Otter. I'm going to want this one off right when I say."

Renny felt the sweat trickling down his back. It itched as it found his spine and coursed down it, soaking his undershirt and his coveralls. The waiting grew unbearable. Just as the chief started to give the order, a new sound cut through the quiet of the sonar shack. "Conn, sonar, torpedoes in the water. Two of them skipper."

"Two, aye. Stand by for evasive maneuvers." Even as the skipper spoke, the submarine leaned steeply to port and tilted forward. "Sonar, no change in the thermal layer?"

"No change, sir. Standing by with decoys."

"You know when, Chief."

"Aye-aye, sir. Renny, watch the contact—I've got the depth gauge—and keep your hand on the decoy."

"Got it." Renny knew what he was doing, had done it so many times in simulators and during REFTRA that the whole thing had a feeling of unreality to it. The chief standing behind him, Otter at his side—how many times had he done this in the last four days?

The chief would be watching the depth gauge. As the submarine approached the isothermal layer, where the temperature of the water was no longer the primary determinant of the speed of sound, the chief would eject the noisemakers. The decoys would churn up masses of bubbles in the water, enough sound to both mask the other sonar's detection and hopefully confuse the inbound torpedoes. If the torpedoes were acoustic or active sonar, the submarine would have an excellent opportunity to make a mad dash to depth, make the ship lose sonar contact, then maneuver back around to take another shot at the ship.

Of course, acoustic blindness worked both ways. If the ship couldn't see them, they couldn't see the ship. No matter—if the decoys didn't work, they'd hear the torpedo itself.

"Now," the Chief said.

Renny slammed up the toggle that released first one decoy, then another. How many did they have? He was tempted to glance over at the status board, but the chief would have already checked.

The two decoys performed as they were supposed to, frothing up the water and blasting acoustic noise across the entire spectrum. The automatic gain controls kicked in, attenuating the noise in his headset down to a manageable level.

The first torpedo on Renny's screen veered off to the right, clearly enticed by the attractive noise source saturating the water with acoustic energy. It reached a point that satisfied some primitive firing mechanism in its brain and it detonated.

The second one wasn't so sure. The detonation of the first torpedo evidently confused it. It wavered along its track for a moment, then started a hard lefthand turn. "Search pattern," the chief announced. "Conn, Sonar— it's lost us. For now."

"Roger," the skipper answered. "Chief, I'm going to make a run for it back toward the contact. You see any problem with that?"

"Couple of ships between us and Sierra two, Skipper," the chief answered. "Any word on their status?"

Renny listened to the conversation, his fingers still on the decoy buttons and his eyes glued to his screen. What the chief was asking made perfect sense, if you had to believe that someone just off the coast of Hawaii was shooting torpedoes at them.

"No information, Chief. Until I hear otherwise, every one of them is potentially hostile. Can you rule any of them out—any positive friendlies?"

"Yes, sir. I have *Jefferson* and her escorts, solid contact. I know where they are."

"Under the circumstances, I'm not sure the carrier would appreciate a high-speed run toward her. Give me a course."

"Two eight zero," Renny whispered before the chief could ask. "That's the straightest course that will leave us well clear of *Jefferson*."

"Two eight zero," the chief immediately repeated. Renny didn't know whether the chief was just relying on Renny's ability or whether he'd done the math himself. Verified it, probably. He'd seen the chief do that sort of instantaneous angles calculation before.

The submarine heeled hard in the opposite direction. She'd backed off on the down bubble and the deck was now almost level.

"Six minutes, captain. Four until we're inside minimums."

But we don't want a max range shot, Renny thought. Not with only two more warshots onboard. No, Chief will want us in a good deal closer, maximize the probability of a kill.

A kill. The word sent fresh shivers down his spine, and just for a moment—not long at all, but enough to make him waver—Renny paused. The kill—it would be either them or the other boat.

The other, he decided on some level, making a full commitment to those two possible resolutions to their tactical situation. The other—and not us.

"Wait for it, now," the chief said softly. "We're safe right now. She's lost us, she can't hear us. She's got to suspect we're coming for her, but she has no idea where we are. Not yet."

Renny found the words oddly soothing. He stole a moment to glance over at Otter and was relieved to see the calm, confident expression on the other man's face. Yes, this was what they'd trained for, this was why they were here. They knew what to do, knew they were good at it. And before the hour was up, someone was going to learn that it was a very, very bad idea to shoot at the USS *Centurion*.

USS Jefferson
0622 local (GMT-10)

"Get them back here," Batman roared, pounding on the TAO's back. "Recall all fighters. Can't you see it? Don't you know what's going to happen?" He grabbed the handset without waiting for an answer. "All aircraft, this is the admiral. Starboard marshall—*now*. If you're getting low on fuel, we'll handle that, but clear the area around the island's airspace immediately. Acknowledge." He dropped the mike from his mouth and waited for the responses.

One by one, the aircraft leads answered up. As they watched, the friendly aircraft symbols that had been boring in on Hawaii stopped, then the pixels pivoted to indicate that the aircraft were headed back to the carrier. Over tactical, it was clear that the operations specialists that normally coordinated the approaches on the carrier were quickly becoming overwhelmed. The airborne E-2C Hawkeye stepped in, assuming control of the majority of the aircraft and vectoring them around the approach radials to a safe distance south of *Jefferson*.

Batman stared at the screen, the color drained from his normally ruddy face. "My god, we almost bought it that time." By now, even the watch officer understood what he meant.

The airspace around Hawaii and the main channel was engorged with a spiderweb of long speed leaders projecting out from missile symbology as the surface ships leaving port opened fire on the hostile aircraft symbols.

Had the *Jefferson*'s aircraft continued inbound on the island, most of them would have become missile sumps for the firepower the cruisers and frigates were unleashing.

Tomcat 201
0623 local (GMT-10)

Lieutenant Hot Rock had been next in line for the tanker when TFCC and the Hawkeye started shouting orders. After an initial period of confusion, he managed to sort out what happened. It was unbelievable, unthinkable— but there it was. An enemy attack on Pearl Harbor. One part of his mind kept insisting it was simply another part of the battle problem that they'd been working all week.

Hot Rock's lead, Lieutenant Commander Lobo Hanson, grasped the situation faster than he did. "Come on, Hot Rock. Snap out of it. I don't have time to baby-sit you. Get your ass up the high position."

He yanked backed, putting the Tomcat into a sheer, bone-crushing ascent toward high position. The loose deuce fighting formation was the one preferred by most American pilots, and consisted of a team of two aircraft. One took high position, guarding the tail of the forward aircraft and providing additional area coverage because of increased radar range with altitude. The other aircraft took a lower altitude, slightly forward, and was usually the first engage the enemy aircraft.

A couple of cruises ago, high position had been Hot Rock's favorite. Although he hadn't been willing to admit to anyone, he had suspected that a deep streak of cowardice ran down his spine. The idea of facing incoming fire, facing it and ignoring it all as he took his own

shot, had seemed beyond him. For a while, he managed
to slide by on his superb flying skills, but eventually even
his backseater reluctantly voiced his opinion.

But finally, when it came right down to it, he found
he had what it took. Ever since that cruise, he'd finally
felt a part of the fighting squadron.

Not that anyone had let on. Even Commander Magruder, CO of VF 95, hadn't suspected just how terrified he
was in the air. Oh, sure, in aerobatics, formation flying
and practice bombing runs—he was above most of them
when it came to that sort of stuff.

But when it came down to actually shooting, to facing
down an enemy and fighting for your own little square
piece of airspace, he backed off. The last time, it had
almost gotten Lobo killed.

But that was behind him now. The squadron seemed
to be willing to let his past go, and God knows for what
reason, Lobo Hanson had decided he was all right. So
when she said take high position, his hands and feet
moved to obey before he could even get out a question.

But what the carrier was saying was insane, wasn't it?
An attack on Pearl Harbor?

Impossible. Absolutely impossible. As he climbed to
altitude, he found himself wondering just how many men
had said that before.

"Twenty miles," his backseater announced. "You got
a visual?"

"Yeah, I got it." The islands of Hawaii stretched out
as green and gray lozenges on the horizon. Even from
this different distance, their volcanic origins were evident. You could see the islands' ancestry in the rugged
jagged peaks climbing up in the sky, the sheer black of
hardened lava as the last of the sun hit it. From this angle,
you could see the difference between the leeway and the
windward sides of the island, with the former covered

with lush green vegetation, and the latter less so.

So who was howling that enemy aircraft were inbound on the island? Boy, somebody was going to get their ass kicked when the admiral figured out who had screwed the pooch on this one.

The more Hot Rock thought about it, the more convinced he was that it was all a screwup. Maybe even part of the training. That had to be the explanation—some stupid-assed junior officer had seen something, maybe a weather balloon, maybe somebody burning trash, and had made the wild leap to assuming whatever it was that he saw was caused by an air attack.

Just then, he saw it, and immediately revised his opinion. Black smoke boiled up, stark and ugly against the verdant hills. He saw fire flashing up at the base of it, obscured higher up by the swirling smoke.

A civilian airliner crash, maybe. Maybe a chemical plant exploding. He was aware that he was grasping at straws now, trying desperately to find some other explanation for what his eyes told him. Anything, everything— it couldn't be what the carrier was now saying.

"Ten miles." Hot Rock heard the tension in his backseater's voiced ratchet higher. So at least one of them inside this airframe believed what the carrier was saying. "Aw, shit! Look at the ships getting under way!"

He could see them now, the foamy wakes cutting swaths through the placid blue waters as the American fleet steamed toward the exit of the harbor. So many of them, crowded so impossibly close, at this distance looking more like light gray swatches against the water than actual Navy ships. But his link data confirmed it. Every combatant and every other Navy vessel capable of getting under way was steaming out from Hawaii.

But where were the other aircraft? He glanced down in his radar tactical display, and saw the picture beginning to build. The aircraft further ahead of him were picking them up on radar now, and as the ships lit off their combat systems and started feeding data to the battle group LINK, they were getting the advantage of the powerful SPY radar system.

Sure enough, there was something that looked awfully much like an enemy fighter pack clustered on the far side of the island. They were in the sort of minor disarray that normally follows a successful bombing run as aircraft break off on their assigned patterns and maneuver to avoid mutual interference. But they were starting to regroup now, probably transitioning from a land attack mode to getting ready for aerial combat.

How many of them were there? He tore his eyes away from the actual island, and tried to take a quick count. Thirty, maybe forty.

They were turning now, flying back toward the island of Hawaii. Another bombing run? Or was it simply a mad dash back to the safety of their waterborne airfield, getting within range so that their ship's automatic weapons defense systems could help protect them.

Or were they after *Jefferson*? The thought made his blood run cold. No matter that they would be able to land on Hawaii if they had to, the audacity of anyone trying to take a shot at his carrier blinded him with rage in a way that the hard evidence of an attack against the ground had not.

Hot Rock pulled up and away from Lobo, throttles jammed full forward and he arrowed up toward the heavens. The enemy aircraft were just nearing the edge of the island now, and he was losing their silhouettes against the night-darkened land. Not that he had to have a visual, no, not with the array of sensors feeding data to him via the HUD and not with a RIO in the backseat making sure he didn't miss a damned trick.

Below him, Lobo's aircraft was boring in toward the island. There'd been a time when Hot Rock would have been silently howling his anguish and fear, a time when he'd thought—no, he'd *known*—that he just didn't have what it took. Sure, he could fly the aircraft, and do it better than most. But when he compared his own courage with that of the other pilots, he'd found himself sorely lacking.

That is, until last cruise. Now he knew he could be part of the team, that he wouldn't let his wingman down. MiG pilots had had to die to confirm that.

"Got a lock," Lobo announced, indicating that her AMRAAMM had acquired one of the enemy fighters and was ready to launch. "Waiting for it, waiting for it—"

"Weapons tight!" a familiar voice commanded over tactical. "Goddammit, *weapons tight*!"

"What the hell—?" Hot Rock's RIO asked. "Admiral Wayne lost it?"

"Sir, I got him." Lobo's voice was angry and anguished. "I let him go now, I'll just have to deal with him later."

"No. Weapons tight, damn you!" Hot Rock heard Batman say. "Think, you idiot. Think. He's right over downtown!"

Cold horror swept through Hot Rock as he realized the choice Batman had been forced to make. The fighters, still wing-heavy with weapons, were in transit over a densely populated civilian area. Tourist, natives, locals, all crowded together in the lush, teaming city. If they took the shot, nailed the bastards—and they would, Hot Rock had no doubt about that—they'd spatter flaming aircraft, fuel, and weapons all over the innocent bystanders. Collateral damage, the military had tried calling it, trying to de-emphasize the fact that it meant civilian deaths.

But the alternative—how much worse would it be for the countless military personnel and their families currently on the base? Was it fair that Batman was choosing to allow the fighters to proceed inbound on military targets in order to spare the civilians outside the gates?

But the military men and women knew the risks, didn't they? And while an attack on Pearl Harbor might not have been the first one they'd be worried about, it was all part of what you signed on for.

And their families, too?

No, not the families. They were no different than the men and women outside the gates.

Yet given the two alternatives, Batman had chosen to engage the fighters on their way out, after they'd dropped the munitions.

They'd be harder targets, too, once they'd stripped off the extra weight of armament and some fuel. Lighter, more maneuverable—were they carrying air-to-air weapons? Or had they been wing-heavy with ground ordnance, certain that they wouldn't encounter any air threats this close to American soil? If so, they'd pay for that overconfidence now, and pay heavily.

"Hot Rock, on me," Lobo commanded. "We're going to take the west side of the island, wait for them to start their egress. Let them get over water first."

"Roger," he answered, already pulling around smoothly to maintain his position. On his HUD, he could see the other fighting pairs breaking off to cover the rest of the sectors, with the majority of the fighters positioning themselves between the island and the carrier.

"Should be ninety seconds or less," his RIO announced. *If they're headed to the base,* was the unspoken qualification.

"I want weapons assigned to every little bastard," Hot

Rock growled. "This isn't going to happen again—not on my watch."

But yet, despite his bravado, it did. He watched, his stomach turning violently over and over as though he were caught in an uncontrolled spin, staring at the HUD then focusing past it on the actual land. The HUD and the radar showed the inching progress of the enemy shapes across the land, the moment when they passed over American coast. The blips suddenly veered off their track and increased speed. His nausea increased to the point that he thought he would puke. To stay up here, wings fully loaded, and watch it happen was the worst experience he'd ever had.

Then past the arcane symbols on the HUD, down on the actual land depicted in dotted green lines, the sudden blossoming of light. Almost pretty, in a way, unless you knew what it really was. Ground attack weapons, meeting dirt, gouting huge fireballs into the air, consuming flesh and metal and wood and brick. What didn't burn was blasted apart into fragments and flung into the air.

Smoke billowed up in ugly black smears of dark against the darker land.

THREE

Rear Admiral "Tombstone" Magruder slung one arm around his wife's shoulder and stared down at her fondly. "This enough like a honeymoon for you?"

Commander Joyce "Tomboy" Flynn Magruder stared up at him, a rapt expression on her face. "It ought to be—we've been waiting long enough for it."

"Two years." He pulled her close and turned to face her. "But I'm planning on making up for lost time on this trip."

She nuzzled up against him. "Two years. I can't believe it." She pulled away slightly and smacked him lightly on the chest. "What would you say if one of your staff officers told you he made his wife wait that long for a honeymoon?"

He sighed and pulled her back in close to him. "I'd say he was a damned fool, if his bride was anything like you. But then, most women aren't."

"Aren't what?"

"Like you."

"Hmmm."

Tombstone knew immediately he'd struck the wrong note, and tried to make up for it. "And there were a few other things that interfered as well, if you'll recall. Blame the Chinese and the Russians, not me. You were there—you know what we were facing."

He felt her head nod against his chest, her breath ruffling the hair on his chest. "Some things I won't ever forgive them for."

"And it's not like we had much of a choice, did we?" he continued. "I mean, you understand what being an officer is all about. That's one way you're different."

"From Pamela, you mean?"

"Among other people, yes. Pamela would be a very good example of what I'm talking about."

"Pamela." This time she did pull back, and Tombstone could see the storm clouds gathering on her face. "Let me get this straight. We're on our honeymoon, said honeymoon having been delayed for two years—six months longer than a normal command tour—we're in Hawaii, at perhaps the world's most romantic tropical resort. You would agree with those facts?"

"Yup."

"Now, given all that, what in the *hell* are you doing mentioning that bitch's name?"

Tombstone stared down at her, amazed at the transformation her face had undergone. He'd seen it before, that legendary redhead temper, but only occasionally had been on the receiving end of it. Her brilliant green eyes were narrowed to mere slits, and the golden-red hair seemed to halo her face like lightening. Her eyebrows were drawn down toward her nose, and her normally full and luxurious mouth had narrowed down to a thin line.

"I'm sorry. I didn't mean it," he said, still confused about what exactly he'd done wrong—hell, he'd been *complimenting* her, hadn't he?—but falling back on a spousal survival skill he'd learned early on.

No matter that his darling wife, the love of his life, was perhaps the best backseater he'd ever flown with, male or female, and a front-running officer in the Tomcat community. No matter that she'd seen her share of combat, both as a regular member of a fighting squadron and in command of a squadron as well. It didn't even seem to dawn on her that he'd picked her over Pamela Drake, breaking an engagement of sorts that spanned nearly a decade to marry the diminutive RIO now virtually spitting her words at him.

No, this was definitely not the time to point those items out. The last thing he wanted to be doing right now was arguing with her, and the fastest route to resuming their honeymoon— He glanced at his watch. Just barely enough time before dinner if he could clear this up now—was to simply shut up and apologize. Later, when she'd calmed down, he could figure out what he'd said wrong.

"I'm sorry, you're right," he said again, putting all the conviction that almost three decades in uniform could bring to bear. "It's *our* honeymoon."

"As opposed to who else's?"

No, he'd missed the window of opportunity, he could see that now. Once Tomboy started spinning up like this, it was damned hard to cycle her down. An apology worked, but only if you could get it in play fast enough.

"As opposed to living my entire life alone, miserable without you." He drew her in close to him and felt his body surge in response. "Have I told you in the last five minutes how wonderful you look in that swimming suit? And how much better you'd look out of it?"

She planted her hands squarely in the middle of his chest and shoved. Not hard, but hard enough to make her point. "No. You haven't. And it won't get you out of this one so easily, Stony. Don't even try." She turned and stalked off.

He followed her into the luxurious penthouse suite that had eaten up a good portion of their savings. "Why are you mad at me?"

"Why?" she echoed, her back still to him. "You start rambling on about Pamela Drake, and you have to ask me *why*?"

"You brought her up," Tombstone said, now resigning himself to the fact that there wouldn't be a sweet session of lovemaking before dinner. Indeed, if things progressed much further, there wouldn't be any afterward either. "I was just saying—"

"You were thinking about her, weren't you?" she shot back. "Don't lie to me, Stony. Don't even try."

He sighed. The bitch of it was, she was right. He'd been watching the sun trek down toward the ocean, wondering whether or not they might see the fabled green flash just as the sun disappeared into the Pacific Ocean, idly considering whether or not he could slip the maitre d' a few bucks to get them a seat next to the window so they could watch for it, wondering how much time they had left before dinner, letting his mind wander through a few sexual fantasies and *bang*—Pamela had flitted across his mind. Not settled in there, not stayed for much more that a microsecond. And honestly, he'd just thought about how lucky he'd been that he was here with Tomboy instead of Pamela.

And she'd heard him. It was spooky sometimes, how she seemed to read his thoughts.

Well, if she was going to read his mind, she ought to at least have the courtesy to read the entire thought, not just pick out one name at random that happened to pop up.

But maybe there was still a way to salvage the evening.

He looked pointedly at his watch. "Hey, about time to eat, isn't it? Hungry? I'm starving." He mustered up his most winning smile and prayed.

For a moment, he thought it wouldn't work. Then he saw it, the beginning of the frost melting off of her face. A smile tugged at the corners of her mouth. He breathed a sigh of relief.

"Cut that out," she said, her voice warm and intimate.

"Cut what out?"

"That. You know."

Safe now, and only because of a quirk of facial muscles that his mother told him he'd inherited from his father, some odd sort of smile that seemed to be his ultimate weapon. "How about this?" he said, stepping close and running his hands over her body. "Should I cut this out as well?"

She moaned softly. "Maybe."

"And this?"

She pressed up against him. "Only if you want to be on time for breakfast."

Come to think of it, he wasn't *that* hungry.

When the hotel management had learned who would be staying with them, the manager had insisted on upgrading them to the best suite in the hotel. He'd also evidently had a word with the restaurant staff—Tombstone and Tomboy had never had to wait for a table.

After dinner, Tombstone ordered a bottle of champagne. He waited while their glasses were charged, then held his up. "To us. And to a honeymoon every moment we're together."

She clinked her glass lightly against his. "To us."

Overhead, the stars were just memories in the gradually lightening sky. The restaurant had all the windows open, and the early morning breeze ruffled his hair gently. He took one of her hands in both of his and said, "There's nothing else in the world except us. Nothing."

She sighed happily. "Us and the stars." She pointed with her chin at the sky outside. "It looks like that sea, too. Even better there, with no ambient light." Just then a light streaked across the blackness. "Oh, look," she exclaimed. "Shooting star—make a wish, quick."

Something about the path the light traced across the sky made him pause. He felt an uneasy churning in his stomach. "That star . . . something's not right."

"Pshaw," she said lightly. "Go ahead, make a wish."

"I wish I'm wrong," he said, talking to himself more than complying with her request. "But—" he was on his feet, moving toward the entrance to the restaurant and the telephone.

"What . . . ?" she started to ask, then a look of dawning horror crossed her face. She was on his heels in an instant.

The peaceful night world outside exploded into blots of light and noise, the light flashing away their night vision just seconds before the sound and fury of multiple explosions reached them. The pressure wave arrived then, blasting the glass out of the windows.

Tombstone grabbed Tomboy and pulled her into the inner entrance to the restaurant. He dove for cover, pulling her down with him and covering her body with his own. Glass and debris peppered his back.

"No," he heard Tomboy wail, then felt her writhing underneath him as she struggled to get free. "No, it can't be!"

He let her up then, but caught her as she started to run for the exit. He pulled her around to face him, holding her just above the elbows and pulling her up on her tiptoes. "It's going to get crazy right now." He pulled her into a hard, brief kiss. "You know what that was, just like I do. We've got to get down to CinCPac Fleet. If we get separated, find a way to get back to *Jefferson*. She's just off the coast on REFTRA."

Tomboy nodded, all trace of panic and confusion gone from her face. "I'll go with you to CinCPac, and we'll figure it out from there."

Camp Smith
0710 local (GMT-10)

As they approached the Commander in Chief, Pacific, headquarters located on the Camp Smith Army compound, it became obvious that there were no answers to be found there. Guards blocked the gate, all with that itchy trigger finger look in their eyes that warned the two Magruders that this was as far as they were getting.

"Anyone know what happened?" Tombstone asked. His tone of voice, that of a senior naval officer who wanted answers—and wanted them now—had the desired effect. Although the soldiers appeared no more likely to open the gates to their rental car, he did see a slight softening in their manner.

"Bombs, sir." The soldier waved in the direction behind him, never completely taking his eyes off the occupants of the car. "Air launched, if it matters."

"Casualties," Tombstone demanded.

"Still sorting it out, sir. It's pretty bad. We can't find everyone, so Captain Smith's taken charge of CinCPac Fleet."

Captain Billy Smith. Well, it could have been worse, Tombstone reflected. A surface sailor, a charter member of the old school club. Billy Smith hadn't changed his conviction since his days at the Naval Academy that there was only one way to do things, and that was by the book. It was an approach that left something to be desired when it came to aerial combat, but worked perfectly fine most of the time. And fortunately, the navy had instructions to cover virtually any contingency in the book. Particularly the book that covered attacks on Pearl Harbor.

"Sir, the other senior officers are mustering at the officers' club," the sergeant said, his eyes drifting over to something behind him. "We're a little busy right now with the rescue and damage control efforts—there'll be someone there organizing transport back to your commands there, sir. And ma'am."

Tombstone nodded. Yes, there would be a plan for everything in Hawaii, and most certainly for getting officers back to their commands. And for damage control.

Still, it was all well and good to say they'd get him back to his command. If you had one.

Tomboy did. As commanding officer of VF-95, they'd slap her skinny little butt onto the first COD bound for *Jefferson*, along with any other spare aviators that happened to have been in port. Probably about two-thirds to three-quarters of her squadron. Only the duty section would have voluntarily remained onboard the carrier, and they were probably in four-section duty. No need to have more people aboard, not when they were steaming in the peaceful waters off Hawaii.

Not unless the unthinkable happened.

Tombstone pulled the Taurus into a tight circle and headed back the way they'd come. For now, the officers' club looked like the best bet.

"Stony?" Tomboy asked. "Drop me at Base Operations."

"Why? He said transport was being arranged out of the officers' club."

Tomboy's face was pulled into the hard mask that he

recognized as her command face. "I'm not relying on somebody else's prioritization of passengers. There'll be pilots and aircraft at Base Ops. That's all I need to get back to *Jefferson*.

"You've got a pilot right here," Tombstone said. "Half the problem solved."

Tomboy nodded. "I'd thought of that. And you're current, aren't you?"

"Indeed I am." Just before departing on their honeymoon, he'd spent a couple of weeks in Norfolk scraping the rust off. "Card-carrying naval aviator, I am."

"I probably ought to take a combat pilot, though, if I can," Tomboy said thoughtfully. "Whatever's happened, we'll need warfighters more than planners."

A cold chill seeped through Tombstone. Had she really said that? Implied that there would be someone more useful to her in the air than her husband? Some twenty-something-year-old nugget with maybe one cruise under his belt? Who'd never taken on a MiG one-on-one, flown combat missions over hostile territory?

"I fly missions," he said thickly.

She shook her head. "No, you don't. The Navy's not paying you admiral's pay to sit in a cockpit. You're the front end of the solution, the one who figures out how to keep pilots from getting killed. Not the one who flies the mission." She glanced over at him, suddenly aware how it'd all sounded. "Not that you're not a fine pilot, Stony."

"Sure. Just not the one you want to fly with." The words he'd intended as a joke came out entirely too harshly.

"Don't be an ass," she said sharply. "You know exactly what I mean."

The bitch of it was, he did. Jobs for a combat pilot got scarce as hen's teeth as you got more senior. You flew a desk more often than a Tomcat. His uncle had realized that, and had come up with the solution that would make best use of his nephew's combat experience and practical knowledge—troubleshooter. Not for paperwork and administrative problems, or for the various political situations the navy faced today. No, Tombstone was the warfighter that his uncle, the CNO, sent into sticky situations and nasty little wars. The sort of problems where nobody could figure out how to achieve their objectives without losing a lot of men and women and aircraft in the process. A troubleshooter who not only knew the enemy, but had killed his fair share in the past decades.

"Let's see if they've got an aircraft," he said, putting aside for the moment the question of who'd actually fly it out to the ship. There was no point in pointing out that he outranked everyone that they were likely to run into at Base Ops, and if he wanted an aircraft, they'd damned well come up with one for him. And no one, not even his pretty little tiger-wife, was going to stop him.

Base Ops
0715 local (GMT-10)

A COD was just pulling up in front of Base Ops as they pulled into the parking lot. A stream of passengers clad in survival gear was already heading toward the loading area.

"Not a full load," Tomboy noted. "If we hurry, we can be on it." She opened the door and hopped out before Tombstone had even brought the car to a full stop. "I'll get our names on the manifest." She was out of sight before Tombstone could get his own seat belt unfastened.

By the time he made it into Base Ops, Tomboy had already filled out their next of kin cards and added their names to the manifest. She tossed him his cranial and floatation vest, then pointed toward the waiting COD. "Two minutes. Let's get our asses in gear." They pulled on the safety gears as they ran for the turbo-propped transport aircraft.

The aircraft was just over half full. An enlisted aircrewman directed them to seats in the middle of the aircraft, then trotted back down the ramp to check for any more late arrivals. He was back within moments. He slipped his headset on, and Tombstone saw his lips moving as he talked to the aircrew up front. The ramp that served as a boarding ladder pulled up and joined with the fuselage of the aircraft. The passenger compartment was plunged into darkness broken only by the feeble overhead bulbs few and far between.

Tombstone glanced over at Tomboy and saw her shut her eyes for a moment. She was a RIO, a backseater, used to having someone else doing the driving, although he thought she probably did understand just how much he hated being a passenger on any aircraft.

He'd been a passenger far too often in the last year, he decided. Enough was enough.

"Listen up, please. Magruder?" an enlisted sailor standing in the aisle shouted. "Magruder?"

"Which one?" Tombstone asked.

"Oh, there are two of you, sir," the sailor said. "I thought it was just a mistake."

"There are two," Tombstone agreed.

"And you're both billeted onboard *Jefferson*?" the sailor asked.

"She is," Tombstone said, pointing at Tomboy.

"And you, sir? Because right here—sir, I'm sorry, but if you're not assigned to the ship, I need to put someone in that seat who is. Mission essential only, it says. Sir."

The sailor was clearly not comfortable making his point to the admiral, but he stood his ground.

Not mission essential. Tombstone stood and coldly stalked off the aircraft. As soon as he'd cleared the flight deck, he pulled out his cell phone. They'd just see who was not mission essential in this Navy.

FOUR

Admiral Thomas Magruder had just finished a hard-fought battle of racquetball when the news first reached Washington D.C. His aide, Lieutenant Commander Henry Williams, tracked his boss down in the shower.

"Admiral! The Chinese have just attacked Pearl Harbor!" Williams was already rustling up towels, making sure his boss's clothes were ready to go as he briefed the CNO. "Evidently three vessels masquerading as merchant ships were actually configured as warships. From all we can tell right now, they launched a missile attack on the harbor followed by a wave of jump jets."

All around the shower area, Williams could hear the water being turned off. Almost every person in that room had the need to know, and he didn't hesitate to continue his brief that inadvertently encompassed a number of other officers.

"I have Rear Admiral Magruder on cell phone, sir," Williams continued. "And the National Command Authority on line two."

Admiral Magruder poked his head out from the shower, then reached out to grab the cell phone. "Stony?"

"I'm here, sir."

"What happened?" the senior Magruder demanded.

"As far as I can tell, a missile attack on Pearl Harbor. I've been seeing something that looks like a Chinese carrier off the coast for the last hour."

"My aide said something about civilian vessels—is that what you saw?"

"I can neither confirm nor deny that, sir," his nephew said. "Tomboy and I were having dinner and observed missile launches from aircraft, but I couldn't determine their point of origin."

The CNO held his cell phone trapped between his shoulder and his ear as he tried to shuffle on his clothes as best he could. All around him, other senior officers were doing the same dance. "Who is there with you?"

"Tomboy caught a hop back out to *Jefferson*," his nephew said. "I'm at the officers' club—looks like a lot of us are stranded here for one reason or another. The Air Force is sorting out transportation arrangements as I speak." The elder Magruder could hear a loudspeaker announcement in the background, but couldn't make out the details.

The CNO took a deep breath, mentally shifting gears as he slipped his shirt on. "Okay, Stony. Here's what I want you to do. I'll formalize later, but we need to get this ball rolling. *Jefferson* is in the area, but she's going to need some help. Check around, see who is in the same situation you are. Pick out the good ones and put together a battle staff. Draw from all the services—make sure you get some excellent logistics people from both the Marines and the Air Force. I have a prepositioned assets ship somewhere in the area that I can divert to you, but you'll need knowledgeable people to get it offloaded and mobilized. And people—you'll need people. Have your experts working on ways to get Marine troops out to you."

"Aye-aye, sir. I understand."

"Anything you need, Stony, you let my office know. My God, an attack on American soil—I don't need to tell you how desperate this situation is. We're not prepared for this—we never have been. Every other asset I've got is deployed overseas, at least three weeks at flank speed away. And if they've got air superiority, there's no way we'll get assets in by CRAF. For now, it's *Jefferson* and whatever other assets you can rustle up there."

Lieutenant Commander Williams tapped the CNO on the shoulder. "Sir? I'm getting reports from intelligence that the Chinese have captured the main communications facility in Hawaii. As well as third fleet and seventh fleet commanders and their staffs. Evidently they were there for a planning conference."

The senior Magruder closed his eyes and groaned. Adrenaline pounded through his veins and if there's one thing he knew, it was that he would need it. "Do we have special forces in the area?" he asked.

Lieutenant Commander Williams nodded. "SEAL Team Seven, Squad Two. According to the CIA, they're deployed in the mountains on Hawaii for an international exercise. They're already talking to them and they've got orders to retake the comm center first. After that, well . . ." The aide fell silent, knowing that "after that" was far above his pay grade.

"Okay, okay, at least that's something," the senior Magruder murmured. "Murdoch, right? Of course it is—Don Stroh would know about this before anyone. Stony, you still there?"

"Yes, Admiral."

"This line isn't secure," the elder Magruder said carefully. "So I can't give you all the details. And from the sounds of it, we won't have secure communications until you get back to *Jefferson*—you understand that?"

"I do, sir."

"This pick-up team of yours—keep a sharp eye out for special forces and intelligence people, particularly those working with civilian agencies. You know who I'm talking about using, I suspect. When you get to *Jefferson*, establish contact with them. Got it?" the CNO asked.

"Understood, sir."

"Very well." The CNO hesitated for a moment as the enormity of the situation overwhelmed him. By now he was dressed, headed out from the shower room. Williams had picked up the CNO's racquetball racket and exercise togs and was dutifully stuffing them into the Admiral's gym bag as he trotted along behind.

As the CNO headed for his office, with Tombstone still on the other end of the cell phone, the corridors exploded into action. People usually walked briskly down the corridors, carrying with them a sense of self-importance in the urgency that affected every detail of duty at the Pentagon. Now, however, everyone was running. Civil servants, the longtime experts who constituted the corporate memory of the Pentagon, were staying close to the walls of the quarters as officers and enlisted personnel ran at breakneck speed. No one waited for elevators—the doors to the innumerable stairways interspersed between the rings shot open like fans.

"Stony, be careful out there, okay? But whatever you need, you've got. You have any problems putting together this team, call me. I'll get you some help out there as soon as I can. For now, do what you can to stabilize things and let the special forces take the lead."

"Yes, Admiral. This seal team squad—how do I talk to them?"

"Satcomm. Lab Rat's still onboard *Jefferson*?"

"I'm sure he is, Admiral."

"Then he'll know. Call me back as soon as you have the people you want and plans for getting out to *Jefferson*."

The senior Magruder terminated the call as he reached the door to his office. He paused for moment outside of it, and took the last slow breath he would take for many days. Then he opened the door, a heartbeat ahead of Lieutenant Commander Williams, and stepped into the storm.

Officers' Club
Hawaii
0720 local (GMT-10)

Tombstone clicked off the cell phone and surveyed the room again with a new perspective. No longer were the men and women crowding into the small room strangers. Instead, they were potential shipmates, officers who had already been drafted to his private staff. Even if they didn't know yet.

But how to sort them out? How to tell which ones had the brains, the fire in the belly, and a technical expertise to make a difference?

The noise level inside the banquet room was growing. An Air Force master sergeant who appeared at the doorway was mobbed.

Tombstone vaulted lightly onto the bar and headed to the corner where a ship's bell was suspended from a metal bracket. It was traditionally used to gong someone who entered the club still covered, and announced that the offender would buy the bar a round for his or her transgressions. Now, he used it for the purpose it was originally intended—to get the attention of his crew.

Tombstone grabbed the bell ringer and slammed it back and forth rapidly inside the bell. The harsh, urgent clamor cut through the noise of the crowd. Seeing that he had their attention, Tombstone jumped back up on the bar. He shoved aside an unfinished drink with his right foot, put his hands on his hips, and said, "Now listen up. My name is Rear Admiral Matthew Magruder. I've just been on the cell phone with the CNO in D.C." He pointed at the Air Force master sergeant. "Am I to assume you're trying to sort out the transportation requirements?"

The Air Force master sergeant slid through the crowd, politely murmuring his excuses as he forcibly parted the waves of people until he stood in front of Tombstone. "That's correct, Admiral."

"Good. Stay right there—I'm going to need you. The rest of you, listen up. At this moment, the only military forces in the area are Navy. We have indications that all secure communications in and out of Pearl Harbor have been compromised. The CNO—and I expect to have the backing of the Joint Chiefs shortly—ordered me to assemble a theater battle group command composed of people here, and then get them out to the USS *Jefferson*. The first question—who's the senior officer here?"

A murmur swept through the crowd, then a tall, bulky man in tan shirts and a brilliant flowered shirt stepped forward. A fresh sunburn was peeling off of his nose and the tops of his ears. Under short clipped hair, his scalp was scorched fiery red. "I believe that would be me."

"Yes, sir. May I have your name?" Tombstone asked politely.

"Major General Bill Haynes," the two-star said. "Infantry."

"Sir, can I impose on you to join me up here?" Tombstone asked, pointing down at the bar.

The army general forced his way forward with much less difficulty than the Air Force master sergeant had experienced. He climbed up on the bar next to Tombstone, and said, "Looks like you've got marching orders right now, Admiral. For the time being, let me know what I can do to support you."

Tombstone nodded, grateful that a pissing contest with a more senior officer wasn't going to happen. In a few sentences, he filled General Haynes in on his conversation with his uncle.

"Sounds like a plan," Haynes said. "Why don't I take charge of assembling the ground force end of it, including the commander of the landing force contingent? You pulled what you need for air operations and sea operations?"

Then Tombstone raised his voice and asked, "Anyone with special forces experience, amphibious experience, or ground intelligence experience, I need you up here."

During the next thirty minutes, the two men methodically worked their way through the assembled officers and staff. They compared notes frequently, and Tombstone found General Haynes to be a reasonable, bluntly competent officer. They passed over most of the personnel and support functions officers, although General Haynes insisted on several more supply people than Tombstone thought they might need. Finally, they had their team. Tombstone dismissed the others with thanks, and took the ten officers they jointly selected to a small conference room located on the lower level of the officers club.

"Introductions first," Tombstone said. "And before you ask any questions, let me point out that the carrier already has a battle group staff on it. We will be their immediate superior, coordinating both the operations of the special forces units ashore as well as preparing for the eventual arrival of ground troops to retake the island. I know who you all are—it's time you met each other."

General Haynes cleared his throat, and addressed the group "Major General Bill Haynes, U.S. army. I was here for a CINCPACFLT briefing prior to assuming duties as Deputy Commander in Korea. Most of my time is in infantry, although I'm very familiar with artillery and armored operations. I attended the Naval War College," he nodded politely at Tombstone, "which is why I decided not to get in the way of the admiral here."

"Thank you, General." Tombstone murmured. "Next?" Tombstone pointed at a Marine colonel.

"Colonel Darryl Armstrong, deputy commander I Corps. Two tours in special operations, including a joint assignment to the Rangers, which is why I assume you picked me, Admiral."

Tombstone studied him for a moment, certain he'd made the right choice. "We will need a commander for landing forces," Tombstone said. "Are you up for it?"

The colonel nodded. He was a powerfully built man a couple of inches taller than Tombstone himself. Maybe 6'4", 230 pounds, Tombstone figured. Muscles rippled under darkly tan skin, and there was an intense, driven air about him that attracted Tombstone's attention immediately. His hair was cut so short as to be almost invisible, but Tombstone could see a few streaks of gray at the temples. Ice blue eyes seemed to absorb everything in the room without actually looking at anything.

The colonel nodded. "Honored to be part of the team, Admiral."

"Lieutenant Commander Hannah Green," the next officer said. She was a tall, willowy blond with a slim, athletic build. Short blond hair framed a classically beautiful face with blue eyes a couple of shades darker than

Armstrong's. A stunner, Tombstone thought, then immediately chided himself for the thought.

"My primary expertise is in support of landing operations," Greene continued, transferring her gaze from one officer to the next as she spoke. Each one met her eyes, saw something there that Tombstone himself had detected, and nodded almost imperceptibly. Whatever gender issues still remained in the navy, they wouldn't be a problem with this officer. "And additionally, like the colonel, I spent time at special forces command. In fact, I believe we met there about eight years ago," she concluded.

Armstrong nodded. "I'm surprised you remember."

"Photographic memory," she said, and left it at that.

"Carlton Early," the next officer announced. In contrast to the two spoken before him, there was a gleeful, almost idyllic look to his face. "KC-135 navigator. No experience at all with special forces or intelligence—that goes without saying, although I am in the Air Force—but I know just about everything there is about getting gas in the air." He cocked a quizzical eyebrow at Tombstone. "I assume you're planning on long-range tanking to support operations in theater."

"I suspect so, Major. Aviation fuel will be the first thing we run out of. From here on out, I want you talking to somebody at Castle AFB every spare second you've got. I don't think coordination will be a problem—at least not when the Joint Chiefs of Staff says for it to happen—but it will be easier if they're talking to someone who speaks their own language."

Early nodded. "You got it, Admiral. There are a couple of other places we'll want to use as well for the other assets when they arrive. But for now, I'll build a permanent Texaco in the air. Get my best people on it, too, then make sure they don't send us any no-loads." For a moment, a dark expression swept across Early's face.

Tombstone let it pass, but filed it away for later investigation.

"Captain Ed Henry," a man in garish shorts said. For a split second, Tombstone wondered just why it was that the most senior officers seemed compelled to don such gaudy gear. "Coast Guard. Ship driver. I'm assigned here."

In short order, the other members of the team introduced themselves. They included every specialty ranging from satellite communications to a SEAL lieutenant who'd been on vacation in Hawaii when everything broke loose. It was the SEAL officer who confirmed Tombstone's conclusions about the SEAL squad now in place.

"That would be third squad of SEAL team seven," the lieutenant said. "I know their guy—Murdoch."

"Is he dependable?" Tombstone asked.

The lieutenant let out a short, sharp bark of laughter. "I think that would be understating it by a factor of ten, Admiral. That is, unless you're the sort of officer who insists on doing things by the book." From his tone of voice, the juniormost officer in the room made clear his opinion of that particular type of officer.

The junior officer's directness amused Tombstone. To be so young, so cocky—had he been like that himself at that age?

"Will you fill us in on this special squad," Tombstone said, "so were all reading off the same page?"

"Glad to, sir. SEAL team seven is based out of Norfolk and comes under Group Two. Squad three is—" He hesitated, and glanced around room, then looked to Tombstone for reassurance.

"Everyone here is cleared for specially compartmented

information," Tombstone said. "By my order, as of now. We'll catch up on the paperwork later."

The SEAL lieutenant nodded. "Squad three works directly for the CIA," he said bluntly. "They do things that . . . well . . . that maybe we don't want people to note that we've done. Sensitive missions, mostly. In countries around the world. They run through a lot of men, sir. They lose a couple each mission, I've heard."

"What communications will they have with them?" Hannah asked.

"Satellite communications. And believe me, they know how to use their gear. Squad three gets the latest in technology even before we even know about it, and they don't worry about using it or breaking it. I'm willing to bet that as soon as they heard what was going on, they were talking to their CIA controller. And by now, they've probably talked to *Jefferson* unless they're under orders not to."

"Why would they be under orders not to?" Tombstone asked, a trace more sharply than he intended. "This is a full joint operation."

"I don't know, sir. I'm just saying it's a possibility."

The last member of the party was the Air Force master sergeant who had been attempting to coordinate transportation requirements with the officers in the club. Tombstone had drafted him immediately as an ad hoc member of the new battle group. As a full extent of the operation became apparent, Tombstone could see that would have taken a crow bar to separate the Air Force master sergeant from his new battle staff.

"Fred Carter," the Air Force master sergeant said. "Logistics—spent some time with KC-135s, sir—and VIP transportation requirements. Mostly that, now," he said quietly. From the little the master sergeant said, Tomb-

stone had the feeling that there was a good deal more to
his career than he was letting on.

"I imagine you could've handled that crowd in there
on your own, Master Sergeant," Tombstone said.

The master sergeant nodded. "But I appreciate your
help, sir. A collar count always helps. I had directions
for my people, but I believe your orders supercede that."

"Now that we've got that straightened out—how do
we get out to *Jefferson*?" General Haynes broke in. "I
saw one of those C-2s taking off not long ago. Is there
another one on deck?"

"I doubt it," Tombstone said slowly. "From what I
saw, the Chinese were moving to establish air superiority
pretty quickly. They're flying their CAP stations right
over the city. The battle group commander out there is a
good friend of mine. He's not going to want ACM over
land. And even if he did, I'm willing to bet that he gets
guidance not to do so."

"But we're not going to just let them have Hawaii,"
somebody said. "And establishing air superiority is the
first step in winning any battle, right?"

"Yes, but to maintain control of the skies, they've got
to keep control of the air bases. In this case, the stations
on land as well as their ships. Destroy the ships and
bombed the hell out of the airstrips ashore, and you've
got no way to maintain air superiority. Besides, I'm to
bet that most of their aviation and munitions are onboard
the ships. They're going to want to be going back and
forth to re-arm, even if they do use the fuel depots at our
bases.

"But for now, at least the short run, they own the skies.
So I suspect that C-2 was the last American aircraft coming or going from the island for a while."

"So we go by ship," the Coast Guard officer said.
"That should be fairly easy to do."

"Yes," Tombstone said, "except for the fact that most of our fleet that was in port is probably either damaged or already under way."

"I wasn't suggesting a military ship, Admiral. There's a large compound lot just south of the Navy base—private watercraft we've seized for possible forfeiture for drug operations. They're not going to be able to cover every bit of the island immediately. I'd bet we won't have a problem getting into the forfeiture shipyard and getting out."

Adding the Coast Guard officer had been a judgment call. For the most part, he didn't possess the areas of intelligence expertise that Tombstone was looking for. Yet, as a service, the Coast Guard was probably more used to doing everything with less than any other service in the U.S. inventory. They faced shortages of assets, personnel, and just about everything else, too. Tombstone had taken a gamble that the Coast Guard officer would have some excellent suggestions. Besides, this one was a surface warfare officer, and would have served on the larger Coast Guard vessels. Since the island had major Coast Guard facilities on it, as well as personnel familiar with the waters in area, it seemed like a logical choice.

"You can get us in there?" Tombstone asked.

The Coast Guard officer smile slightly. "No problem."

"All right, then, Coastie," Tombstone concluded. "You're in charge of shore to ship movement. Let's get going before they seal the base off completely.

An hour later, the eleven officers walked down the pier surveying the impounded boats, looking for one that suited their purpose. The Coast Guard officer had the final call. "That one," he said, pointing at a luxurious cruiser with blue trim. "Furuno radar and it looks like she probably carries a fish finder. Sonar," he added, seeing the puzzled expressions on a couple of faces.

"What do we need a sonar for? And a lot of good sonar will do us without torpedoes," one officer said.

Captain Henry shook his head. "Almost anything can be a weapon, if you think enough about it. Besides, I'm not saying that there are submarines involved, or if there are, that we'll find them. But it pays to be prepared for every possibility, don't you think? Would *you* mount an operation like this without submarine support?"

The more Tombstone heard from the Coast Guard officer, the more he liked his style. "So what are you suggesting, Commander?"

The Coast Guard officer led the way to another boat nearby. It was a sharp contrast to the one he'd selected, it was battered and rusted, evidence of years of hard use in every line of her. "This," he said. "Her name is *The Lucky Star*. Might be an omen, you think?" He pointed to the aft deck. There were mounds of nets and cables. "I can get a couple of sailors to help us move this gear and to crew our boat."

"You're going to attack a submarine that we don't even know exists with fishing nets?" someone asked incredulously.

"A submarine can drag a fishing boat under, if I remember news reports correctly." They had all heard stories about U.S. nuclear submarines on covert missions snagging fishing nets.

"Only if the nets are still attached to the fishing boat," the Coast Guard officer said quietly. He looked over at Tombstone as though checking for the admiral's comprehension rather than asking for agreement. "You understand what I mean?"

Tombstone nodded. "A submarine with a fishing net wound around her propeller isn't going to do much tracking of anyone, is it? And even if it just fouls the sail, it will make it noisy enough that it'll be easier for air assets to attack. That about it?"

The Coast Guard officer nodded. "Additionally, if you checked the aft deck closely, you'll see that it's capable of handling a small helo. The sort fishing vessels use. And I think I might just be able to rustle one up."

"But who's going to fly it? And what about the maintenance?" the Air Force officer asked.

"I believe I might be able to handle the helicopter myself," Tombstone said quietly, well aware of the fact that it had been years since he'd flown rotary wing. But under the circumstances, who would quibble about his lack of current quals? Besides, he spent enough time recently flying his Pitts Special to feel fairly confident he could handle any civilian aircraft. "And maintenance—well, maybe we can draft a Coast Guard sailor who knows something about helicopters."

"I can handle that end of things, Admiral." The Air Force master sergeant stepped forward. "Before I got too senior to turn wrenches, I worked on rotary wing." Something in the master sergeant's voice left Tombstone with no doubt that the Air Force technician was more than up to the task.

For the first time in several hours, Tombstone felt the beginning of hope. He'd run the gamut of emotions during the day, from the exhilaration of starting his honeymoon with Tomboy to the agony of watching Pearl Harbor bombed. Now, listening to his team gel, coming up with solutions to problems he hadn't even anticipated, he started to believe success was possible.

FIVE

IWA Captain Henry Mitchell stared down at the fuel indicator and ran the figures one more time. It was hopeless. Back in the old days, he would have had enough fuel to divert completely out of the area. But cost-cutting measures and penny-pinching bureaucrats had set up a new protocol. After examining the weather between San Diego and Hawaii, and allowing a comfortable margin for safety, the flight was fueled with a partial load.

Mitchell's second in command, Commander Liam Nevins, glanced over at his captain and said, "It's not like we have a choice, is it?"

"No, it's not." Captain Mitchell resigned himself to the conclusion both of them had reached independent of the computer program. "We'll divert sixty miles north of Oahu and come in from the west. It's the best I can do."

Landing at another island wasn't something that either of them felt comfortable with at all. But certainly they couldn't go into their primary divert since there wasn't enough fuel left at the time they first heard the news to divert back to San Diego. Consequently, after discussion with his ops center in San Diego, Mitchell made the decision. He would try to stay clear of the area with the fighter aircraft, consistent with fuel constraints, and still land somewhere in the windward chain. Over the last hour, the possible landing sites had been narrowed down to two.

Additionally, during his discussions with flight control, another problem had surfaced. His hydraulics indicator light was flickering and the computer printout indicated that there might be a problem with the braking system. Of course, there were backups upon backups, but if he couldn't say for sure that he had a functional braking system, there was no way he was going to divert to any shorter airfield. Regardless of the military situation, he was responsible for these passengers and he needed safety equipment, foam trucks, and immediate repair parts and expertise available.

How was this all possible, anyway? Captain Mitchell had grown up during the days of the Cold War when there were still generations of soldiers who remembered Pearl Harbor. Hell, even today, there were people around who were there during the first attack. If asked, he would have said that foreign troops would never set foot on American soil. It was, even after Pearl Harbor, simply inconceivable.

Still, there had been indications throughout the world that the concept of the all powerful United States, respected throughout the world and virtually invulnerable, had been crumbling. It had begun, he thought, with the taking of the U.S. Embassy in Iran. It had degenerated since then, as America expended her military might on a series of small conflicts that really made no major differences he could tell in the state of the world. For every ethnic conflict that the U.S. or NATO stopped, another one sprang up. The much-publicized activity in Kosovo had gone on while the world ignored decades of ethnic cleansing operations in Africa. Now, with its assets and energy frittered away on inconsequential causes, the United States no longer demanded the respect of the rest of the world.

"Why did they do it?" he asked, shooting a look over at his younger second in command. "Why?"

Nevins shook his head. "I can see no good reason for them to do it," he said. "And I wouldn't be surprised if there are recall orders waiting for me when we get back to the U.S. mainland." While Captain Mitchell was a re-tired Air Force fighter pilot, Commander Nevins still had a few years remaining on his reserve commitment. As often as his civilian flight schedule would allow, he flew KC-135 tanking missions for the California National Guard.

The National Guard was completely funded by the federal government, although nominally under the command of the governor of the state of California. If so requested, however, the governor was obliged to federalize the troops immediately and transfer them to the Department of Defense. During any conflict, the tankers were among the first units recalled, as they had been in Kosovo.

"I don't like it," Mitchell said flatly, voicing the concern that was on both of their minds. "This aircraft has no business being anywhere near the combat region. We've got 320 souls on board—and they don't even know what happening." At the first hint of the conflict, Captain Mitchell had elected to terminate direct feed of news radio channels into the passenger compartment. "We're taking them into a danger area, and they don't even know it."

Nevins smiled wryly. "Well, it's not like we give them a vote, will we? Besides, no matter what they want—or what *we* want—fuel is still the main constraint. We're out of options, Captain, and we both know it."

"Don't remind me. So, just for the sake of argument, what do we do if we run into any hostile activity? Or even a Chinese air patrol?" Mitchell's voice had taken on a more strident military tone. It was the voice of a senior officer quizzing a junior one, not of one uncertain as to what he himself would do.

"Evasive maneuvers first," Nevins said promptly. "We go low, get down to the surface of the ocean. Hope we can distract any missiles by wave action. In a worst-case scenario, at least that gives the passengers a better chance of survival, too. At low altitude, we can ditch fairly safely."

They spent the next ten minutes discussing the unthinkable, planning how they would react if they ran into what they were beginning to call delicately "any problems." Finally, when they both were certain they'd exhausted the short list of possibilities, they fell silent.

"Keep an eye on the radar," Mitchell said, knowing that every moment he'd been talking to Nevins the man had had his eyes glued to it anyway.

"Roger, sir."

Mitchell kept his hands poised lightly over the throttle quadrant, his gaze roving over the compartment and the airspace around him in a continuous scan. Old habits were coming back quickly, and he could feel the familiar thrill of adrenaline surging through his body. This might not be a fighter aircraft, but he was still a combat pilot. If there was anything that could be done to keep their passengers safe, it was up to him.

MiG 33
0745 local (GMT-10)

Chan leveled off at 31,000 feet. The MiG-33 felt superbly responsive under his hands, as though she had no need of the powerful engines to remain airborne. This was her natural element, where she belonged. Not sweltering on a hot deck of a merchant ship deck outfitted as a combat, nor baking on the tarmac under the sun. The MiG belonged airborne, far from the surface of the earth.

He would have thought of her as a butterfly, had she not been so deadly. Antiair missiles bristled under her wings, each one with a range of almost sixty miles. They were fire-and-forget weapons, each with miniaturized computers on board as well as a radar seeker that kept them "on target on track" even if the firing platform lost radar contact. Once launched, the missile would proceed to the designated contact, or, if contact lost, the last known position. It would then execute a search pattern, looking for its quarry, until it found an appropriate target or ran out of fuel.

Chan's mission orders had been relatively simple—prevent any aircraft from entering the airspace around Oahu. Exactly what comprised the interdiction airspace, or how Chan should handle intruding aircraft had not been explicitly defined, but Chan was capable of determining his superior's orders. When his boss said no incoming aircraft, that's exactly what he meant.

His fingertips caressed the throttles, feeling the sheer raw power surge through the fuselage and linkages and up to his fingertips. It was by far the sweetest aircraft he'd ever flown, and this airframe in particular was the best of all onboard the ship. He made certain of that, watching carefully the technicians who maintained her, ensuring that no speck of corrosion or grease was allowed to mar her aerodynamically perfect form. Sure, there had been some resentment, criticism from the other pilots, but he made sure his bird got attention first, even if at the expense of others.

A small blip crept onto the edge of his heads-up display. Simultaneously, a soft chime warned him that his radar was holding a new contact. A blip appeared on his HUD. Next to the tactical symbol was the transmission from the contact's IFF. Passenger liner, according to its modes and codes.

Or was it? The United States had made no secret of its ability to commandeer civilian aircraft to transport troops into troubled areas. An aircraft that size could hold nearly a brigade.

But that was unlikely, wasn't it? He did the mental calculation quickly. Just barely enough time—*if* the United States had had any advance warning, had known what was coming, then they could have gotten the troops on the aircraft in San Diego and sent them enroute the Hawaiian Islands.

It wasn't likely. Every aspect of operational security had been closely monitored. There had been no warning, none. The contact was really what it seemed, a passenger liner plying the airways between mainland and the most distant state.

But what about the position? The contact was well north of the established international airways transiting at speeds and altitudes lower than that allowed for westbound aircraft, according to the briefing that he received before launching.

No, no, part of his mind argued. *You know what is happening here.*

For most of his life, Chan had been a civilian aircraft pilot himself, and he knew well the dilemma the captain of the IWA flight would be facing. All those passengers,

fuel constraints—perhaps he had no choice but to continue on to the Hawaiian Islands, diverting from his original destination tour more distant—and perhaps more
secure—location. Yes, that is exactly what Chan himself
would have done, had their positions been reversed.

But the obvious wasn't always the correct answer, was
it? Yes, with a bit of warning, the aircraft could very
well have been converted to military use. Not that that
mattered, in the end. Chan had his orders, and they were
explicit. The United States had been warned, and it chose
to ignore that warning.

Just then the modes and coats radiating from the contact's transponder changed to 7777—the international
IFF signal for air distress. At the same time, his ESM
gear picked up the weak pulse of the civilian airborne
radar. So the airliner had detected him, and was now
radiating the distress frequency.

*Or trying to deceive me. Pretending to be on an in-
nocent, peaceful mission, even as the pilot ferried troops
into Hilo for a short hop over as part of an assault force.*

Though Chan understood his superior's orders, one
part of him quailed at what he knew he must do. He knew
too well what the missiles under his wing would do to
the airliner, no matter how solidly built. It would sheer
through metal and the delicate contents like chopsticks
through rice. The missile would find a heat source, one
of the engines. It would spiral part of the way up the
intake, destroy the turbine before it exploded. Shrapnel
from both the missile and the engine turbine blades
would spin outward, penetrating and shredding the fuselage. Most likely the aircraft would break into two
pieces along the line of the initial explosion, probably
fracture along its upper surface before the lower edge
gave way. It would spill its human contents into the air,
and at least a portion of them would still be alive. Many

of them would be unconscious within seconds, those who were already seriously injured or dying from the explosion. The oxygen was simply too thin to support life. They would tumble helplessly down toward the surface of the ocean, completely oblivious to what lay below them, accelerating at thirty-two feet per second squared.

The aircraft might remain nominally intact for a few seconds later, but soon the fracture in its sides would meet on the underbelly of the aircraft. Then it would most probably break in half, dumping the contents of the passenger compartment into the air. By then, if not earlier, a spark from metal scraping across metal would ignite the now free-floating cloud of aviation fuel into an all-encompassing fireball.

By then, the true horror would be taking place 10,000 feet below. As it plummeted through the atmosphere down into thicker air, any passengers or flight crew still alive would begin to regain consciousness. They would have seconds, maybe even a full minute, to watch the earth speeding up gracefully toward them, growing ever closer and closer. Swaths of color would become mountains, trees and structures. Their view of the islands would grow smaller and smaller as they descended, until eventually the horizon shrunk down to a few square miles of land. By then, they would be able to see the details clearly. But they would have only seconds to appreciate the view before they smashed into the hard, unyielding earth.

No, better to die as a fighter pilot would, merging with his aircraft and in an instant of eternity, obliterated before he ever knew what was happening.

Chan pushed the thoughts away as he pressed the firing trigger. It was dangerous to be distracted, even with easy targets such as this. Although the sky around him was clear, there was still the American aircraft carrier to contend with. Traveling at speeds in excess of Mach one, well over six hundred miles an hour, an American fighter could be in the game at any time. Any time.

Get it over now. Do it. He felt a surge of sympathy for his American civilian counterpart, then pressed the trigger.

The missile leaped off of his wing, arrowing straight for a moment before it curved off to the right. He heard the tone in his headset telling him it knew where it was going, had activated its own radar seeker head, and was hungry for prey. Chan avoided the temptation to become fixated on his own missile's exhaust, and instead kept up a scan of both cockpit and sky.

His ESM warning gear caught the first sign of trouble, and its strident, insistent beeping soon confirmed his worst fears. He glanced at the signal parameters display, and agreed with the classification that the system had assigned it—it was an AWG-9, the tracking and targeting radar associated with the F-14.

And how far away? He resisted the urge to scan the sky around him, and instead kept his gaze fixed on the heads-up display. The computers onboard were capable of detecting and classifying the targets far more quickly than he could.

Two seconds later, he saw it. It popped up on his display, already labeled with a track number and a hostile symbol. Chan banked his aircraft away from the airliner. The missile was on its own now, a fire-and-forget weapon that require no further guidance.

The American pilots normally fought in a loose deuce position, one high, the other low and forward. The formation had proven its worth in countless battles, enabling the high position to keep a close eye on the overall picture and back up the low aircraft as necessary.

In aerial combat, altitude was safety. As the situation

warranted, he could quickly exchange altitude for speed, and sometimes that was all it took to make the difference between life and death.

So where was the second Tomcat? He pointed the nose of his MiG back toward the American, hoping to increase radar coverage slightly. It should be somewhere along the same line of bearing.

There. Another blip, another warning from the ESM. The pulses were coming tighter now as the Tomcat switched from search to tracking and targeting mode.

Where was the rest of his squadron? The last thing he wanted to do now was take on two Tomcats by himself. Although the MiG 33 was lighter and more maneuverable than the Tomcat, more like a Hornet in performance characteristics, the Tomcat was a formidable foe.

He could see them now, two silver blurs flashing against the sky. He took his eyes off them for a moment to glance down, and was horrified to see how far out over the ocean he was. How could he have been so careless? They had briefed safety precaution endlessly, and certainly the range of his missile had not required him to move in so close to the civilian airliner.

What had he done? Professional suicide, or some deeper need to actually have a strong visual on the civilian aircraft he was about to destroy?

A new tone beat in the cockpit, and simultaneously a missile symbol flashed up on his heads-up display. AMRAAM—the new, long-range replacement for the Phoenix. A fire-and-forget weapon, one with an improved secret head.

He thought he could see figures inside the black canopy of the American airliner. There was a pale oval as the pilot turned to watch him, and Chan even imagined that he could see the man's mouth open slightly as though in protest. Against the bulk of the airliner, the missile seemed minuscule, a mere sliver of metal that posed no threat to the complicated airframe it was tracking.

Chan knew better. And, he suspected, so did the airliner pilot.

For the merest second, the missile was a bright white lozenge against the side of the silvery body. Then it penetrated the fuselage and it was all over.

IWA Flight 308
0746 local (GMT-10)

Captain Mitchell saw the white contrail crawl across the sky toward him and knew immediately what it meant. He jammed the yoke forward, putting the airliner into a steep dive. The airframe shuddered, protesting against G-forces it had not experienced since the days of its final acceptance trials. Loose gear in the cockpit slammed forward against the windows, virtually obliterating his view.

The needle on the altimeter unwound at a furious rate. Auto-alarms and indicators howled their warnings. The only thing silent in the cockpit was his copilot, who knew as well as Mitchell did just how close they were to dying.

They had no chance, absent divine intervention or serious mechanical malfunction in the missile. Even if it didn't detonate, it would surely crack open the fuselage and spill both cargo and passengers into the thin air. Mitchell could see in Nevins's pale face a full acknowledgement of that fact, and he saw Nevins's lips moving silently as though in prayer. He hoped his copilot offered up one for him as well, and he hoped whatever God Nevins prayed to would understand just why Mitchell was a little too busy right now to ask for help himself.

Even with no possibility of survival, though, he had to try. Had to challenge the fate that was looming up in front of him, blocking out any possibility of a future. His wife, his children—they flashed through his mind for a split second, and then he concentrated on watching the altimeter and the alarms. If the wing nuts held, if he kept power and hydraulics for just a few seconds more—*now*.

He stamped down on the controls, throwing the airliner into a hard, breaking turn to the right. For just a moment, he thought he'd overdone it, and that she'd go into a wingover. But the control surfaces bit into the air and hauled her around in an impossibly tight turn. The debris that had crowded his windscreen now pelted Nevins.

Descending again, with no spare time to try to catch a glimpse of the missile headed their way. Heat-seeking? Would it find the jet exhaust or would it impact the fuselage? For some reason, it seemed important to know that.

As the ocean rushed up to meet them, Mitchell pulled up hard, manhandling the airliner out of both the turn and the dive simultaneously. Air speed peeled off at an alarming rate, and he caught the look from Nevins that warned him to avoid a stall. They were three thousand feet above the ocean, still descending as they waited for a miracle.

In the last few seconds, a strange peace swept over the captain. He looked up at the voice recorder microphone mounted high on the cabin and said, "I love my wife, my children, and my country. God bless us all." Perhaps, he thought, the message would be of some small comfort to them in the days that would come.

Nevins started to speak, but too late, far too late. A sharp *crack* interrupted him, followed immediately by the *whooshing* as the air spilled out of the cabin. The airliner slued around in mid-air, pivoting on its center of gravity.

The aft section spiraled off to the left, the forward part
to the right. Whatever message Nevins had wanted to
leave was lost in the fiery incandescence of the explosion
that followed.

SIX

Hot Rock stared in horror at the picture unfolding on his heads-up display. The MiG, the civilian airliner, the missile—a simple, uncluttered geometry, entirely too elegant to result in the death of almost four hundred civilian passengers.

He could see in the first instant that he was too late to stop it. Too far away, too out of position—even if he had wanted to drive his Tomcat into the path of the missile, take the hit to save innocent lives, he couldn't have. The inexorable equation of time, speed and distance wouldn't allow it.

Fury boiled in his veins. They were going to die, right there while he was watching, and there was nothing he could do about it except avenge their deaths.

"Lobo—you see that?" Hot Rock demanded, anger searing in his voice. "Come on, let's go get the bastard!"

"In case you hadn't noticed, there's a little problem with doing that," Lobo said acidly. "Like an island. Like a couple of Chinese ships probably loaded with surface-to-air missiles. Like the MiG himself, who's bound to have some more buddies out here to play patty cake with. In case you haven't checked recently, maybe I ought to let you know—it's you and me, and that's it."

Just then, a black spot appeared on the horizon. It mushroomed immediately into a boiling cloud of orange, yellow, and black. Smoke billowed up as well, quickly obscuring the flames. It streamed out behind a central mass, evidence that even though the aircraft as such had ceased to exist, its shattered remains were still traveling south at about three hundred knots.

Hot Rock swore violently. This wasn't a war. It was a massacre.

He yanked his Tomcat into a hard turn, heading directly for the MiG. Three miles of island lay below him, and he offered up a silent prayer for forgiveness, knowing that he was violating orders. But anyone would understand, under the circumstances—there was no doubt in his military mind.

Within seconds, he was feet dry, streaking over the island like a silver rocket. Over tactical, he heard the startled yelp from the *Jefferson* air controller, then a hard command from Lobo as she turned to follow him.

"Tomcat 207, this is the admiral. Just what the hell do you think you're doing?" an all-too-familiar voice demanded over tactical.

Hot Rock winced, then answered, "*Jefferson*, I'm having some communications difficulties. Will contact you when back in range. Out."

"That's not going to work, son," the same voice continued calmly. "Anything you can think of pulling at this point I've already used in every part of the world you can think of. I know what you're thinking, but you're not being paid to think. You get your ass back to the carrier this instant, you hear? There's nothing you can do about it now."

Lobo—was she in or out? Hot Rock switched over to ICS and asked, "Do you see her?"

The answer came quickly: "She's going buster to catch up with us."

USS **Jefferson**
0748 time (GMT-10)

Batman paced the small compartment that housed TFCC like a caged lion. "Get his squadron skipper up here— and I mean now!"

He turned and faced the carrier Air Wing Commander, who was just entering the compartment. In a glance, CAG took in the situation with the Tomcat.

"Dammit, why can't I have a pilot that obeys orders." He fixed CAG with a steely glare. "Do you know why, Captain?"

The CAG, never one to quail in the face of an angry admiral, nodded gravely. "Yes, Admiral, I think I do."

"Then tell me—why? Weren't they briefed on no overland operations? Don't they know that those Chinese ships are probably carrying surface-to-air missiles? Those pilots were smart enough and tough enough to have gotten through the entire Tomcat training pipeline," Batman raged. "So tell me, mister—why?"

"They're doing what you would do, Admiral, were the situation reversed. That's all."

The silence in TFCC was absolute. Batman paused in his facing and turned to look back at the display. "There's one big difference, mister. We all made it back." He pointed at the tactical display. "And right now, that's looking like a distant possibility for Lobo and Hot Rock."

MiG 33
0749 local (GMT-10)

As he watched the Tomcat race forward, Chan continued to climb. It would be altitude that he would later convert into speed, trying to entice the heavier Tomcat into an altitude game. Finally, he converted into level flight, and waited there for the Tomcats to catch him.

Just then, he got a call over his own communication circuit. He breathed a sigh of relief as he felt the sense that it was all futile lift. If he could hold on for five minutes, maybe a little more, he would have reinforcements. Four more MiGs were launching off the third Chinese vessel.

Tomcat 207
0750 local (GMT-10)

"We've got company, Lobo," Lobo's backseater announced. "Four more playmates inbound—let's get the hell out of here. As it is, we're not going back overland— we'll have to circle around seaward to get some support."

Lobo acknowledged the pronouncement with two clicks of the mike. Her attention was elsewhere, as she took station on Hot Rock's position, coming in high as he automatically took the low position.

"How much time have we got?" she asked.

"Three minutes, maybe."

Lobo nodded. It would be enough, especially with a two-on-one engagement. Especially now.

There had been a time when she wouldn't have been so certain, when Hot Rock was facing demons of his own, learning that being a fighter pilot was more than just fast reflexes and good eyesight. He'd come to terms with it several cruises ago, and since then his attitude equaled if not surpassed his technical flying capabilities.

"We're going in. Kill him now," she ordered.

Tomcat 201
0750 local (GMT-10)

Hot Rocks barreled in ahead of Lobo, slipping into the low position that was usually hers. He expected to hear a sharp reprimand over tactical, but she simply took his normal position above and behind. Somehow she knew how much he wanted this kill, how intensely personal it was for him.

The MiG was slightly above him, just starting to turn away. Hot Rock ascended, calculating the vector that would put him square on the other's tail in perfect firing position. While the envelope for an air-to-air shot was increasing every day with the advanced avionics and independent seeker heads in the AMRAAM, he wanted this kill to be up close and personal. If there was a way he could have made it a slow, painful death, he would have.

"Take him with AMRAAM," his backseater ordered. "Don't screw around with this."

"I can't. We're too close to land. Can't take a chance of overshooting and collateral damage," the pilot answered. Collateral damage—a cold, passionless word for the death of civilians, the exploding cement and bricks, the shattered bodies and lost lives.

"We don't have time for guns," the backseater argued.

Hot Rock ignored him. If there wasn't time to avenge this atrocity, then time had no meaning at all. He kicked in afterburners and rapidly closed the distance between them. Just as he settled in within range, the MiG jinked violently upward, using its own afterburners to achieve a sheer vertical climb with no movement forward. It was an impressive display of power and airmanship, had Hot Rock been in the mood to admire it.

But he'd seen the maneuver too often at airshows to be distracted by it now. Reacting instantaneously, he slammed his Tomcat into a similar maneuver, starting well before he reached the MiG's last position of level flight. No, the Tomcat couldn't duplicate the maneuver, but it could come damned close.

"Back off, Hot Rock," Lobo snapped. "You're interfering with my shot!"

"Not a chance," Hot Rock grunted, straining against the G-forces slamming him back into his ejection seat.

"Break right!" Lobo ordered. "Break right, or you're going down with him."

Hot Rock ignored her, fine-tuning his approach on the rapidly ascending MiG. Sooner or later the bastard would run out of airspace and be forced to turn out of the climb, and Hot Rock was making sure he had just enough reaction time to roll into level flight behind the MiG and blow it to Kingdom Come.

"Out of time!" his backseater shouted. "Hot Rock, we gotta get out of here, buddy! His playmates will be within weapons range in fifteen seconds, and I guaran-damn-tee you they're not going to give a shit about firing over land or collateral damage."

Hot Rock swore violently, and just for a split second considered ignoring the unfolding geometry. A few more seconds and the MiG would have to turn out of the climb, just a few more—

"Now!" his backseater screamed. "Break off *now* or I punch us both out!"

Finally, the hot red rage flaming behind his eyes loosened its hold on his brain. If he got the MiG, but added to the loss of civilian life, what was the point?

He pulled out of the climb and looked for Lobo. She was eight thousand feet below him, waiting on him.

"Buster, asshole," she snapped. "Follow me this time." She peeled off and headed back for the boat without another word.

Hot Rock followed, but snapped his head around to get one last look at the MiG as it escaped.

I'll be back for you, you murderous bastard. And next time, no power on earth is going to stop me from smearing you and your aircraft across five acres of sky.

SEVEN

Heaven Can Wait
0800 local (GMT-10)

Adele Simpson stared dumbfounded at the black smoke rolling up from the city. The transmissions on bridge-to-bridge radio onboard *Heaven Can Wait* were incomprehensible. Everyone with a radio was trying to talk at once and give the definitive and only report of what was going on ashore. Each party on the circuit seemed convinced that he and he alone had the truth. As a result, every channel normally used around the Island was completely clobbered.

"Honey? Got that chart?" a voice from overhead asked.

Jack Simpson, her husband of three days. After a long engagement and quiet wedding in San Diego, they had flown to Hawaii and rented *Heaven Can Wait* for seven days of utter solitude. Adele had grown up around water and was an excellent sailor. Her husband, Jack, a senior engineer with McIntyre Electronics and a Naval Reserve captain, was a fair hand with larger boats but that didn't necessarily mean he understood the intricacies of driving anything without missiles or a flight deck.

She reached into the chart table and pulled out a fresh

copy of the harbor chart. She used tape to hold down the corners as she centered it on the plotting table. "Got it," she reported, and then went back up to the flying bridge to check their situation.

"So what do we do?" she asked quietly. Adele was not one given to panic, and she found that panicking usually made a bad situation worse.

From the moment they heard the muffled distant explosion, they had both known something was terribly, terribly wrong. Unlike many of their fellow sailors, however, they did not try to pretend that whatever had happened ashore was none of their business and simply continue their cruise or jam the airwaves with rumors. Duty ran deep in each of them, and that had been one of the first things that had attracted her to Jack.

As a result, Adele immediately turned over ship-handling responsibilities to Jack, and gone down below to pull out a chart. What exactly he intended to do, she had no clue, but Jack seemed to think it was important.

"Okay, honey, you know where we are?" Jack's voice floated down. "Take a few bearings, and get us in as close as you can."

Adele peered out a side window and took a hasty bearing with a handheld compass. That lighthouse there—and on the other side, the jagged stack of rocks. She slid a ruler across a piece of paper, lined up the bearings, and drew in a small circle where they intersected. Just for accuracy's sake, she checked against the GPS. It was dead on.

"Got it, on both GPS and visual bearings," she reported. She hadn't questioned his request that she take visual bearings, as both of them knew that the global positioning satellite system would be one of the first ca-sualties of any real—

Any real *what? War?* How had she come to that conclusion so quickly, she wondered.

"Keep track of where we are. I'm going to call off
anything of interest, and give you a range and bearing
from our position, okay?"

"Okay. But even assuming you turn up something of
interest, how are you going to report it to anyone? No
traffic is going to get out on any circuit we've got," Adele
pointed out.

"Cell phone," her husband answered. "If I can figure
out who to call. Then there's one other option as well."

Adele took a few steps back and popped her head up
out of the hatch to look up at him. "What do you mean,
another option.?"

"This." He extended the small, black radio about the
size of the cell phone. "It is a PRC seven, an emergency
aviation radio. Saltwater activated so that if it gets wet it
broadcasts a constant beeping. It's also got a direct transmission limited range." He pointed at a toggle switch on
the side. "If I switch to military frequencies, assuming
there's someone with a receiver in range, I should be able
to talk."

"Where did you come up with this?" she asked.

"I borrowed it from my office," he said calmly. "Just
in case."

And if any one phrase characterized Jack Simpson, it
was that one. Just in case.

USS Centurion
0810 local (GMT-10)

Petty Officer Jacobs felt the foam of the headset wearing
down the skin on his ears. It had been over four hours

without a break. A couple of times, he felt his attention start to wander, just as it had during refresher training, but after a few moments, he remembered exactly how things were.

Centurion had come shallow and attempted to communicate with the naval station, with no luck. Dead static echoed over every official Navy circuit they tried. The harbor channels suffered from exactly the opposite problem—voices shouted in screams, clamoring to be heard over each other. Just outside sonar, in the control room, Jacobs could hear Captain Tran discussing their situation with the navigator.

"I recommend we make a slow, deep approach on the harbor, then come to periscope depth and see if we can figure out what happened," the navigator said crisply.

The skipper was a good man, probably one of the best officers Jacobs had ever met. But for all that, he was an officer—maybe a little too strict sometimes, maybe a little too prone to worry about things that didn't make a difference.

Still, since the situation seemed to be going to shit, Jacobs was glad to be serving under him.

"It sounds risky, coming shallow in the harbor," he heard the captain say. "There's no way sonar can keep everything sorted out to make sure we don't surface directly under a small craft."

"We'll come up slowly," a navigator said. "Our bow wave will push them away from us."

"Probably. I don't imagine they'll like it any better than I do," the skipper said.

If it were only a small boat running an engine, they would hear the vessel in plenty of time to slow their upward motion and avoid crashing into its keel. No, the problem wasn't motorized boats, although their speed could put them in danger's way. The problem was sailboats. There was simply no way to accurately detect them by passive means and nobody wanted to put an active sonar tone in the water. Counter detection considerations aside, they'd be lucky if they didn't fry a swimmer.

"We'll come to periscope depth now," the skipper said, making the decision that Jacobs had hoped for. "We'll assess what the situation is, then decide whether we're going to proceed in the harbor. If we do, it will be at periscope depth."

From a sonarman's point of view, that was the preferred alternative, but the thought of having anything just above them when they didn't know what was going on ashore made him excruciatingly nervous.

EIGHT

Batman paced furiously along the side of the island, stomping down hard on the flight deck as though to punish it instead of the pilots. There was no way he could damage the nonskid, but oh, Hot Rock and Lobo were in for it. They'd be lucky if they ever saw the inside of a cockpit again, much less flew combat missions from *his* carrier.

He could hear the calls now, with the team of two inbound on *Jefferson*. Lobo was in the lead, her Tomcat lined up hard and righteous on the flight path. He felt a moment of appreciation at the lineup, rock steady, on course, on altitude, then pushed the thought away. She might be in the lead in the air, but god knows she'd just failed every definition of good leadership he could think of.

Being an officer meant more than flying a hot aircraft and shooting down MiGs. It meant following orders, fitting your aircraft's mission into the overall battle picture, making sure that your wingman and the rest of the junior officers were also onboard with the program. And no matter how hot a pilot Lobo was, no matter that she'd earned the respect of every pilot in the Navy, she'd just screwed up big time, just as much as Hot Rock had. Oh, sure, he'd taken the chase on, but it was *her* flight, *her* mission. She knew as well as the admiral that it was her responsibility.

Can't you cut her some slack? After what she's been through?

He considered that for a moment, tempted. One part of his mind would have given anything to avoid the action he was about to take against the two, and trotting out Lobo's career would be justification for just about any breaks he wanted to cut her. During a mission in her nugget year, Lobo had been shot down. She'd spent a couple of months in a POW camp, abused, raped and generally tortured beyond anyone's understanding. That she'd withstood it, then had the sheer guts to recover and get back in a flight status—well, he wasn't so sure he would have made as good a showing, had he been in her shoes.

It's an out. Take it.

But no, he couldn't. Not if he wanted to do his duty. This was why they'd made him an admiral, given him command of a battle group, to make the calls like this one.

And to use your discretion. For a moment, Batman thought he heard the sternly lecturing voice of Tombstone. *We've pulled our share of shit, shipmate. Find a way out of grounding those two. Because in your gut, you know that's what you want to do.*

Batman sighed, frustrated. Tombstone—or at least the Tombstone he was talking to inside his own head—was right. Lobo and Hot Rock had done what every man and woman on board the carrier had wanted to do, tried to take out a MiG that had attacked an innocent, unarmed civilian aircraft. Yes, it had been too damned close to Hawaii, and yes, it could have gone brutally wrong if they'd sent the MiG spiraling into the hotels and tourist facilities crowded onto the shoreline.

But they hadn't. Lobo had waited for the shot, held Hot Rock in check, from what he'd been able to tell. They'd maneuvered the MiG out over open ocean and away from the harbor.

She used her good judgment—now you use yours.

"They're not getting off scot-free, Stony," Batman said out loud, his voice lost in the cacophony of the flight deck. "I can't let that happen—you know that."

I know. Rip 'em each a new asshole, nail them in their fitreps, give them every shitty little job you can think of. But keep them in the air. That's where they belong.

Lobo's Tomcat called the ball, indicating that the pilot had a visual on the meatball, the Fresnel lens located on the starboard side of the stern. Batman heard the voice of the LSO, the landing signals officer, chime in on the circuit.

"Tomcat 201, say needles."

"Needles say on glide path," Lobo replied.

"Roger, 201, fly needles," the LSO concurred, indicating that he agreed with her instruments' assessment of her approach on the carrier.

Lobo didn't need instruments, Batman thought. She didn't even need the LSO, not really. Rock steady on approach she held the Tomcat so steady in the air that you could almost believe it wasn't flying at all, that it was a giant balloon being towed aft of the ship.

But a balloon wouldn't make that much noise, wouldn't be howling in toward the deck with low-throated thunder. It wouldn't be getting larger every second until it looked so large that a civilian would have

thought it impossible to fit that much aircraft onto the
deck of the carrier.

Tomcat 201 slammed down on the deck with a squeal
of tires and a puff of vaporized rubber. The engines
howled as Lobo slammed the throttles forward to full
military power, insurance against an arresting wire breaking or a kiddy trap when the tailhook appeared to catch
and then skipped over the arresting wire. Without full
military power, the heavy aircraft would lack sufficient
speed to launch again off the forward end of the carrier
and would simply dribble off the end of the ship and
smash into the ocean. Missing the arresting wire and taking off again was called a bolter.

The tailhook caught the three wire neatly, pitching the
nose down hard on the deck of the carrier. The arresting
wire spun out against the hydraulic pressure with a harsh
keening noise, slowing the Tomcat from landing speed
to a dead stop. Lobo kept the Tomcat at full military
power until a yellow shirt stepped out in front of her and
signaled her to reduce power. No sane pilot reduced
power until the technician in charge of that portion of
the flight deck felt confident enough about the landing to
stand in front of the aircraft himself.

The Tomcat backed down slightly, and at a signal from
the yellow shirt, the tailhook lifted up and dropped the
arresting wire. Lobo taxied forward confidently, following the flight deck technicians as they directed her aircraft
to its spot.

Batman stood motionless, his hands on his hips, as he
watched Lobo roll her bird to a gentle stop. Behind him,
he could hear the next Tomcat approaching the stern, but
his business was with Lobo. His anger rose as he watched
the canopy slide back and saw the plane captain mount
the boarding ladder to assist Lobo and her RIO in un-
strapping their ejection harnesses. The plane captain sig-

naled that the retaining pins had been placed in the ejection seat, rendering it inoperable. Only then did Lobo rise from her cockpit and swing one long leg down over the side of the aircraft, her foot finding the boarding ladder without even looking.

Slam! The deck under Batman's feet quivered as Hot Rock's Tomcat made the controlled crash that passed for a carrier landing.

Lobo stopped next to the aircraft and spoke with the plane captain, pointing back toward the right wing control surface. The plane captain nodded. Lobo started to lead him around to the far side of the aircraft when Batman saw the plane captain point in his direction.

Lobo looked over at him. Even from a distance, Batman could see the adrenaline tide surging in her face, the joyous look of a pilot who's just done what she's trained to do, done it very well, and then pulled off one hell of a three-wire trap just to top it off. It was a look that went past glee into something divine, invincible and holy.

And it was a look he was about to wipe off her face. For a moment he wondered whether he ought to wait, let her enjoy these few minutes when, orders or no orders, she was a hero.

No. He might let her continue to fly, but that was the most she could expect under the circumstances. It was time to get this show on the road.

He waited impassively as she approached, hands still on his hips. When she came up, she said, "Good afternoon, Admiral. I guess you want to talk to me."

"Talk isn't the word I would have used," Batman said. "What the hell do you think you were doing up there? And don't give me any shit about a communications problem. Just don't even try."

"Sir, that MiG—"

"What were your orders, mister?" Batman snarled,

completely oblivious to the gender question. "What the fuck did I tell you to do?"

"You told us not to engage the MiG, Admiral."

"And what did you did?"

"Went after him sir. Over the water."

"And do you see any little problem with that? Other than the fact that I told you not to?"

Lobo paused for a moment, clearly coming down from the adrenaline high. She must have known—how could she not?—that she was going to get her ass chewed for the stunt she'd pulled up there. But it always took a few moments for reality to seep back into a pilot's brain. Batman waited until he saw the smug smile disappear from her face.

"You getting the picture now?" he continued. Over Lobo's shoulder, he could see Hot Rock taxiing into his spot. Hot Rock was dividing his attention between the plane captain directing him and Lobo popped tall in front of her admiral. "You and that little shithead wingman of yours are in deep shit. Disobeying a direct order, endangering civilian lives unnecessarily, and I can think of about four other articles under the Uniform Code of Military Justice to charge you with, but that's just for starters. A court-martial, at the very least a FNAEB—that's what you're looking at."

Hot Rock was walking over toward them now, worry on his face. Batman pointed a finger at him and shouted, "Stay right there, asshole, until I've dealt with your lead." Turning back to Lobo, Batman said, "You want to ruin your career, go ahead. But what you did also put his on the line. You think about that, if that's the kind of officer you want to be. Now get out of here before I have your ass tossed into the brig to think this over."

Batman waited for her to turn and leave, but to his

surprise, Lobo stood rock steady in front of him. "Permission to speak, sir?"

"Hell, no. You heard me."

Lobo ignored him. "If I let that MiG live, my career would have been over anyway, sir. I couldn't walk away from it. You wouldn't either, if you'd been the lead." Lobo's voice was calm but unrepentant. "If you ground me for that, I can live with it." *But not easily, the look of anguish on her face told him.* "It's the MiG that screwed up, sir. I saw people falling through the air—and parts of people. Some of them were on fire. I though—I thought I saw one of them screaming. I couldn't walk away from that, Admiral. No fighter pilot worth his salt could."

Hot Rock was out of earshot, braced at attention, the concern deepening on his face. Lobo was also standing stiffly at attention, her eyes focused on something no one else could see. Batman started to wonder what she saw, then forced himself back on track.

"Suppose you were right this time," he said, his voice colder than an arctic sea. "Suppose you were. What about next time? You get away with this, you'll think you've got a double-oh-seven license to kill in the sky. Wars aren't fought like that, lady. And the sooner you figure that out, the sooner I'll reconsider letting you fly off my carrier."

"Sir—" Lobo began. Batman cut her off.

"You and Hot Rock are grounded. Your RIOs too, for not having the good sense to talk you out of this. When you find a way to convince me to trust you again, I'll reconsider."

"But—"

"Get the hell out of my sight, Commander. Now." There was no mistaking the menace in Batman's voice. "Do you have any idea how serious a situation we're facing? Any idea of what happens outside your own little cockpits? Do you know what this all means for the United States? You couldn't possibly, otherwise I would not be having to take time to deal with your disobedience of a direct order. That's the kind of conduct that gets people killed. Now, if we're clear on what I mean, I need to get back to the war."

The full force of her predicament sunk in with Lobo. The color drained out of her face. "Aye-aye, sir," she said quietly, and then executed a perfect about-face. She walked over to Hot Rock, spoke a few words, and then the two of them walked to the island and inside the skin of the ship.

Batman watched them go. *How'd I do, old friend? I had to take them off the sked for a few days. Now the ball's in their court to figure out how to convince me to let them fly again. Shouldn't be that tough for a couple of pilots who can trick a MiG into flying out over the water, can it? Sound fair to you?*

NINE

Petty Officer Tanner walked forward until he found Captain Henry, who was deep in discussion with the two flag officers. He waited a polite distance away until the Coast Guard officer acknowledged him.

"Yes, Petty Officer Tanner?"

"The engines, sir—they've been rode hard and put away wet. I need about three days to get them in proper shape, sir. Been run low on oil for way too long and they're a filthy mess."

Captain Henry nodded, waiting. Tanner knew the score just as well as he did.

"But I can keep 'em running for a while longer, sir. Ninety percent sure of that—they'll get us out to the carrier, probably," Tanner continued.

"That'll do, then," Henry said. "It'll have to do."

"Yes, sir. When would you be wanting to get under way?"

"As soon as we can."

"Fifteen minutes, then, sir. Long enough to warm 'em up and make sure we're not going to bust apart as soon as we clear the harbor."

"Very well." Henry turned his attention back to the flag officers. "Fifteen minutes, General, Admiral."

General Haynes's eyes were still fixed on Tanner's back as the man walked back aft. "Good man, that."

Henry nodded. "That's the thing about the Coast Guard. They get responsibility early. Tanner, there—he's already been in command of one of our smaller rescue ships. He can anticipate what's on my mind because he's been there himself. By the time he makes chief and senior chief, he'll be looking at command of a larger vessel or of a shore station."

General Haynes merely nodded, but he was clearly impressed. "Fifteen minutes, he said?"

Henry chuckled. "I'm willing to bet it's closer to ten. Tanner always builds in some slack time."

The throaty roar of the diesel engines thrumming under their feet increased in both volume and pitch. There was a slight unevenness to the rhythm, a protesting, grinding noise that worried Henry. He could see that both General Haynes and Admiral Magruder heard it as well.

"Things break when they sit," Tombstone noted.

"If Tanner says he can get us there, he means it," Henry noted.

Just then, Tanner's head popped up from a hatch located on the forward deck. He shouted to be heard over the noise pouring out of the compartment behind him. "You hear it, right, sir? May settle down some as we run, may not. It's not good, though. A cracked head and bad seals."

"You still think we can get there?" Henry asked.

"Eighty percent now, sir."

Henry nodded. "Good enough," he said, his voice grim and decisive. "Under the circumstances, it's a lot better odds than those ships still at the pier had."

With the assistance of a small Coast Guard contingent, the lines holding the vessel to the pier were quickly singled up, then cast off. Henry himself took the conn, and quickly demonstrated his ship-handling skills were superb. Using a combination of rudder orders and engine orders, he twisted the stern of the ship out from the pier smoothly, then eased her into an ahead knot as soon as they were clear.

Two petty officers took bearings and plotted their position on a chart both visually and from picking off landmarks from the Furuno radar screen. A third manned the fish-finder now doubling as a sonar suite. They sang out routine reports, position recommendations and contact intercepts as though they'd played this particular pickup game every day. Lieutenant Command Hannah Green slipped behind the plot table and quietly took over navigator duties without being asked. Tombstone and the other nonsurface types did their best to stay out of the way.

"Be nice if we had a position on *Jefferson*," Henry said. "But I can't imagine she'll be too tough to find."

"Watch for any American aircraft—follow their direction back out to sea," Tombstone said. "I don't think she's far off shore—no more than thirty miles, if that. I'd want to be just far enough off land to be safe."

Tombstone had spent so much of his life inside the skin of *Jefferson* that he thought he could almost feel her out there, just out of sight, prowling the horizon like the deadly ship she was. He kept his eyes focused on one bit of the horizon, feeling an overwhelming pull, as though *Jefferson* were trying to reach him.

"Contact, possible U.S. aircraft carrier," a lookout sang out. "Bearing one seven niner, range twenty thousand yards."

Yes, she's right where I thought. Hold on, Jeff—I'm on my way.

"At last," Tombstone said, as he studied the smudge

on the horizon. *Jefferson* was far enough off shore that only a portion of her island was visible above the horizon. "That's her."

After a brief discussion with Petty Officer Tanner, Henry eased the throttles to just below full open and made a slight course correction to put the bow of the vessel dead on to the aircraft carrier.

"Let me see if I can raise them," Tombstone said. He picked up the microphone attached to the ship-to-shore radio set and turned up the volume.

A babble of noise, squelches, and at least five different languages filled the bridge. Tombstone depressed the transmit key and said, "USS *Jefferson*, USS *Jefferson*, this is—" He paused for a moment, trying to decide how to identify himself. This was not a secure channel, and the location and intentions of the senior naval officer in the area were most definitely classified information. Finally, he said, "This is Tomboy's husband. Do you copy, over?" As soon as he released the transmit key, the noise flooded the small bridge again. He tried several times but if there was a response, it was indistinguishable in the babble.

Finally, he gave up. "Be nice to let them know we're coming," he said. "*Jefferson*'s not likely to appreciate being approached by a small, unidentified boat right now."

Henry considered the matter for a moment, then said, "You remember flashing light or semaphore?"

"Not hardly. I haven't used it since the Academy."

"Me neither. Let me check with the crew."

Hannah Green spoke then. "It's not even taught in school anymore. But I can handle it."

"That photographic memory you mentioned?" Tombstone asked.

She nodded. "I won't be fast, but I'll be very accurate."

"Fine." Tombstone thought for a moment, then scribbled out a message on a piece of paper. "Send this."

PASS TO ADMIRAL WAYNE: PER CNO, REQUEST PERMISSION TO APPROACH AND DEBARK PASSENGERS. TEN SOULS ON BOARD. STONY SENDS.

"Nothing fancy, but he'll know who it is," Tombstone said.

"This isn't exactly set up for speed," Green murmured as she examined the spotlight mounted on the side of the ship. "Just an on-off switch, no shutter rig. But probably fast enough for me."

Tombstone watched her set up to send flashing light and listened to her talk herself through it. She mouthed the letters of the alphabet first, her fingers twitching on the light as she mimed the movements required to transmit each letter. Tombstone had the impression that this was how she recalled information, translating it from data into usable information by pairing it with a physical movement. Her eyes were slightly unfocused. He felt as though he were eavesdropping on some private conversation between Green and her innermost self.

Amazing, the amount of information that must be stowed beneath that pretty face. Anything she'd ever seen, anything she'd ever heard, it was still lodged in there somewhere, just waiting for her to call it up. For a moment he wondered whether it would be overwhelming.

"Here goes nothing," she said finally. Her fingers curled around the shutter mechanism, rock steady on the handle. She started blinking the light off and on.

USS **Jefferson**
Bridge
0945 local (GMT-10)

At first, the lookout thought it was just the tropical sun glinting off the ocean. The pattern was irregular, but there was definitely a pattern to the short flashes that caught his eyes as he scanned his sector of the ocean. Then he noticed that the flashing seemed to shift in a linear pattern, proceeding in a straight line directly for *Jefferson*.

The submarine? Sun on the periscope and maybe I get lucky? Without taking his eyes off the contact, he reached down and pressed the button on his sound-powered phone.

"Combat, starboard lookout. I'm holding a contact," and he reeled off a relative bearing and range, and then added, "Can't see anything yet except the sun reflecting off anything."

"Roger, starboard lookout, wait one." Silence on the line for a moment, then, "We hold a small contact doing 22 knots along that bearing. It looks to be headed directly for us."

The lookout felt a small shiver of disappointment. Not a submarine—but the next words perked up his spirits again.

"She's BCRD—bearing constant, range decreasing. Keep a close eye on her. Could be a terrorist attack of some sort."

"Yeah, that's what I'm seeing. It's not changing bearing much but it's getting stronger," the lookout said, now excited again. Then he heard "Conn, Combat. Recommend you deploy the surface gunners. Small boat, potentially hostile, inbound BCRD."

"Roger," the officer of the deck acknowledged. Seconds later, the lookout heard the 1MC spring into life.

"Secure from flight quarters. Red deck, I say again, red deck. Now man all fifty-caliber gunnery stations for surface action on the starboard bow."

"Combat, I'm coming left slightly to open up gunnery stations," the lookout heard the OOD say. "Keep me advised."

For a brief moment, the lookout wished that he'd taken his recruiter's advice and gone into a weapons specialty instead of a deck rating. If he had, he could be one of the people racing through the passageways right now to get to the fifty-caliber gun stations.

Not that being a deck rating was that bad. With some time and study, he'd probably become a quartermaster or a signalman. Hell, he was already making good progress on learning—

"Combat, starboard lookout!" he shouted, forgetting to push the button down. When no one answered, he repeated the call up, this time activating the button. "This flashing—I don't know for sure, but it looks like it could be flashing light."

Silence for a moment, then, "Lookout, Combat. Hold on, we're getting the signalmen on it."

"You can't shoot at him until you know," the lookout blurted out. Sure, he was just a junior seaman, but this was *his* contact. He'd found it, he'd noticed the lights, and he'd been the one to figure out it might be important. Even the officers on the bridge hadn't noticed that.

"Stand fast, lookout," a new voice said over the circuit, slightly amused yet chiding. "You did a good job. Now let us do ours. TAO out."

The tactical action officer. A shiver of pride ran up the lookout's spine. Usually he only talked to the petty officer running the surface plot, maybe occasionally the chief if he screwed up. But an officer!

Heaven Can Wait
0946 local (GMT-10)

"You getting anything, honey?" he asked.

"Nope. The radio's clobbered," she answered. "Everybody with a radio's screaming for information. Even if the carrier's listening, she's not going to be able to pick us up out of the noise."

He swore silently. Maybe they should just head back into port. But no, he couldn't see that as an option, not until they knew what was going on. They had food, water, enough fuel to survive out here for a week if they had to. He'd head for another island before he'd put in to home port.

"I see the carrier," he said out loud. "She's headed toward us. And something else—there's a small craft headed directly toward her. And what the hell—is that flashing light I see?"

"Does the carrier see it?"

"She has to by now. They've got a lot more lookouts that we do."

"You complaining about my performance, Skipper," she asked with a slight smile.

"Of course not. It's just that—"

"I know. You want to do something and you can't."

"Yeah. Listen, let's make another circuit a little closer in to land. Try to gather some intelligence. With a little luck, a lot of these weekend boaters will start heading in and clear the frequency," he said.

A weekend boater, he thought. *A foolhardy one, if they're headed toward the carrier at a time like this. Those gunner's mates have got to have itchy fingers right now. I wouldn't want to be the poor SOB that makes them the slightest bit nervous.*

TEN

USS Centurion
0948 local (GMT-10)

It had only taken a quick look at the entrance to the harbor to dissuade Captain Tran from even considering entering it. If the long-range view of smoking ships half-sunken in the water and otherwise empty piers had not convinced him, the message traffic that they downloaded from the satellite would have. One message sent over the battle group's dedicated circuit was of particular interest—and oddly enough, rather than go through the communications facility on the island, it came over the LINK.

Centurion was directed to break off training and independent operations and support the battle group in ASW. Admiral Wayne had assigned her a wide swath of water between the carrier and the shore, postulating that any diesel submarine in the area would most likely be lurking around the entrance to the harbor, acting as a gate guard or early alert platform.

None of the higher-level planning made much difference to Otter and Renny. Searching one piece of ocean was pretty much like searching any other spot, except for a few local differences. For the most part, it was as exciting as watching grass grow.

After another hour on the sonar stack, Jacobs finally heard a sound that brought him bolting upright in his chair. He shut his eyes and concentrated for a moment. "Bilge pump," Jacobs announced confidently. "No doubt in my military mind."

"Let me double-check with engineering," the chief said, nodding his agreement. "Make sure they haven't got something lit off we don't know about."

"I think I'd know if it were ours, Chief," the sonarman said, his voice slightly offended. "I mean, after all."

"I know, I know. But it never hurts to double-check." The chief turned away and spoke quietly into the sound-powered phone. A moment later, he left the sonar shack for a few moments, then returned with a satisfied look on his face. "General Quarters and quiet ship," he said. "Skipper wants to track this baby down and get her moving. If it's a nuke, it'll make enough noise for us to get a good classification on her. And if it's a diesel, we'll force her to suck down some battery power. Sooner or later, she'll have to snorkel and light off her engines to recharge the batteries. Then we'll have her."

There was nothing noisier beneath the water than a diesel submarine recharging batteries.

"She's coming left," the sonarman said. "Down Doppler." The chief relayed the information to the OOD. "Losing contact—damn! I think she's cross layer now."

"Let's follow her," the chief said, still holding the sound-powered phone up to his lips. A moment later, the deck tilted down at the bow slightly. "Sing out when you regain contact."

The sonarman shut his eyes, concentrating on the flow of noise into his ears. Off in the distance somewhere, a pod of whales were singing quietly to themselves, the eerie wail of their song echoing through the ocean. Closer by, shrimp snapped and popped, chittering away at their mating rituals.

The submarine herself added a bit of noise to the spectrum, although filters in place reduced known frequencies emanating from her hull. Still, even apart from the discrete frequencies, the flow of water over the hull and the limber holes, the holes through which water was pumped out, increased the overall ambient noise.

Just at the edge of his hearing, he caught the faint hum of the bilge pump. It was a slow, methodical thump punctuated by a whine between strokes as the slow speed pump drew water up from the bilges and forced it out of the submarine. Not his, no—their submarine never needed to pump bilges, or so the engineers claimed.

It was getting stronger now, easily discernable over the noise of the biologics and the distant shipping. It beckoned to him like a drumbeat.

"He's moving to the left," he said quietly, hating to even make that much noise for fear of losing the sound again. "Stern aspect." He heard the chief repeat the words.

Next to him, Pencehaven was setting up a firing solution, inputting the contact into the fire control computer, coordinating the actions with the torpedo room. Soon, very soon.

"Open outer doors. Flood tubes one and two," he heard the chief say quietly, and swore silently as the words forced him to miss a few beats of the bilge pump.

"I have a firing solution," Pencehaven announced. "Ready for weapons free."

"Hold fire, weapons tight," the bitch box over their head said quietly. "We don't know for sure who it is yet, but I'm going to try to spook him. The second you have a refined classification, you yell."

Yell. Right. Like there was going to be any yelling on

a submarine at quiet ship. Still Jacobs held his tongue and waited.

A quiet shudder ran through *Centurion* as her propeller speed increased. Noise, more noise, and Jacobs quailed involuntarily at it. It went against every instinct ingrained into his body since the first days of sub school. He looked over at Pencehaven, and saw that his friend was shaking his head.

"She's got to know we're here," the chief said. "Unless she's deaf or stupid."

"And if she's deaf or stupid, she ain't ours," Pencehaven replied.

The bilge pump ceased abruptly.

"She's gone quiet and is running. That clinches it," Jacobs said softly. "Whoever she is, she's not on our side."

Tran's voice came over his headset. "Good work. We'll check in with the carrier and let them know that they've got more to worry about than Chinese fighters."

USS Jefferson
0950 local (GMT-10)

Bam-Bam stared at the tactical screen, trying to force meaning out of the movements he saw shown there. The *Jefferson* was in the center of the formation, her escorts arrayed around her. Cruisers to port and starboard, a destroyer closer in to land, and two fast frigate astern, one in position to serve as plane guard, the other conducting an ASW search. They were still south of the island. To the northeast, a submarine datum reported by *Centurion* was getting staler as each hour passed. The *Centurion* was also still in the area, patrolling the area between the carrier and the island.

Over land, picked up by the powerful Aegis radar, six MiG-33s flew CAP stations. Satellite intelligence revealed that another ten were parked on the runway radiating heat signatures from their engines. Warmed up, then, on alert and ready to launch given the slightest provocation.

How could it happen like this? Aren't there island defenses or something—there have to be, on Pearl Harbor of all places! But who would have suspected the unthinkable? Evidently not Pearl Harbor, no more than Russian security had been able to explain the small private aircraft that somehow sneaked through their defenses to set down in Red Square.

Jefferson had two sets of fighters deployed in forward CAP stations between the carrier and land. Four Tomcats and four Hornets were in alert five on the deck, their pilots and RIOs ready to launch and one positioned on each catapult for immediate launch. Another eight fighters were in alert fifteen, with the balance of the squadron in alert thirty. Except for the hangar queens, every aircraft was ready to launch immediately.

But from the looks of it, the biggest problem wasn't airborne right this moment. The contact the lookout had spotted was still bearing down on the carrier.

At first glance, it would seem to be no contest. Tons of aircraft carrier, the mightiest fighting vessel ever built, against a small boat whose displacement could be measured in the low thousands of pounds. The airwing with its potent fighters, S-3B antisubmarine and surface capabilities, not to mention the helos and the electronics and refueling support versus a rich man's toy built for fishing, cruising fast, and pleasure.

But modern technology made evaluating the threat based merely on size a problem. Stinger missiles, with their two-mile and extended ranges, were available to anyone with the right contacts and sufficient cash. In recent years, there'd been reports of Soviet-made antiair systems flooding the weapons markets of the world, along with small and deadly torpedoes and a host of electronic jammers. Even nukes—he shuddered at that particular thought—were reportedly available in small launch containers that could easily be stowed on the deck of a boat the size of the one homing in on them. War had become a wildly chaotic matter of trying to assess threats in a world where everything was a threat.

"Anything from the signalman?" Bam-Bam asked.

"Not yet," the watch officer replied. "He just got on station."

"Keep me informed."

"Roger. How close will you let him get?"

"Three miles," Bam-Bam said without consulting his standing orders signed by the captain. "No closer."

Even that was taking a chance. While the maximum range of the new extended Stingers was reportedly slightly less than that, who knew what changes and updates could have been made?

One small missile from a shoulder-held missile tube could wreak destruction if it hit the right spot. Say the hangar bay, launched from sea by a fast and highly maneuverable boat into the massive opening below the flight deck that opened onto the hangar bay. One missile—yes, that would be enough. One burning aircraft under the flight deck, the heat stress on the flight deck and associated gear, the conflagration billowing up into the stored AVGAS and weapons stacked in piles near the island— one missile would be enough if it hit in the right spot in the hangar.

And who would be foolish enough to fire just one?

"Three miles, aye, TAO," the watch officer echoed. "Weapons free?"

Bam-Bam hesitated for a moment. Giving weapons free would leave the power to decide to fire in the hands of the petty officer manning each fifty-cal gun site. Better to hold weapons tight, deny them the right to fire until he gave the order.

Unless things got busy. Say, with air combat and a splashed bird. Did he really want to risk the delay that weapons tight would involve.

"Yes. Weapons free on any contact designated hostile within three miles of the carrier," he said finally.

Bam-Bam heard movement behind him and turned to see Admiral Wayne slipping into his chair behind the TAO station. Bam-Bam gave him a brief rundown on the situation, concluding with his decision to grant weapons-free status to the gunnery crews.

"Good call," the admiral grunted.

Bam-Bam felt a sense of relief—he'd known it was the right thing to do, but even a mighty Navy lieutenant commander didn't mind having a little positive reinforcement by the man who wore the stars on his collar. "Sir, I'd like permission to set a green deck while we've got gunnery stations manned," he said, aware that it was outside the usual safety regulations. But then, by definition, so was most combat. "A helo and a fighter paired up together might be more useful against a maneuverable target."

"Go ahead," the admiral said after a second's reflection. "But call a check-fire while you're actually launching. I don't want to lose a pilot because a gunner got too eager for a shot and forgot about the Tomcat crossing his field of fire after launch."

"Aye-aye, sir." The TAO briefed the gunnery crews over his coordination line, affirmed that there were no questions about his orders, then switched channels to the Air Boss. "I'd like to go ahead and put one section of

Vikings and one section of helos in the air," he said. "Helos are already fitted with their side door guns, right? That's after you launch a section of alert five Tomcats."

"That's affirmative on the helos," the Air Boss answered.

"Good. Green deck. Brief the aircrew that the gunnery stations will be on check-fire until they clear the area, but they better go buster once they're airborne. Launch when ready."

"Roger, copy all. Ready now, TAO." As the Air Boss spoke the words, a low rumble built through the compartment, shaking and shivering every piece of loose gear. The noise built until the edge of the TAO's computer stand jittered. A Tomcat, first, then, he could tell without even looking at the plat screen. The helos would cause barely a ripple within CDC and the Vikings barely shuddered the coffeepot. Even the potent Hornets couldn't match the low-throated roar of a Tomcat on the catapult.

A second Tomcat howl joined the first, then the higher-pitched distinctive whine of a S-3B Viking. The S-3B was nicknamed the Hoover, since it sounded like a vacuum cleaner.

Just as the first Tomcat howl started to fade away, there was a soft thunk—the catapult reaching the end of its running and releasing its aircraft off the forward end of the ship. A second thunk followed quickly, and then a softer noise as the S-3B on the waist cat launched. Then two helos taxied forward to launch spot, shuddered and lurched as they built up rotor speed, then quietly lifted off the deck and slid out over the sea. As soon as they were clear, the second set of Tomcats taxied forward to the cats.

On the tactical screen, the symbols were popping into being superimposed over the symbol for the carrier itself, slowly drifting away from the ship and vectoring in on the contact marked as a hostile surface target. The helos followed behind their faster fixed-wing brethren, but soon the air around the one contact was cluttered with air symbols.

Still the contact maintained its course and speed, still headed directly for *Jefferson*.

"Sir," the watch officer said, "lead Tomcat is requesting weapons free on the contact." The pilot, the TAO knew, would want to take the contact with his nose gun.

"Range from Jefferson to the contact?" the TAO asked.

"Five miles, sir."

"No. Tomcats are weapons tight. Gunnery stations, weapons free inside two miles. Have the Tomcats ready to go, but for now, tell them simply to stay overhead. And to make *sure* that boat *knows* they're overhead."

"Roger, sir." The stations answered up one by one.

Just who the hell are you and why are you so damned determined to make it out to my ship? the TAO thought. "Where the hell is that signalman?" he asked out loud, his gaze still fixed on the interval between the carrier and the contact. "I want an answer on that flashing light question *now!*"

The Lucky Star
1000 local (GMT-10)

"Hey, we got us an escort in," Major Carlton Early, the KC-135 tanker pilot, crowed. "Couple of Tomcats, right? Nice, real nice of the carrier."

"I'm not so sure about that," Lieutenant Commander Green said. She turned to Tombstone. "They haven't acknowledged any of my transmissions, sir."

"You sure you're sending right?" he asked, then immediately wished he hadn't asked. Green's face went still and cold.

"Yes, sir," she answered calmly, her voice matching her expression. "I've transmitted your message five times with no response."

"Keep transmitting," Tombstone ordered. He looked up at the sky, his eyes following the movements of the Tomcats, the way the helos were standing off between his vessel and the carrier, the low altitude wobbles of the Tomcats as they cut tight station-keeping arcs overhead. One broke off and jogged off five miles, then a small geyser erupted underneath it.

"Shit. They're test-firing nose guns. Green, keep transmitting. General, take another shot at the bridge-to-bridge radio. Try channels eight, nine, ten, and thirteen. Keep trying until someone answers up. The closer we get to the carrier, the more likely they are to hear us through the noise."

Heaven Can Wait
1001 local (GMT-10)

"So what're they doing now?" Adele asked Jack. She'd just come up from below for another short break only to find her new husband studying the other boat in the area through binoculars.

"Still sending flashing light, still heading toward *Jefferson*," he said without taking his eyes away from the binoculars. "I wonder if—*hey!* The cell phone—you've got it, right?"

"Of course."

"Would you get it, please?"

And that, she thought, as she headed back down to

retrieve her cell phone from her luggage, was another thing you could count on with Jack Simpson. A thank-you. Courtesy ran as deep in his bones as the reflex to prepare for potential emergencies.

"Thanks," he said as he took it from her a few minutes later. "You take the conn for a moment, would you?"

"I have the conn," she acknowledged.

Jack punched out a series of numbers on the cell phone, and then grunted impatiently as he got a busy signal. He hit redial, then entered another number.

"Who?" she asked finally.

"The Reserve Center first, then a couple of my reserve buddies if I can't get through. Somebody, somewhere, has a cell phone number for the *Jefferson*, and I think it's time we got it."

"What for?"

He grinned, a devilish look on his face. "Under the circumstances, seeing as we're mobile and in the area, I want to check in and see what we can do to help."

"How could we possibly help?" she asked.

The smile faded from his face and he put the cell phone down carefully. "You know, I didn't mean for it to be like this," he said soberly. "It's our honeymoon, after all. And you're a civilian—you didn't sign on for any of this. I'm not sure it's fair to risk you at all, not at all. In fact, I'm not sure I can bear the thought." He started slowly down the steps to the lower level of the boat.

"Jack Simpson, you get right back up here," she shouted. "Right now."

He popped back up, a look of surprise on his face.

"When I married you, I married all of you. That includes the part of you that's in the Navy. Part time, maybe, but it's there."

"No," he said immediately. "If the Navy had wanted

me to have a dependent—and that's what you are now,
my dear; it's the new politically correct term for wife—
they'd have issued me one."

"To hell with that," she said forcefully. "The Navy has
got nothing to do with it. It's my country, too, Jack. And
if there's anything we can do to help that carrier out
there, then you better count me in. Because you military
types don't have a monopoly on serving your country.
You think you do, but you don't." She paused for a moment to let that sink in, then said, "Pick up that phone
and get us some sailing orders, mister. *Now*!"

USS **Jefferson**
TFCC
1004 local (GMT-10)

The small boat inbound on the *Jefferson* had gone from
being a minor issue to the primary focus of Bam-Bam's
attention. How many times had they run through this scenario in drills? Not exactly like this, of course. The usual
scenario was a new helo flying in too close to forces in
combat, and the checkpoint of the exercise was to see
how close the TAO would let them get before they'd
shoot them down. But always in the scenario, they'd had
some way of talking to the inbound helo, of trying to
warn them off. Not like now, where he had no way to
tell the foolish—or was it treacherous?—skipper of the
boat that Bam-Bam was prepared to have him blasted out
of the water.

Still, he had to know that, didn't he? That to come
barreling up on an aircraft carrier after everything that
had happened ashore was a sure invitation to disaster.

"Range?" Bam-Bam asked.

"Seven thousand yards," the watch officer said. "Still doing twenty-two knots. Less than a minute before she's in range of the fifty-five cals."

Damn it! You're going to make me do this, aren't you? For just a moment, he wished that he could see the skipper right in front of him, right now. It would be far easier to strangle the guy himself than order what he was about to order.

"Six thousand yards—no closer," Bam-Bam said. He felt a cold sense of finality as he heard the order relayed to the aircraft overhead and the other ships around them.

And yet if he'd learned anything at all in the Navy about responsibility and warfare, it was that once a decision was made, it was futile to keep second-guessing himself. There was too much danger that you'd get fixated on one small part of the problem and miss the larger threat developing, and right now he had more than enough on his plate.

"The SEAL team—have we heard from them yet?" he asked.

The watch officer shook his head. "The Marine detachment keeps trying, but they think the team may have secured their radios."

"And if they've done that, then that means they're too busy to talk. Or it's too dangerous. Have the Marines continue to monitor the assigned frequency, but cease all callups. We'll wait for them to call us." And with another decision on the table, he dismissed the SEAL team from his mind and moved on to the next problem.

Signal Bridge
1005 local (GMT-10)

"Come on, hurry up," the lookout said, his voice sharp with urgency. "What's taking so long?"

"You think you can do any better, you step up to the plate, asshole," the signalman muttered. Binoculars were glued to his face as he stared at the incoming vessel. "Assuming I've got the right contact, then whoever's running the signal light is about as ham-handed an operator as I've ever seen. I'm not entirely sure it's not some kid playing with switches or a short in the circuit somewhere."

True, but not entirely true. Signalman Second Class Avery Hardin hadn't read light since A school, and he was finding it damned difficult to keep up with whoever was on the other light. He ran through the letter combinations, wondering if he'd gotten it right, if the guy on the other end could even spell. If he'd been entirely certain of his read on the flashing lights, he'd have smacked the lookout to kingdom come for giving him a hard time.

He could have called for help—any one of the signalmen would have been glad to come up and help him out. But admitting that he couldn't do what he was supposed to be able to do was just a little more than Hardin was capable of doing. He was the signalman on watch—he would break the light.

"They got the guns out," the lookout reminded him. A pattern of bullets stitched the water alongside the carrier as one of the fifty-cal teams limbered up. "They got helos with guns. You take your sweet time, they're going to kill that boat."

"I got it," Hardin said finally. *At least, I think I do.* "Give me that." He snatched the sound-powered phone from around the lookout's neck. "Combat, this is Signal Bridge. Flashing light from unknown surface contact garbled on other end. Best translation reads as follows:

PASS TO ADMIRAL WAYNE: CHINESE REQUEST PERMISSION TO APPROACH AND

DEBARK PASSENGERS. TEN SOULS ON BOARD. SOMEONE SENDS.

With a sick feeling in the pit of his stomach, Hardin passed the message on to the watch officer, suspecting but not knowing for sure that he'd garbled it very badly.

TFCC
1006 local (GMT-10)

"They wouldn't dare," Admiral Wayne shouted. "By god, I'll fry in hell before I see one of them bastards on my ship!"

"Sir, the signalman did say the transmission was broken and garbled," Bam-Bam pointed out. "That might not be an accurate translation. It sounds like we're supposed to understand what that means."

There was a brief pause, then Admiral Wayne said, "Ask the boat who Stony's wife is."

"What?"

"Just do it, Bam-Bam," the admiral said. "Tomboy told me Stony was going to try his best to get out here, and if that's him, we need to find out pretty damned fast. Otherwise, we blow that piece of shit out of the water."

Signal Bridge
1007 local (GMT-10)

"Ask him who Stony's wife is," the lookout repeated. "You can do that, can't you?"

"Sure, sure—hold on a second." Hardin shut his eyes,

desperately dredging up his rusty signal skills. It was taking too long, too long. He made a silent vow to himself that if he just didn't screw this up, if whatever god looked after sailors and fools let him do okay, he'd get right to work on his Morse code skills. Never again would he be caught so rusty in what he was supposed to know.

Hesitantly, he flapped the shutter on the signal light, pumping out a series of dots and dashes that he was pretty sure made up the question the admiral had asked him to ask.

"Dit-dah-dit. Not dit dit dah," the lookout said suddenly. "You screwed it up."

"Who the hell are you?"

"A striker. One who learned Morse code in four years of high school ham radio. Dit dah dit—trust me," the lookout answered. He looked deep into Hardin's eyes, saw the fear and uncertainty there, and felt a wave of power surge through him. It was his contact—his. He would make sure this was done right.

The lookout put his hand over Hardin's and clicked the shutter open and shut, moving precisely but faster as he picked up the feel of the mechanism. He blinked out the end transmission signal and then moved his hand away. Hardin said nothing.

The lookout squinted out at the vessel, still difficult to make out in the water. He saw the first flash, puny and barely detectable.

"Here." Hardin pressed his binoculars into the lookout's hands. "You talk—I'll copy." He held the grease-pencil board steady on the stand. "Go ahead. You're better at this than I am and I don't want to screw it up." It hurt to admit it, but he knew immediately that it was the right thing to do.

The lookout started echoing the blinks and flashing, mentally translating them into words as he did so. By the time the other vessel reached the end of the transmission, he'd already broken the code.

"Tomboy," he said confidently.

Hardin nodded. "That's what I got, too." He picked up his sound-powered phone and relayed the message to CDC. Then he turned back to the lookout. "Thanks, man. You know what I mean. You ever need something, you come see me." He paused for a moment, a look of shame on his face. "Everything that's at stake—I mean—hell, we're at war. I could have screwed it up big time, gotten some people killed. Thanks. Like I said—you need anything, you come see me."

"Actually, I do need something," the lookout said, still staring out at the contact—*his contact*—in the water so as not to miss any more transmissions. "I got to get someone to sign off on my watchstanding qualifications so I can take the signalman third class exam. But with the four on four off schedule, I haven't had time, and the deadline is tomorrow."

"Consider it done." Hardin smiled. "On the condition that you never screw up and get out of shape on flashing light like I did."

ELEVEN

Heaven Can Wait
1015 local (GMT-10)

Jack kept up a constant scan of the water around them
as he sat on hold, scribbled numbers down, and then re-
dialed the cell phone, but it was Adele who saw it first.
It was an odd streak of white water moving at a direction
different from the whitecaps, and at first she couldn't
figure out what was causing it. A whale immediately below the surface? A reef that wasn't on the charts?

Then it hit her, and she turned immediately to tug on
Jack's arm. "Look," she said, pointing to the east. "That
water."

Before he could answer her, a thin black metal pipe
poked up from the surface of the water, swiveled about,
catching the sun in a quick flash as it faced them, and
then disappeared. It was followed shortly by the entire
upper deck of the submarine emerging from the water,
then quickly disappearing. Jack's mouth dropped open
for a minute, then he resumed dialing even more desperately.

"Submarine," Adele said, awed. It gave her a creepy
feeling, knowing that it was cruising through the water

below them, silent, deadly, and could surface underneath them at any moment. "Ours?" she asked.

"No. Not ours. And if they don't know it's here, they've got to be told immediately." He snorted in frustration as he encountered another busy signal on the eleventh number he'd dialed. "If only I can find a way to get a message to them."

As he continued dialing, Adele kept her gaze on the sea around them.

USS **Centurion**
1018 local (GMT-10)

"Conn, Sonar, regain of contact on Sierra two," Jacobs said. After an hour of slowly quartering the strip of ocean assigned to them, he'd finally caught the first hint of the other boat.

Captain Tran leaned over Jacob's shoulder, studying the signature coursing down the waterfall display. The submarine had just executed a turn to starboard and was proceeding slowly back toward them.

"Clearing her baffles, I'd say," the chief remarked. "Just making sure no one's following her."

"Always a good idea," the captain said. "It just doesn't work if the boat following you is a lot quieter than you are."

"We might know more about her if she'd put some knots on," Jacobs said. Even with the familiarity the crew and officers developed living in close quarters, he still was uneasy venturing his opinion. "If I could get a propeller count, maybe some main propulsion, it might refine the classification."

The captain smiled, a faintly wolfish expression on his

face. "When in doubt, take the offensive. One ping."

Pencehaven toggled over to the active mode and considered his options. Ranging or targeting? The long, slow ping that they used for open area search, or the short, tight burst that would tell the other boat that someone was getting ready to shoot a torpedo up her ass? He glanced up at the captain.

"Targeting, I believe," the captain said softly. "We want her to move, that's the fastest way to get her attention."

"One ping, targeting mode," the sonarman said happily. He selected the mode then depressed the button that activated the transmitter. "Next thing we hear will be the crappers flushing as they start shitting their pants."

A hard, short burst of acoustic energy rattled the speaker overhead. It was pure tone, as solid as slamming on the hull of the other boat with a two-by-four.

The reaction from the other boat was immediate and dramatic. A low frequency line snaked up the spectrum, evidence of the diesel's increasing speed. A host of other lines appeared on the display as she started maneuvering, the up and down Dopplers gyrating wildly on the screen.

"Bet she dives," the chief said. "Try to get the layer working against us."

"Five bucks," Pencehaven said promptly, his earlier reluctance gone completely. "She's been down a long time. She's headed for the surface to recharge her battery. She might take a little excursion descending, but she's got to head for the surface real soon."

The skipper nodded. "Let's put the hurt on her for a while. Drop the tail down below the layer, but keep us shallow. I want to be waiting for her when she comes up to light off. We'll take her out then."

"What's to keep her from taking a shot at us now?" the chief asked, already reaching for his wallet.

"Because she's going to need targeting data on us," the skipper said. He shook his head slowly. "I don't think her skipper is going to risk going active, not now. Not low on batteries with a hostile on his tail. He'll try to clear the area, get up to the surface and snorkel quickly, then come back after us." He clapped the sonarman on the shoulder. "Good job. Now be ready for her when she comes shallow. They may have taken the first shot in this war, but as far as that boat's concerned, we're going to take the last."

The chief tweaked up the volume on the speaker in the sonar shack. Underneath the sea noise, the discrete frequencies of the biologics and other ship, the random noise generated by undersea wave action and oil rigs, he could hear it. A faint rub-rub-rub sound, accompanied by a slight hiss. Classic propeller noises, moving higher in pitch and frequency as he listened, indicating that the contact was picking up speed.

"You're certain it's the sub?" the chief asked.

Jacobs nodded. "It's got this *hiss-whoosh* you always hear off diesels—something about the way their propellers are configured. There's nothing surface about that noise at all. And listen—there! A slight rattle, like a baby's toy shaken underwater."

The look on the chief's face confirmed the sonarman's classification. He reached for his wallet and extracted a five-dollar bill. "Periscope rattling in the shaft," he confirmed. "She's getting ready to come shallow and take a look around."

"Flood tubes," the skipper said. "Let's finish this now."

Just then, a faint serpentine line traced its way down the screen. "Shit," the sonarman said. "It's aircraft—sir, I think the carrier's somewhere nearby. That's one of her SAR helos."

"That's what she's after," the skipper said, his voice

deadly. "The carrier. And she's just tracked out of our area. We can't follow or we'll risk bringing down one of the helos on us. OOD, come to communications depth. I'll let the carrier know that they've got company."

Heaven Can Wait
1019 local (GMT-10)

It took Jack Simpson another ten phone calls, but he finally extracted the telephone number he needed from a bored watch officer. He punched the numbers in and glanced over at Adele. "Hope they're not tying up the line." His eyes widened slightly as someone on the other end answered.

"Hi. This is Jack Simpson, skipper of the *Heaven Can Wait*. We're the small boat ten thousand yards off your port bow."

"What the—how the hell did you get this number," the voice on the other end asked.

"D.C. gave it to me," Jack answered. "Ship-to-ship is clobbered, and I had to get in touch with you. I want to report a submarine sighting."

"Listen, mister, I don't know who you are and what you want, but we're a little busy right now," the voice continued, clearly exasperated. "Now get the hell off this line and—"

"No, wait! You don't understand! D.C. gave me the number—there're no other comms right now, not secure. Listen, I saw a submarine out here. It's headed for you."

Silence from the carrier for a moment, then, "Hold on. Just—just hold on for a moment." Static crackled across the line. A new voice said, "Hello? This is Commander Busby, *Jefferson*'s intelligence officer. What's this about a sighting report?"

"That's what I was trying to tell you," Simpson said.

"We're off the coast of Hawaii," Busby said. "Not surprising."

"Not ours. A small diesel, Russian-built by the looks of it."

"How do you know?"

Simpson briefly sketched in his background, then said, "I know the difference between a U.S. sub and a Russian diesel, Commander. This one started life as a Russian, but someone's made a lot of modifications to it."

"Okay, thanks. I'm not saying I believe you, understand. But we'll be on the lookout for it. In the meantime, if you've got any more information for us, call this number." Busby hesitated for a moment, considering the possibility that the Simpsons weren't who they claimed to be. But the circumstances were so dire that he had to take the chance. He rattled off a new telephone number, then added, "That's my direct line."

"Hold on!" Simpson said, as he heard Adele shout from the aft of the ship. "Just—shit! You want to see a submarine, Commander, you look aft. I've got a snorkel mast just coming up out of the water. And from the looks of her periscope, she's up for only one reason, sir. To take a final bearing on the carrier."

TWELVE

Rising Sun
1020 local (GMT-10)

Communications Specialist Wang slid one long, delicate finger under the foam rubber earpiece and scratched. Cool air crept under the pad, reducing the heat generated by the close-fitting earpiece.

He sat in front of a bank of advanced electronic equipment, most of it cobbled together from different pieces of U.S. gear. Thanks to the Clinton administration, they'd had no problem assembling the highly specialized equipment needed to detect and monitor a vast range of frequencies in the electromagnetic spectrum. The entire system was modeled on the U.S. Echelon program, a systematic way of monitoring every form of electromagnetic transmission for key code words and names.

But while funds had extended to the latest in electronic wizardry, his government was not as concerned about creature comforts as the Americans were. The earpiece he used was of the cheapest foam rubber available, hot and cloying over ears rubbed raw from hours of monitoring voice transmissions.

How did the Americans stand it? he wondered. By all

reports, they had neither the dedication nor the patriotism of the crew on board this ship. They'd all been specially chosen, they were told, for this most dangerous and honorable mission. Wang tried to believe that himself, but he couldn't help noticing, as did a number of his crewmates, that the thrill of danger wore thin after hours of staring numbly at the electronic console.

Still, his job was a vital one. While the gear could detect voice transmissions and sort them out into separate conversations, it could not tell what was important from what was trivial. Even if it had some rudimentary analysis capabilities, those would have been useless under current conditions. In the hours since the first launch, every radio frequency had been filled with the babble of a thousand voices. It took every bit of his concentration just to flip through the channels, continually scanning for anything of interest, simultaneously translating while trying to keep track of a hundred different circuits.

Wait—what was that? His hand froze over the frequency selector button. Something from the aircraft carrier? Yes, that was it. A cell phone communication, something about intercepting a stone. Or was it stony?

Without looking behind him, he raised a hand and motioned to his supervisor. He heard a slight click as the more experienced linguist started monitoring the frequency as well.

"Is it important?" Wang asked softly, careful not to disturb his supervisor's concentration.

"I do not know. Keep listening." In the background, Wang could hear his supervisor speaking to the watch officer, careful not to disturb his concentration. How the man could manage it, he had no idea. In the next few seconds, he realized they'd hit a gold mine.

Stony. That was one of the words, along with the variation Tombstone, that Wang had been told to listen for.

Was it possible? His breathing quickened slightly.

His supervisor broke in immediately. "You have done well."

Wang heard him passing the information over the tactical air circuit, vectoring one of the potent MiG-33s in toward the location they'd triangulated on.

The Chinese carrier had a series of electromagnetic receivers mounted along the deck, each one looking like a small chock or deck fitting from a distance. In reality, the system had a sensitivity that rivaled the U.S. Navy's own passive intercept capabilities. By positioning different receivers at different places on the ship, one vessel could accurately triangulate the location of any transmitter.

Wang listened carefully, but there were no further transmissions over that circuit for *Jefferson*, nor were there any mentions of Stony or Tombstone. But it did not matter. The one brief transmission was enough to enable them to pinpoint the location of the vessel fairly accurately. The MiGs would do the rest.

Wang felt a moment of pride, realizing that he was indeed performing as vital a mission as his supervisors had claimed. He felt a fierce thrill of anger through his body, and wondered if the Americans on board the small Coast Guard vessel would ever know that it was he, Wang Su, who had been responsible for their destruction.

Heaven Can Wait
1021 local (GMT-10)

"That's what I'm trying to tell you, sir," Jack Simpson said, frustration in his voice. "I don't give a damn what all your sonars tell you. I saw the periscope right off my starboard bow. Now what are you going to do about it?"

Normally, the reserve officer was a quiet, easygoing man. His subordinates hated playing poker with him, because they could never tell when he held a good hand. And indeed, his ability to remain calm when everyone else was losing their perspective was one of the reasons he'd risen so quickly through naval ranks. In addition, within his own intelligence community, he had never had to deal with people who doubted his technical competency. Not after the first time they'd met him.

"Look, what did you say your name was again?" Simpson asked. "Do I need to get out the lines that the CNO himself can call you and tell you to listen to me?"

"You know we don't pass names over an unclear circuit," the intelligence officer on the other end replied coolly. "And I think I'm capable of evaluating your information without the CNO's oversight."

"Then you'd damned well better get moving, mister," Simpson snapped. "I make the distance between that submarine and your aircraft carrier less than eight thousand yards right now. Unless you've got two helos airborne right now, enroute his datum, you'd better head to your abandon-ship positions."

Silence on the other end for a moment, and he could hear muffled voices on the other end, as though a hand were covering the receiver. Watching the carrier as he waited, he saw a helicopter aft of her, which had clearly been in plane guard duties, veer away sharply and head toward *Heaven Can Wait.*

"I see your helo," Simpson said, his voice now calm and collected. At least they were doing something. It might not be enough, but at least they'd go down fighting. "Tell him to come to his left a bit more—yes, that's it," he said as the helicopter corrected its course. "He should be overhead the location in about five seconds. There."

A thin sliver of metal separated from the undercarriage of the helicopter and fell blunt end down toward the water. The splash it made was quickly lost in the gentle swells.

"All right, *Jefferson*!" Simpson howled. He turned to face his wife, glee on his face. "He listened to us—that asshole finally listened!"

A look of stark horror swept over Adele's face. Her face was pasty white, her finger trembling as she pointed toward the water behind Jack's back. "How—how far away from us is it?" she asked, her voice quavering.

Jack felt like a heavyweight champion had just landed a punch to his gut. He felt his own features start to mirror hers as he turned around to look. "Maybe two thousand yards," he said, already running for the controls.

"And what's the max range?" Adele asked, close behind him.

"Too much. If it doesn't find the submarine right off, it'll start circling for another target. Depending on whether it's a wake homer or an acoustic homer, it will try to acquire an acceptable target."

"Like us?" Adele asked.

Jack shook his head. "Most torpedoes have a depth setting on them. They won't attack a surface ship."

"Most. Not all." It was clear from Adele's voice it was not a question.

Jack nodded once, his hand already rock solid on the throttle controls, his other whipping the wheel around. "Most."

He kicked *Heaven Can Wait* up to top speed, and felt the boat surge powerfully under his feet. Adele, forewarned by watching him, was firmly anchored with her hands clamped down on the railing.

"Not to worry," Jack said, with more confidence than he actually felt. "We'll soon be out of range."

"How fast do they go?" Adele asked.

"Later, Adele," he said, casting an anxious look back over his shoulder.

"How fast?" she insisted.

"Fifty knots, some of them," he shouted, the noise from the water and the engine already drowning out his voice. "Some of them."

He saw Adele brace herself against the vibration of the boat as it slammed up and down violently against the swells. The gentle water that had rocked them into their afternoon nap was now hard as cement as the boat accelerated rapidly to its top speeds of forty-five knots. *Heaven Can Wait* was a capable ship, but she was not built to endure high-speed chases through these seas for too long. She'd be all right for a while, though—long enough for them to clear the area.

Jack heard a tinny voice speaking somewhere in the area, and he glanced down at the cell phone in his shirt pocket. They were calling him, asking him something, but right now he couldn't take his hands off the controls long enough to answer. Adele solved his problem for him, plucking the cell phone out of his pocket, keeping one hand firmly in place on the railing. "You'll have to speak up," she shouted into the phone. She held it close to her ear, nodded once, then looked over at Jim and smiled. "What's the depth setting on the torpedo, sir?" she asked into the phone.

The answer came, and was evidently satisfactory. Despite the pounding of the boat, she relaxed ever so slightly. "I understand—yes, we'll keep the line open."

She looked up at Jack and smiled. "He said it's set for forty feet, shallow for a diesel submarine, but still deep enough to avoid most of the pleasure craft in the bay."

Good thinking, Simpson thought. And just how the hell had they managed to put the pieces together so quickly and change the depth settings on a no-notice submarine problem?

Maybe it wasn't as no-notice as you think, one part of his mind suggested. *After all, they are the United States Navy, and you're just a reservist.*

"He said keep an eye out for any explosions or debris," Adele shouted, clearly relieved that they were outrunning the torpedo. What she didn't know, Jack thought, was that a margin of error was built into every intelligence estimate of their range.

He concentrated on ship handling while Adele kept a sharp eye aft for any information that could be related to the carrier. Five minutes later, he was relatively certain they were out of danger. He throttled back into a comfortable cruising speed and changed course slightly. "Still talking to them?" he asked in a more normal tone of voice.

Adele nodded. "But he said he might be too busy to talk to me for a few minutes. Jack, they're talking about MiGs." Her deep blue eyes pleaded for reassurance.

"MiGs are fighters," he said, drawing her close with the hand that had been on the throttles earlier. "They're interested in other aircraft, not little pleasure boats like us."

"But what if they know? What if they know that we're the ones who reported the submarine?"

"They won't." For the second time in as many minutes, Jack had spoken with more confidence than he felt.

"But look," Adele said, pointing back toward the vessel they'd seen heading for the carrier. "Somebody is shooting at the water, aren't they?"

A slight buzz, barely at the edge of their perception. Aircraft unlimbering their nose guns.

"Yeah, they are," he admitted reluctantly. "But those aren't MiGs, honey. Those are Tomcats—F-14s. The good guys. And just to be safe, I think we'd better get out of the area," he said, releasing her to goose the boat back up to a higher speed, settling it in at around thirty-five knots, well below maximum but still faster than was comfortable.

"If those are Tomcats, then who are those?" Adele said, pointing back toward the mainland.

Sunlight glinted off four sets of wings as new aircraft barreled directly toward them.

"Let's not wait to find out. Hand me the cell phone." Jack reached out and took it from Adele. "You still there?"

"Yes, Captain, we are." There was a new note of civility in the other officer's voice. "Any reports on our torpedo run?"

Jack refrained from pointing out that he'd been a little busy getting out of range to watch carefully, but said, "No sign. No explosions, no water spouts, no debris. I'd count this one a miss, sir."

"I was afraid of that. Well, you've got the number, now."

"Wait. That small boat that's got Tomcats overhead— if you haven't seen it already, I think they're about to have playmates. Four other aircraft, look to be MiGs, maybe a twenty-nine, maybe a thirty-three, I can't tell, yet, but they're headed directly for your Tomcats."

"Got 'em," the voice from the carrier said. "We're going to be a little bit busy here for a while. Suggest you clear the area. You don't want to be directly underneath—well, just clear the area. Check back in with me when you're at a secure location."

The line went dead. Jack pushed the OFF button to conserve energy. Sure, now they tell him to clear the

area. Even if it was too little too late, it was still good
advice.

"You watch the aircraft, I'll watch the water," he said,
handing over the steering to Adele. "Just stay to this
heading until we're out of sight of all of this."

TFCC
USS Jefferson
1030 local (GMT-10)

The helo attack on the submarine first reported by *Centurion* had taken up most of Bam-Bam's attention for the
last several minutes. While he waited for damage reports
or any indication that the sub had been hit, he turned his
attention back to the two small boats converging on the
carrier. The lead helo reported that the submarine contact
had not been hit, and that it had turned tail and was
running back into the *Centurion*'s area of responsibility.
Bam-Bam ordered them to break off prosecution and
leave the bastard to *Centurion*'s tender care. Now, with
one of the small boats identified, he turned his attention
back to the one still in doubt.

"What the hell's going on out there?" Batman roared.
"That can't be Stony, not if the Chinese are so eager to
keep us from taking a shot at that boat."

Lab Rat shook his head. "But why would they be sending a small boat out toward the carrier?"

"Hell, I don't know," Batman raged. "Spotter for the
submarine, maybe a kamikaze-type suicide mission.
We've been over the scenarios often enough, over the
damage a small boat can do to this bird farm. You're the
intelligence officer—you tell me why!"

Lab Rat felt a slight shiver run through his fingers, and

clasped his hands in front of him to keep it from showing. Too many hours, too many long hours crouched in front of consoles, hot air blasting down his neck while the metal in front of him radiated heat, trying to sort through the often contradictory indications and warnings, electronic intercepts, and other intelligence that came pouring into SCIF. The first strike on Pearl Harbor had only been days before, but already he felt twenty years older, the sheer horror of it, the unbelievable anger raging through the ship that anyone would dare reach out and touch American soil.

"Well?" Batman demanded. "Who is it, Lab Rat? Stony or some Chinese deception plan to get in close to the carrier?"

"It's ours," Lab Rat said.

"You certain?"

Lab Rat shook his head. "There aren't any certainties in this world. You know that, Admiral." He raised his head, clenched his hands even tighter, and stared at the more senior officer.

Batman looked astounded. Lab Rat was normally the most calm and confident of all his officers, invariably quiet and well-spoken. It was unthinkable for him to be anything but completely courteous. *But what do you expect,* one part of Batman's mind asked. *You ask the impossible. Just because the impossible has happened—this whole attack—you expect equal miracles for your side?*

"So how do we tell?" Batman said in a more reasonable tone of voice. "Within the next three minutes, I mean." He pointed at the screen. "Because when that blue gaggle intersects that red gaggle, we've got no more choices left to make."

"I have an asset in the area," Lab Rat said immediately. He fished his cell phone out of his pocket and punched in the number that Jack Simpson had given him. "I don't know if they're close enough to tell, but maybe. Hell, there's even a chance that they're not who they claim to be. But under the circumstances, it's worth a shot." He plugged the jack in the back of the phone into a patch panel nearby, circumventing the carrier's electromagnetic shielding by wiring its small internal antenna to one of the massive arrays atop the carrier's mast. He listened to the ring signal, and then said, "This is the carrier. I've got a question for you to answer for us."

Heaven Can Wait
1031 local (GMT-10)

"You want us to what?" Jack Simpson asked. "Conduct an intercept?"

"That's right," the other voice said firmly. "We have to know who's on that pleasure craft—good guys or bad guys. And as you might notice, our fighters are otherwise engaged at the moment."

"Yeah, but—" Jack glanced over at his wife. An offended expression started to cross her face. She reached out and grabbed the phone from Jack.

"What is it you need to know?" she demanded.

There was a pause, then the voice said, "As I was telling your husband, we need to know who's on that pleasure craft. Can you get back in and see if it's Americans or Chinese?"

"Of course we can," she said firmly. "My husband is an officer—and I'm an officer's wife. We're on our way." She handed the phone back to her husband, a fierce expression on her face. "Don't ever let me catch you pulling that shit again, you understand?"

Jack could only nod, speechless and overwhelmed by

his admiration for the fierce warrior he'd married.

Before Adele had even hung up, he'd turned toward the small boat that they'd seen flashing light at the carrier. Within five minutes, staring through the binoculars, he had his answer.

"Hit redial," he said, as he approached the other vessel. "Tell them that whoever is on that boat, they're not Chinese."

Tomcat 201
1035 local (GMT-10)

"That's it," Bird Dog said. "Little bastard's at two and a half miles. He's toast."

"Hey," Gator protested. "Two miles. And we're weapons tight."

"And he's not. Look." Bird Dog rolled over inverted and stared down—up—at the surface of the water. "You see that group up forward? Ten gets you twenty that's a Stinger they're holding."

"Bird Dog, you ass. Roll this bitch back over before I puke." The sight of the sea rushing by, seemingly just outside the canopy, was disconcerting.

"Did you see it?" Bird Dog asked, swiftly rolling back into the proper orientation.

"I didn't see shit that looked like a Stinger."

"You weren't looking hard enough."

"Hard enough to see that that looked like Navy uniforms they had on."

"Bullshit. Just tan pants and shirts. And there was a guy in BDUs, too. Carrying a machine gun."

"I didn't see a machine gun, either," Gator argued. "For all you know, that's a charter out of the Officers'

Boat Club that got caught out on the harbor when it all went down. It could be that they're *trying* to get *back* to *Jefferson* because that's where they came from.

"Bullshit," Bird Dog repeated. "By the time I come back around and get in position, they're going to be at two miles."

"I know. Okay, line up on them, but you're still weapons tight, remember," Gator said.

"Weapon's tight my ass. Lobo wasn't all that weapons tight the other day and she went after a MiG," Bird Dog muttered.

"Oh, so that's what this is about? Your girl chases a MiG, you gotta chase something?"

"No."

"You happen to see Lobo's name on the flight line when we launched?" Gator pressed. "Or Hot Rock? Or their RIOs?"

"No," Bird Dog said, doubt in his voice now. As he talked, he put the Tomcat in a hard bank, crossed over the bumpy stream of his own exhaust, descended another hundred feet and lined up on the stern of the boat. He toggled off a short burst of gunfire, the rounds striking the water two hundred feet off the starboard side of the boat. Every tenth round was a tracer. Even if the boat had missed the sound of the Vulcan canon or the stitches of water, they would have seen the tracer rounds.

"Stop that right now," Gator snapped.

"Just verifying that I'm mission capable, RIO," Bird Dog said innocently. "What's your problem?"

"The reason you don't see them on the flight deck is because they're grounded, asshole. Maybe permanently. And Batman didn't take any prisoners—he grounded the fucking RIOs too, for not having the balls to keep their pilots under control. So hear me when I tell you this— you fire off one round, one single round, before you're weapons free and I'm punching out. By myself. You can hightail it back to the carrier and explain to Batman and CAG why you came back without your RIO and your canopy, and why you fired on an unarmed civilian boat. You got that?"

"If I hit it, it's because I'm weapons free and it's inbound on the carrier,"

"Fine. Find yourself another RIO," Gator snapped.

"You're always threatening me like that, and you haven't punched out yet," Bird Dog observed. He was now barely a quarter mile astern of the boat. He jogged back slightly on the throttle and retrimmed the aircraft for level flight. "You don't have the balls to do it. And there are sharks down there."

"Sharks, hell. I'd rather face them than Batman if he's pissed at you. I get a leg bit off, at least I'll get a medical discharge instead of a court-martial."

Bird Dog fell silent. The warm throb of the Tomcat's engines wrapped around them like a muffling blanket. "Call *Jefferson*, ask them what the status is," he said finally, a note of resignation in his voice.

Gator breathed a sigh of relief. He toggled over to Tactical and contacted the operations specialist who was acting as air intercept controller. "Interrogative the status of that boat inbound," Gator asked.

"Check fire, all stations, all aircraft," a new voice said over tactical. "This is TAO *Jefferson*—boat inbound on *Jefferson* is friendly, repeat, friendly. Check fire all stations, weapons tight."

"Holy shit," Gator breathed, "A friendly."

"You copied that, Tomcat 201?"

"Roger, copy redesignated as friendly. Who the hell's on that boat?"

"Admiral Tombstone Magruder and escort," the AIC said promptly. He paused for a moment, then said, "TAO says for you to stay overhead and make sure no one bothers him on his way in. You copy? Escort duty, 201."

"Roger, copy all," Gator acknowledged. He switched his mike to ICS from Tactical. "Bird Dog, we've got five minutes to get our story straight. Start talking."

Lucky Star
1100 local (GMT-10)

The ass end of the carrier loomed up out of the swells like an improbably massive cliff jutting up out of the middle of the ocean. Even though Tombstone had seen it many times from this aspect, mostly from liberty boats launching, the sheer size of the carrier always awed him. It seemed so small when you were airborne, vectoring in on final approach, your balls climbing up into your stomach every time as you wondered how in hell you were going to get sixty thousand pounds of Tomcat down onto a deck that looked like a postage stamp. It never got any bigger in the air, not unless you were unlucky enough to come in too low—unlucky or just plain not good enough, although they never thought of it in those terms. From the air, it was always too small, too far away, the gray tarmac rushing up to you at impossible speeds as you tried to maintain altitude, pitch, and orient on the center line and the three wire.

But here, looking up at the bulk of the ship jutting up from the sea, it was as though it were an entirely different ship.

"Big bastard, isn't it?" the general asked.

Tombstone nodded. "She packs enough firepower to get the job done. No more."

"Well, then." The general moved over to the side of

the small craft and started expertly handling the lines. A couple of the junior officers jumped to assist him, along with a Coast Guardsman. He accepted help from Captain Henry, but waved the others away. Tombstone watched his smooth, sure movements. "Done this before, I take it?"

"I've sailed all my life," the general said.

"Maybe you joined the wrong service?"

The general shook his head. "Even if I thought that, it's a little bit late in my career to be changing services, don't you think?"

On board *Jefferson*, the fantail was flooded with sailors, all of them clad in safety gear. The controlled chaos took shape into a receiving party under the direction of a crusty old chief petty officer.

The Coasties edged the boat in, then tossed the lines to the waiting sailors. Soon the boat was snugged up against the bumpers, and the team prepared to depart.

"Right behind you, Admiral," the general said, solving the delicate question of who was senior and who would debark first. Tombstone appreciated the courtesy, but reflected that they would have far too little time in the coming weeks to worry about seniority among admirals. Besides, once they were aboard *Jefferson*, it was all Batman's show, anyway.

Tombstone climbed handily up the ladder, returned the salutes from the waiting officer, then said brusquely, "No bells. We've got work to do."

The commander standing in front of him nodded. "If you'll follow me, Admiral." He saluted each of the more senior officers as they came aboard and then led them forward toward the interior of the ship.

Five minutes later, they stepped into the admiral's conference room just off TFCC. A meeting was in progress, led by Batman.

"—until we get some reinforcements," Batman was saying, then broke off his sentence. He stood, rounded the table, and approached Tombstone, holding out his hand. "Good to see you again, Admiral. I understand you've come to help us out?"

Tombstone nodded. "Not that you need it." He turned and introduced the rest of his team, following in his footsteps like a path of ducks.

Batman nodded. "Find a seat if you can." He pointed to a ring of chairs around the outer bulkheads of the compartment. "We're just going over the situation as it stands now. Just got some interesting news from the guys on the ground. There's a SEAL team in there—you may have heard of them. Second squad from SEAL Team Seven."

"Man, that was fast," Tombstone said.

"Fast, no. They were up in the mountains doing some cross-training with the British SAS when the world went to shit."

Batman looked somber. "It's a helluva thing, Stony. Who would have thought we'd see it in our day?"

"I'd have thought you already got the story from Tomboy."

Batman nodded. "She briefed me as soon as she got onboard. But is there something more to it?"

Tombstone shook his head. "Surely you're not accusing me of planning my honeymoon around national security, are you?"

"No, I guess not. Still, mighty odd coincidence."

"That's what it was—a coincidence."

"Well, like I said—pull up a chair and let's get started."

Batman briefly filled in the newcomers on the situation in the air, ending with, "Hard as hell to do anything about it while they're over the island. We run the risk of killing more Americans than they already have."

"So I take it the SEALs have some plans?" the general said, the first words he'd spoken since his greetings to Admiral Wayne and his staff. "They usually do."

"We're talking to them on SINCGAAR, and comms have been good all day. They're going in tonight to take care of the hostage situation at the Comm Center. I don't expect to hear from them during the operation—they're operating on red signature orders—but we may see some fireworks."

"And then what?" the general asked, his voice almost demanding.

"There's an amphibious task force sitting off the coast," Batman said. "As soon as we get the go order, we're in."

"Without air superiority?" Tombstone asked sharply, visions of metal shards in the air, fragments of flesh burning as jet fuel exploded around him, companies strafed into oblivion as they made the beachhead filling his mind. "It'll be a disaster if we do that."

"I know. That's what we're talking over right now—how to take those damned skies back from those bastards. Any ideas you've got, speak up."

"Let's see what you've got so far," Tombstone said. "Then we'll talk."

THIRTEEN

USS Centurion
1105 local (GMT-10)

A submariner from even five years earlier would not have recognized the periscope operations now under way on board *Centurion*. There was no black pipe protruding from the water, no telltale fan of disturbed seawater or rooster tail behind it. Instead, a tiny black bump barely marred the surface of the ocean, extending up only far enough to clear the tops of the waves.

The boat was equipped with the latest in fiber optics technology, and a single thin thread mounted on a stiffening support rod allowed complete flexibility in periscope operations. There was no more sluing the periscope stand around to take a three-hundred and sixty degree view, no manual changes of the resolution, and no switching between the search scope and the attack scope. Instead, the fiber optic line supplied a highly digitized picture that looked oddly clean to the team in the control room.

"At least we know where the good guys are now," Captain Tran said. He tapped one slim finger on the profile of the USS *Jefferson*, now centered in the scope. "I don't like being this close to her, but it's not like we have much choice. Not with the other submarine in the area." He glanced over at the sonar gang, his eyes asking the question he didn't need to voice.

"Nothing yet, sir, but sooner or later she's going to have to come up to snort," the chief sonarman said. "Odds are she'll run back away from the carrier to do that, and as soon as she does, she's in our area."

Tran nodded. The inherent limitations of the diesel submarine made her most vulnerable to detection and attack at nighttime. Still, they'd seen more than their share of unusual capabilities on this contact. And if it was really determined not to be detected, it might find a convenient hole to lie up somewhere for the night, running on minimum hotel power and conserving its batteries. Maybe stretch it to one, two days without snorkeling. More than enough time to creep silently through the clear waters and make a run on *Jefferson*. And if that happened . . .

No, it wouldn't. Because he, Captain Franklin Tran, was going to shove a torpedo up its ass so hard and true that there'd be nothing left of the other submarine except some scattered fragments of metal on an ocean floor already littered with the remains of too many hulks.

Captain Tran was a second-generation American. His grandparents and parents had fled Vietnam during the war. Their first years in America had proved hard for all of them, with a society seething with prejudice and anti-war sentiments hardly the ideal culture to yield up such a warrior as he had become. Indeed, if he thought about it—which he didn't—Tran would have wondered whether it was a wise decision at all on the part of his country.

But from his earliest years, Tran had known that he wanted to join the Navy. Join the Navy, and earn his way into the most elite fighting force the service had to offer. He'd been entranced with submarines from the very beginning, even as a child, marveling that so relatively small a ship could be such a potent force. During the Cold War, his admiration for the submarines increased as he understood the terrible pressures under which the captains and their crews operated.

His grandparents had been rabidly patriotic Americans, grateful for the chances their adopted country would give them and their progeny even as distant relatives and cousins who had not made it out were slaughtered in their homeland. His parents had been slightly less enthusiastic, deeply encultured in the anti-war sentiment that had sprung up during the Cold War. Their son's preoccupation with entering the Silent Service had at first bemused and then irritated them.

Despite their efforts, he'd applied for and been accepted to the Naval Academy. He'd earned his class standing of three out of his graduating class by dint of sheer efforts. There were other Asians in his class—three, to be exact. They'd all majored in mathematics, but his closest racial counterparts had shown no interest in submarines. For the most part, they'd gone into staff positions rather than front-line warriors.

But Franklin Tran was a warrior. It was in his blood, rooted so deeply in his genes that he had been able to conceive of no other career in the United States Navy. He'd applied for, been accepted in, and survived his interview with Admiral Rickover with flying colors.

His early career had gone much as any junior officer's would, marred by a few ugly racial incidents in the wardroom. Still, he had ignored the slights, seeing them as merely another obstacle he had to overcome to fulfill his dream—command of a United States Navy submarine.

Now, twenty years later, serving in a Navy in which

the role of submarines had varied greatly over the decades, he had his own ship. He had been in command three months, just long enough to get her through workups and a nuclear reactor inspection, and they were just preparing for their first patrol when the orders had come. When the tragedy had occurred.

Even now, he was not entirely sure what had transpired ashore. He only knew that there was trouble, big trouble—and he was on scene.

"I want that submarine," he said quietly, his voice carrying to the farthest reaches of the control room. "She's got no business in our waters—no business at all." He looked around to ensure they were paying attention. "We find her, we kill her. Any questions?"

"No, sir!" the chief of the boat, or COB, said enthusiastically. He thumped one of the sonarmen on the back. "And this here's the guy who's gonna do it for you, sir." He turned back to the sonar screen, as if there were some way he could will the enemy into sight.

Heaven Can Wait
1115 local (GMT-10)

"There she is again," Jack shouted. He reeled off a range and bearing, and Adele relayed the information to Lab Rat over the cell phone. "Turning to meet us, honey. Tell them I think—oh, *shit*." In one quick motion, Jack bounded down the ladder and to the stern of the boat. He whipped out a knife and cut the mooring lines holding the lifeboat to the stern of the ship. It smacked down in the water with a sharp smack.

"Jack, honey? What's happening?"

"Stay at the stern," Jack ordered. "Don't leave here,

okay? I'll explain in just a minute." His words drifted back to her as he darted back forward.

"I don't know what's happening," Adele said to Lab Rat on the phone. "Jack's got the dinghy in the water and he's in a hurry. This might be—" She broke off as she saw Jack anchor the wheel in place with two bungie cords and then slam the throttle all the way forward. *Heaven Can Wait* leaped forward.

A moment later, Jack was by her side. "Come on— we need to get to the lifeboat," he said.

"Jack, exactly what is—"

Adele never had time to finish the question. Just as she started speaking, her new husband shoved her overboard.

USS Centurion
1120 local (GMT-10)

"Torpedo in the water," Jacobs sang out, his hands flying over his console. "Russian-made, acoustic and wake homer. Bearing one seven nine, range—*sir*. It's headed away from us!"

"Away?" Tran asked. "You're certain? The carrier the target?"

"Yes, sir. And from the looks of it, it's going to be close."

Close, hell. That bitch has all the maneuverability of a broached whale. By the time she gets up to speed, the torpedo will be on her.

Just as suddenly, a new acoustic signature arced across his green display. It showed a small propeller churning frantically as it headed at right angles to the torpedo's path. It looked like—

Tran confirmed Jacobs's suspicion a moment later.

"She's a decoy," he said unbelievingly. "Her skipper's got her cranked up loud enough that the torpedo is going to make a run on her instead of the carrier. If it works, it's got to be one of the bravest things I've ever witnessed."

They watched in silence, almost afraid to breathe, as though the sound might distract the valiant race to death being played out before them. The torpedo continued on its course, making one small turn as it evidently found the carrier's wake. They all heard the seeker head come on then, the small targeting sonar filling the water with its chillingly high chirps.

But then the small vessel made one final leap out in front of the torpedo, its acoustic signature completely drowning out that of the carrier. The torpedo seemed to hang in the water for a moment as though confused, and then made a sharp turn to the left.

"It took the bait!" Tran said, his voice almost loud for a submariner. "It's going for it."

It was a short, futile chase. Despite the small craft's speed, the torpedo easily overtook it. The sonarmen took their headsets off in anticipation of the detonation. They heard a dull thud outside the submarine as the torpedo found its mark.

"No firing solution," Pencehaven announced. "Captain, I've lost contact on the other sub."

"Find her," Tran ordered.

Heaven Can Wait *debris*
1125 local (GMT-10)

Jack swam up next to her. "You okay?"

"You bastard, you could have warned me," she sputtered.

Jack nodded. "I could have—I didn't." He pointed toward the lifeboat. "We can fight about it once we're onboard."

Jack struck out for the life raft, Adele close behind him. Within a couple of minutes, they'd closed on it, and were hanging on either side of it as they gathered their strength to pull themselves into it. "Let's not wait around," Jack said. "Warm water."

His last comment needed no explanation. While the warm waters off of Hawaii meant that they certainly wouldn't die of hypothermia, it also provided its own hazards—sharks. Many varieties swarmed through these waters, and the noise from the torpedo would have undoubtedly attracted them if the Simpsons' flailing through the water hadn't.

She turned back to look at *Heaven Can Wait*, now bearing down on a steady course and speed as she had been when they'd left her.

The noise itself was just a dull thud, as much felt through the water as heard borne by the air. The boat seemed to shudder, then she spun around violently to port. For a moment, Adele thought the boat would bear back down on them and run them over, as though some unseen hand were at the steering wheel.

Then *Heaven Can Wait* slammed over to her right, whirling quickly through forty-five degrees, then ninety. A huge hole gaped in her exposed hull, and seawater washed in hungrily. There was another series of short, sharp explosions as cold seawater hit hot diesel engines. For a moment, Adele thought that the boat would simply sink quietly, but then it exploded.

"Down." Jack yanked Adele down under the water momentarily, but his strength was insufficient to keep them down with their personal flotation devices. She looked up through the water and saw debris shooting over them. God, if it hit the life raft, what if they were trapped here in the water with sharks? They popped up to the surface and saw that the life raft was still intact.

Heaven Can Wait was now a smoking, flaming pit of debris scattered across the surface of the ocean.

FOURTEEN

Aside from launching the rest of her USW assets and moving further out to sea, there was little that *Jefferson* could do about the enemy sub that had the sheer audacity to launch weapons at the carrier. The contact was clearly inside *Centurion*'s zone of safety, and while *Jefferson* could patrol the edges of that zone, no weapons could be launched inside the box. There was too much danger of taking out the *Centurion* instead of the Chinese boat. As much as he wanted to throw every torpedo he had into the water, Batman was forced to stand back and let the sub do her job. Besides, he had other things to worry about right now.

The compartment was beginning to smell of too many people too long between showers. Batman surreptitiously checked the odor emitted by his own armpits and winced. No matter—they'd all been there before, and a little body odor wasn't going to keep anyone from doing their duty.

And he was willing to bet that the guy on the other end of the SINCGAAR line smelled even worse. Yet, there was not even a trace of exhaustion in the calm, confident voice coming over the circuit.

"Nukes—no doubt about it. The Chinese have demanded that we withdraw from the area or they'll detonate one on the CINCPACFLEET compound. Sir, there's no doubt in my military mind that they mean it." There was no panic in the SEAL's voice, just sheer, gritty determination. "Give us twelve hours, Admiral. I think we can solve this problem."

Batman swore silently, then picked up the mike. "You have RADIAC equipment?"

"Negative, sir. But we've got other intelligence that tells us it's stashed in a truck. We know where to look, and we know what we're doing. It's not like there's many other options, sir. As long as they've got that nuke ground zero at CINCPACFLEET, we're short on options."

No mention of the hostages, Batman noted. It gave him a brief chill. But the SEAL officer was right—the probability was not high that anyone located within the compound would survive the conflict, anyway. Odds were that when the Chinese got ready to pull out—and pull out they would eventually—the hostages would be executed. There was little or nothing that they could do about that, but they could lose that battle and still win the war. And the key to that was eliminating the nukes.

Air superiority—that was the other problem, Batman reflected wearily, running one hand over the slightly gritty, greasy skin on his forehead. No matter which way he turned the problem, he didn't see much of a way around having to engage the Chinese directly over the city. And that meant casualties, lots of casualties, and most of them civilians. There was absolutely no way to evacuate the island, especially not after the demonstration of power involving the airliner as they'd taken possession of the island. No, the people that were on the ground would have to remain there for the duration, although Batman would do his damnedest to try to avoid collateral damage.

"Twelve hours, you say?" Batman asked again.

"Yes, sir. If we're not clear by then, the admiral may wish to consider a surgical strike on the compound itself. Kill the bomb the hard way." No trace of fear showed in the SEAL's voice.

Batman ran the list of hostages' names through his mind again, recognizing that most of them were old and dear friends. They'd all started out together in the Navy, some in the surface pipeline, some in the air pipeline. But the more senior you got, the fewer peers you had, and he knew each one of those men well. Could he order their death?

Of course he could, just as he ordered pilots into the air every day, knowing that they might not come back. But this had a different feel, that the men on the ground would die without having a chance to fight back. "Twelve hours," he said finally. "After that, we're coming in."

Batman clicked the microphone off and then hauled himself out of the elevated chair that was his in the center of TFCC. "I'll be in the conference room if you need me," he said to the TAO. "Get the rest of my staff in there."

Heaven Can Wait *Lifeboat*
1140 local (GMT-10)

Adele felt the deep, hard ache in her muscles as she wielded the paddle. They'd only been at it for thirty minutes, yet the aircraft carrier seemed no closer than it had when they'd started. The seas were running against them, not a good sign. Yet Jack's face was a mask of grim determination as he relentlessly dipped, pulled, and swung the paddle back over for another stroke. The muscles in his back bulged, and Adele could tell from the slight angle on the lifeboat's bow that he was doing more work than she was. She threw herself into paddling with renewed determination.

Aircraft and helicopters from the carrier were filling the air over them. At first she thought that they were the rescue forces, but Jack explained that they were all antisubmarine assets. They might catch the attention of one of the pilots, but rescuing the Simpsons would take a distant second place to tracking down the sub.

Suddenly, Jack stopped paddling. He leaned over the rubberized bow and peered at the water ahead. Then he turned back to Adele, an expression of disbelief on his face. "There's someone in the water ahead," he said.

"Another boater?" Adele asked.

Jack turned forward, then motioned at her to keep paddling, picking up his own paddle at the same time. "We have to pick him up," Jack said. "Of course we do."

Adele groaned when she saw how far off their course the rescue mission would take them. Every foot lost in the battle against the waves was a foot that would have to be regained later if they were to make safe haven at the aircraft carrier. Yet Jack was right. The international law of good seamanship said that every vessel—and that would include their life raft—was obligated to assist in rescue-at-sea operations. She put too much force into her next stroke, broke the rhythm of the movement of the boat through the water, and silently offered up a prayer and a request for forgiveness.

Within five minutes, they closed on the figure in the water. Adele could see that he was almost unconscious, floating partially on his back and held aloft by a personal flotation device. She slowed her strokes in time with Jack's as he maneuvered the life raft upwind of the figure. When they were within ten feet, she gasped.

"He's—he's Chinese!" she said.

Jack nodded but didn't answer. She saw his knuckles turn white on the paddle.

And what the hell were they supposed to do with a Chinese? Had he been part of the crew responsible for directing the submarine to attack them? Had he fueled an aircraft that now flew over Hawaii, or loaded the weapons that had killed so many already?

She could tell that Jack was going through the same thought process. Finally, he sighed, and laid his paddle down in the boat. "Hold me steady," he ordered.

Adele dipped the paddle into the water with delicate sculls, holding position on the man in the water. Jack leaned over the rubberized side and grabbed the man by the back of the personal flotation device. She saw him jerk upward, drawing the man partially out of the water, the corded muscles along his back and arms standing out like iron. With one final, massive heave, he pulled the man into the lifeboat.

The man was on the smallish side, even for a Chinese. His eyes were half closed, his face badly burnt and blistered. He was talking quietly, mumbling, incomprehensible in his native language. Jack ran his hands over the body, checking for breaks or wounds. Finally, he leaned back on his heels and said, "He's been out here a couple of days, I'd say. Amazing that the sharks didn't get him. Nothing seriously wrong that I can find with him, other than exposure and dehydration."

"I wish the sharks had gotten him," Adele said bitterly.

"I know." Jack gazed off into the distance, as if wrestling with his own conscience. Finally, he sighed. "Well, they didn't. And he's here now." He reached behind him and drew out a water bottle. He uncapped it carefully, then tilted the mouth of it up to the sailor's lips.

Fresh water cascaded across the man's burnt and swollen lips, and the sensation appeared to revive him slightly. His eyes were slightly wider open, and with an effort, his eyes focused on them. He tried to lift one hand to assist and hold the bottle, but he was too weak. Jack shook his head, said, "No, just drink."

Jack held the bottle at the man's lips and gently sloshed the water into his mouth. The man started coughing, deep, chest-wrenching spasms that kept him from drinking. Finally, when the last cough subsided, he drew in a deep, shuddering breath and motioned for the water bottle again. This time, he was able to take small sips. Jack held the water back when he tried to drink too deeply all at once.

"Slow at first, fella," Jack said. "You drink too much too fast and it'll all come back up again."

The man reached for the bottle again, this time taking smaller sips. Jack poured some onto a cloth and wiped it gently over the man's face. Then he applied an antiseptic ointment to treat the sunburn. "He needs medical care," Jack remarked. His gaze drifted away from the man and back to the *Jefferson*, still so far away. "And there's only one place to get it." With a sigh, he picked up his paddle again.

Adele picked up hers as well, already feeling the blisters rising on her palm. The man said a few words in his own language that she could not understand. But the meaning was clear from the tone of his voice. Thank you sounded the same in just about any language, no matter what words were used. She nodded in response, but refused to look at him.

"Do you speak English?" Jack asked him.

"Yes." The word was soft and hesitant. "I understand better, but I can speak."

"Which ship are you from?"

The sailor rolled over to a sitting position and pointed at a ship in the distance. It was the massive vessel that Lab Rat had called the *Rising Sun*.

USS **Jefferson**
TFCC
1145 local (GMT-10)

The room boiled with seething frustration, coming equally from Batman's staff and the pickup crew Tombstone had brought along. Tombstone stepped to the head of the table, greeted the two senior flag officers, then said, "All right, people. We need a plan, and we need it now." He briefly sketched in the details reported by the SEAL team on the ground and concluded with, "I want some options. Everything from soup to nuts, people. We don't know what we're going to be ordered to do, and I sure as hell would like to have a plan that doesn't require me to send MiGs down in flames right over the city."

There was silence for a moment, then the army general spoke up. "Sooner or later, we're going to have to put troops on the ground. Air power alone never wins a war, regardless of what you've been told about Kosovo."

Batman nodded. "Point well taken, General. But before we start transshipping troops, we're going to want to have air superiority." He pointed at Tombstone. "My old lead is going to have to worry about the bigger picture, along with the rest of your team. My question at this point is how do we most effectively use our air power under these circumstances?"

"Where is the amphib ship, Batman?" Tombstone asked. "How many days before we can have troops in the area?"

"They should be in area tomorrow," Batman replied. He glanced over at his Marine commander to confirm the information, who nodded. "How and when we deploy them is another matter altogether."

General Haynes chimed in with, "The Marines can take the beach, but we're going to have to have regular Army to secure the rest of the island, I suspect."

"Maybe, maybe not," the Marine countered. "As long as we can keep the division from getting ashore, we ought to be able to handle it. The airport is the key, along with the communications center. Once we control the airport, we can bring in your additional assets as needed." He paused for a moment, then admitted grudgingly, "Sure wouldn't hurt to have some of your urban warfare folks, though."

Haynes smiled grimly. "You'll get them."

The discussion that followed centered on the logistics involved in first securing air superiority and simultaneously denying the Chinese amphibious forces access to the beach. Tombstone was struck by the cold professionalism that developed so quickly. Just hours before, they'd been strangers, but in almost no time, when confronted by an operational problem, they'd melded into one of the finest fighting teams he'd ever seen.

And he'd picked them. Along with General Haynes, of course, but it was essentially his team, his planning that brought just the right combination of characters, specialties, and training together. He was the one who led the problem solving, drawing out opinions from the quiet special forces intelligence officer they'd picked up, tamping down the exuberant Air Force KC-135 pilot when he got out of hand, mining the depths of Hannah Green's seemingly bottomless wealth of information, guiding the discussion and making the decisions at the key points. *He* had been the one to give Coast Guard Captain Henry full go-ahead on what had seemed like a risky scheme. In the end, although he was drawing on the talent of the men and women he'd assembled, it was his war.

He felt a surge of vindication, and wondered a moment at its source. Then it came to him, dawning gradually with a sweet feeling. Tomboy's comments about needing a combat pilot rather than a planner had cut deeper than he'd thought. Yet, he had to admit, she'd been right. And now, looking at the results of his work, he knew that what he did was just as valuable—more so, in the long run—than strapping his ass into the cockpit of a Tomcat and howling off toward the horizon with his hair on fire.

Finally, Tombstone cut off the discussion with a wave of his hand. He leaned forward over the cheap metal table, his elbows planted firmly on it, his dark, somber eyes burning in his tired face. "I don't see any way around it, Batman," he said softly. "The Chinese are using our desire to avoid collateral damage against us. As long as they think we are afraid to act, our hands are tied. So, at least in this room, I think we need to come to a conclusion about that. In the end, it's going to be sheer, brute force air power that wins the day in this one."

Batman sat silent for a moment, then nodded. "We're going to take some civilian casualties," he said heavily. There were a few groans around the room, and Batman quelled them with a harsh look. "I don't like it any better than you do, but until we come up with another plan, there's no choice."

"We wait until the nuke is neutralized, then we pound them out of the air." Batman slammed one hand down on the table. "If I get enough tanking support, I can run every one of those little bastards back all the way to the mainland. And by God, that's just what I intend to do."

"We have to consider the possibility that the nuke may be detonated as well," Lab Rat said. A horrified hush fell over the room. Lab Rat shrugged. "We're trying to consider all scenarios, right? Well, I'd say it's a little premature to assume that the SEALs will pull this off." He held up one hand to forestall protest. "I'm not saying they won't, mind you. God knows that particular team has pulled off the impossible too many times for me to count them out entirely. Still, we're dealing with an enemy that may not hesitate to waste that many of its people to prove a point. When it comes right down to it, we have to be able to take the hit and keep on ticking." He glanced around the room, meeting everyone's eyes with his own stern look. "What I mean is, we need to completely assess our EMP hardening. Take the precautions now that you would in the event of an actual detonation. Be ready for it, people. I'm not going to say it's going to happen, but if it does and we're not prepared, it's too late to do anything about it."

Tombstone sighed heavily. Had it come to this? Contemplating the detonation of nuclear weapons on American soil? He shook his head, trying to pretend he didn't believe it was possible, but he'd dealt with the Chinese too many times in too many scenarios to believe otherwise. In the Spratly Islands, they'd killed their own people just to make it look like they were under attack. In too many theaters of war around the world, he'd seen the difference in the mentality between the Chinese and the American forces. The use of the manned torpedoes, for instance. Even the Russians were more understandable than the inscrutable Chinese.

"Perhaps," a small voice said from the back of the room. Tombstone turned to see who had spoken. It was his Air Force tanker toad. "Perhaps, sir—Admiral, I mean—well . . . I can coordinate the tanking problem for you," the Air Force guy continued. "I speak the language, sir. I'll put gas in your sky all day long if you want. But on the other thing—well, the Chinese are new to this whole carrier aviation thing, aren't they? And they're flying VSTOL aircraft, not conventional launch, right?"

"Stating the obvious, young man?" Batman asked.

"Maybe so, sir," the Air Force officer said, his voice gaining confidence. "But a lot of this is foreign to me. Right now, I'm the best example of ignorance you've got on this boat. Ship," he corrected hastily when another Navy officer jabbed him in the ribs with a sharp elbow. "Anyway, I was thinking about the last time Pearl Harbor was attacked, and some of the strategies used then. I think, knowing what I've heard about your ships and your aircraft, that there might be a way to lure them out into the open."

Tombstone and Batman exchanged incredulous looks, then Tombstone said in a suspiciously mild voice, "Why don't you tell us what you've got in mind?"

The Air Force officer did, sketching in a broader plan, then filling in details as he went along. Soon other staff members were chiming in, and a murmur of excitement grew in the room.

Finally, Tombstone cut off the discussion and turned to Batman. "You know, we pulled something like this before. It worked out then, didn't it?"

Batman nodded. "Damned if it didn't. But what makes you think it will work twice in a row?"

"Because it has to." Tombstone turned back to the assembled group. "It's a go."

Heaven Can Wait *Lifeboat*
1240 local (GMT-10)

As the minutes turned into hours, their passenger steadily regained consciousness. By the time she could tell that they were finally making some progress toward the aircraft carrier, Adele could tell that his eyes were focused, he was paying attention, and he understood what they were trying to do. He took small sips of water, carefully rationing it, and offering it every so often to one of the others. He'd made motions as though he would take her place in rowing, but he was clearly too weak to be able to do so. Adele thought she detected a note of relief in his face when she refused his gestures.

The aircraft carrier seemed to grow larger all at once, and she could see the fine details on the side of it, the rivets holding the plates to the strakes, men moving around inside the hangar bay, and the discharge of water from scuppers located along the edge of the flight deck. How had they managed to gain on it so fast? And then suddenly the explanation struck her. Jack must have known it all along. Of course, the aircraft carrier was not stationary in the ocean, waiting for their poor little life boat to make its approach on her. She'd been maneuvering the entire time, at first steaming away from them, and now coming at an angle toward them. How stupid of her not to have figured that out—no wonder it had seemed that they were making no progress toward the carrier. Now, however, it was a different story.

"Got the flares out?" Jack asked.

She held up one for his inspection. "Right here."

He took it from her, and started to light it. "No guarantee that they'll break off what they're doing and come pull us out of the drink," he said, watching her face carefully for any trace of fear.

"I know that." Involuntarily, her eyes strayed to their passenger. Not everyone was as diligent about following the rules at sea. But dammit, they were American citizens, and they had lost their boat while trying to protect the aircraft carrier. Surely that ought to rate some consideration for pulling them out of the drink.

But the aircraft carrier didn't know that the two—make that three—occupants of the international orange lifeboat on their beam were the same ones that their intelligence department had been speaking with earlier. The cell phone had been one of the casualties of the sinking.

The helicopter that had been trailing behind the aircraft carrier now took a slight tack toward them. It maintained its distance, hovering in the air approximately six thousand yards away. Adele could see the glint of sunlight off the canopy, off binoculars peering out at her.

Jack put the flare aside and picked up the flashlight. He blinked out SOS, the international signal for distress, and then the Morse code word for medical. There was no response from the helicopter.

For a moment, Adele despaired. Then, as she watched, another helicopter launched from the deck of the aircraft carrier.

Of course the plane guard helo wouldn't conduct SAR, not when flight operations were under way. Safe recovery of the air crew was the helo's first priority. The helo had vectored over to take a quick look at them, and then had clearly reported its findings back to the carrier for dispatch of a second helicopter.

Fifteen minutes later, a second helicopter was hovering over them. The air crew lowered a horse collar, and a swimmer dropped into the water beside them to assist them into it. One by one, they were winched up into the belly of the helo.

"Anyone hurt?" an air crewman shouted at her, striving

to be heard over the noise of the helicopter.

"Exposure," she shouted back, pointing at their passenger.

The air crewman did a double take as he noted the identity of the sunburned, exhausted passenger. She saw his lips form into an O, as if he were whistling. "Friend of yours?" he asked.

In brief, shouted phrases, she relayed how they had managed to pick him up out of the ocean, and filled him in on their earlier communications with the carrier. She saw comprehension dawn on his face, and one hand stole up involuntarily to cross himself. After she'd finished, the air crewman left them with the corpsman and made his way forward to talk to the pilot. She could see the pilot glance back at them, then pick up the microphone.

The air crewman came back to them. "Be a translator waiting for us when we land, ma'am."

She nodded, vaguely irritated that the status of their passenger was of more interest to the aircraft carrier than the rescue of its two spies. Still, she could understand their concern.

As they settled onto the deck of the aircraft carrier and a crew of people came rushing out to meet them, Adele noticed a small boat tied to the stern of the carrier. It was smaller than *Heaven Can Wait*, but she had a foreboding feeling as she looked at it.

FIFTEEN

Renny shut his eyes and leaned back in his chair. He clamped his hands over the headset, pressing the foam surrounding the earpieces into the sides of his skull. There, almost at the edge of his hearing—no wait, it was gone again. He sighed, and looked over at Otter. "You got anything?" he asked, taking a look at the passive display as he asked the question.

Otter shook his head. "You're hearing ghosts, man," he said.

Renny started to argue, then froze as a familiar sound came peppering his ears through the earphones. "Helicopter," he breathed, his voice almost a whisper.

"I got it, too." Otter toggled the sound-powered phone on. "Conn, sonar. Hold incoming helicopter."

"Classification?" the OOD asked.

"Not ours, that's all I can tell you." A seriously worried expression spread itself across Otter's face. "I don't like the feel of this at all, buddy," he said softly to Renny. "Not one little bit."

As they listened, the sound of the helicopter both in

Renny's ears and as translated on the passive acoustic display became louder and louder. The increase in frequency indicated that the aircraft was approaching them directly. Finally, the up Doppler stabilized, then began wavering up and down in frequency.

"It's directly overhead," Renny said, now whispering for certain. Around him, the rest of the crew were setting quiet ship stations, and he noted the red light flashing to indicate general quarters. "Right above us," he whispered.

A small splot then, a second motion in the ocean, the noise that a drop of water falling into the bathtub makes. Renny came bolt upright in his chair. "Sonobuoys, I think," he said, his voice barely audible. "Whatever it is, they're tossing something in—" A massive explosion rocked the water around the ship. Renny screamed, ripped the headphones off and bent over, moaning. The automatic gain control had managed to block out most of the noise, but still enough acoustic energy had made it into the headsets to feel like an arrow lancing straight through his skull.

The ship rolled hard to port and then back to starboard as the OOD fought to stabilize her. A down angle on the deck developed almost immediately. Renny felt the nauseating motion of the ship going into a hard lefthand turn while still unstable from the explosion, and diving at the same time.

"Depth charges," he said, barely able to hear his own voice. Behind him, his chief tapped him on the shoulder and nudged him out of the chair. Renny's earphones were already on the chief petty officer's head. "Depth charges, goddammit, who the hell uses depth charges anymore?"

A second explosion answered that question quite handily.

The ship dove more rapidly now, but it was controlled

movement from the ship seeking out a deeper layer of
water rather than a submarine damaged by the blast. The
further down they got, the further away from the helicopter overhead they'd be. Still, submerging held its own
dangers. As the pressures increased, so did the potential
consequences of even a small pinhole leak in any gear.
Outside the submarine, the water pressure was increasing
rapidly, bearing down on every square inch of the hull.
Since water was thicker under pressure, it also served as
a better medium for conducting acoustic energy. A blast
at this depth would be amplified, not only in the amount
of energy that hit the submarine but in the damage that
any breach in hull integrity would pose.

"How the hell did they find us?" Otter demanded. His
hands were dancing over the passive acoustic display,
checking out different frequencies, searching frantically
for any hint of a threat around them. They both knew the
answer to his question.

"Nobody was active, and there were no sonobuoys in
the water," Renny said. "It was the other submarine—he
must have heard us on his passive gear, then surfaced to
radio in a position report."

"But when? When!" Otter demanded. He scrolled back
to the time on the display. "When was it that you heard
something?"

Renny leaned over and pointed to a spot on the graph.
"There. Right about then."

"That was almost thirty minutes ago," Otter said. "You
certain about that?"

Renny shook his head. "Not entirely, but the time fits.
He would have had to be fairly close to us to have heard
anything at all, and you know he wouldn't want to be
anywhere around if they were going to drop depth
charges. So he crept up, took a listen, then sneaked back
out of area before he came shallow and radioed in a po-

sition report ... By now he's at least ten miles away, maybe more."

"All hands, this is the captain," Tran's voice said over the loudspeaker. Every section of the submarine had been turned down to minimum volume, but the boat was so quiet that his voice was easily distinguishable. "It appears we have evaded the helicopter, and I'm going to be bringing the ship back to a shallower depth. Maintain silence about the decks, even after I secure you from general quarters. It looks like we had the bad luck to be directly under that helicopter while he was dumping garbage or something."

Renny grinned, admiring Tran's ability to stay so calm during a crisis. It had been exactly the right thing to say to the ship and crew.

"And I figure we got us a little score to settle with the submarine we left alive back behind us," Tran's voice continued, the slightest hint of a Southern drawl in it now. "So suck it up, stay quiet, and I promise you— we'll get that bastard snitch before he pulls back into port again."

There were no cheers, no applause, but everyone in the submarine could feel the invisible surge of enthusiasm that rallied through the crew. "We'll move back into position on the Chinese aircraft carrier."

As the ship maneuvered, a loud, clanging noise reverberated throughout the entire hull. It seemed to saw at Renny's bones, sink through his flesh, and then fade away into nothingness. Without having to ask, he knew what it was. The ELF antenna wire that they had been trailing had been severed. Their submerged communications with the outside world had been cut off. Sure, they could still come to communications depth and receive and transmit messages, but that would mean giving up the cloak of invisibility that was the submarine's primary defensive weapon.

TFCC
1255 local (GMT-10)

The call came from the SEAL team just as Batman was mobilizing his forces to deal with the troop carriers headed for shore. Tombstone's pickup team jumped as the speaker crackled to life.

"Bad news, sir," the remarkably clear voice of the SEAL team leader said. "We found the weapon—but it's inaccessible. The Chinese dumped it in the shallow water. I've got some plans for getting to it and disarming it, but it's going to take a little while to set up. In the meanwhile, if your sub could keep the area clear around it, it might lessen the chances of detonation. Over."

"Roger, copy all. We'll do what we can, Murdoch." Batman's voice was grim. He turned to Bam-Bam. "Get off a message to *Centurion*."

USS Centurion
1300 local (GMT-10)

Captain Tran fought his impulse to pace, schooling himself to stillness that rigged for silent running required. He would not allow himself the luxury of expending some energy through pacing the small compartment. Not only would it not have achieved anything, but it would set a bad example for the rest of the crew. Silent ship meant just that—no unnecessary movement, no talking, and above all, no pacing the deck.

This was the hardest part of submarine warfare, probably the reason that the men who served on these ships bore the name "silent service." It was a game of cat and mouse, of waiting, of staying submerged and hidden while you waited for the other fellow to make a mistake. Captain Tran held this as an article of faith, that there was no crew as superbly trained as the one on board an American fast attack submarine. Granted, the equipment gave them every edge as well, but it was the crew rather than the steel that encased them that he placed his trust in.

A movement aft caught his eye, and he turned to see the sonar chief holding one finger up in the air. Slightly ashamed at the relief he felt to be moving, Tran padded silently over to the console. He studied data displayed there before asking in a whisper, "Is that her?"

Jacobs nodded. "Bilge pumps, I think," he said. "It's faint, and intermittent."

Tran reached for a spare set of headphones jacked into the input line and slipped them over his ears. He was always surprised at how much more quiet it was with the headphones on, even on a submarine at quiet ship. He could hear his own heartbeat, hear the steady rhythm of his own breathing as blood coursed through his veins. And, just at the edge of perception, he heard the sound that had alerted his sonar team. There it was again—a faint *hiss, whine* followed by a *thump*. Bilge pumps or some other slow rhythm machinery on board. It didn't matter exactly what—the important point was that it wasn't one of theirs.

"Not as watertight as we are, perhaps," he said, making an old joke. Bilge pumps weren't normally run for leaks inside a submarine—any leak would be almost instantly fatal, as high pressure water rocketing into a hull would probably precipitate cascading casualties faster than any crew could keep track of them. No, bilge pumps were used to pump over the small discharges that steam, an occasional leaky pump, and just sheer spillage accumulated in the lower parts of the ship. Still, his joke was met with a slight smile from the crew.

"Targeting solution?" the sonar chief asked.

Tran nodded. "Completely passive. No one is supposed to know we're here until the carrier is ready to move." He could see by the expression on the chief's face that this didn't sit well. They had contact, albeit a tenuous one. They would have a firing solution within seconds. Every second that they let pass with this submarine still alive in their home waters ate at them. He now regretted the one ranging ping that he'd ordered earlier. That extra bit of uncertainty might have now worked in his favor.

"We can't do anything right now with the situation as it is on the land," he said, and briefly debated with himself just how much to explain to the crew. He knew about the nuclear weapon located on the island, but was it necessarily something he needed to tell the rest of the crew? Most of them had families, girlfriends, even parents on the island. Would the additional worry about the families distract them from the job at hand? And more importantly, would knowing that their friends and loved ones were in such mortal danger improve their performance at all?

No. Tran decided to keep the information to himself. "It's all part of a plan," he temporized, not entirely comfortable with the withholding of the information, but certain in his heart it was the right thing to do. This was what he was paid for, to carry the burden of knowing such secrets without allowing them to distract his crew.

That was evidently enough for his chief. He nodded, then pointed to the attack console immediately to his right. "Firing solution, Captain, anytime, anywhere." A quiet smile betrayed the pride behind his voice.

"Captain—she's increasing speed. Look." Jacobs pointed out some acoustic components on the display, then tweaked an automatic gain control knob. "I hold they're headed directly for us, sir, although she's still shallow."

"She can't know we're here," Tran said confidently. "Maintain firing solution."

"And now she's turning away," the chief said softly. Not that he needed to announce the fact—the downward shift in the submarine's frequency had already told Tran she was maneuvering.

Now why is she doing that? Charging straight for us, then turning and heading in the opposite direction. And why the relatively high-speed run now? Tran glanced at the chronometer and verified that it was indeed still daylight on the surface above.

Nothing about the submarine's conduct had made much sense thus far, and this high speed charge was just the latest anomaly. Creeping in too close had put *Centurion* far closer to the rest of the Chinese forces than he was comfortable with, and now it seemed that their positions had been reversed. Was the diesel trying to tempt him into giving chase, hoping to lure him into a trap?

"Sonobuoys!" the chief said, his voice marginally louder than it had been before. "Who the hell is—"

Suddenly the sonarmen ripped off their headphones as a violent explosion rocked the submarine. It was too far away to do any real damage, but the downward force from the explosive rolled the submarine slightly, an odd sensation for those used to working on a virtually motionless platform.

Tran had it on the speaker now, the faint *splash-gurgle* of something large and metallic hitting the water, the hiss as air escaped from it and it bubbled down through the water. Then the explosive crump before the pressure wave reached the submarine.

A second, then a third, a fourth explosion, each one progressively closer to the submarine. Captain Tran's mind was racing. *They can't know where we are, it's impossible. This was sheer bad luck, nothing more—wait it out. They're guessing now, but if you come up to high speed and make a run for it, try the noisemakers, they'll know for sure they've got you.*

Even though his cold intellect advised silence and waiting, every atom in his body screamed for speed. As the explosions came faster and closer, he had an overwhelming sense of the vulnerability of the steel hull that protected them from the deep. Most of the time, he was simply unconscious of it. He lived in the submarine, and everyone else did that you knew, too. No big deal—that's just where you were.

But now, hearing the violent echoes crash against his hull, he felt a sense of vulnerability and frailty. Around him, he could hear the uneasy stirrings of the crew, as their iron discipline cracked slightly under the strain of the noise.

"Not sonobuoys. Depth charges," he said. Tran stepped to the middle of the control room and raised his voice slightly. "They're guessing." He looked around the room, careful to catch each gaze, willing his confidence in his own abilities out in a stream of courage to each of them. "They're guessing—they don't know where we are."

He could feel the tension in the compartment ease slightly. Then the next explosion came, this one farther away than the previous ones. Another, then another, all walking away from the boat. He heard a collective sigh issue out from ten pairs of lungs, and said a silent prayer to the god that watches over submariners that he had been right. Finally, the explosions were muted, more like the far-off rumble of an undersea earthquake than what they really were.

"How many years has it been since anyone used those?" his executive officer said, his voice still low and soft. "We don't even carry them in the inventory."

Tran shook his head. "Maybe we ought to. It might be effective as a scare tactic against someone who didn't have our technology."

"Are we still holding contact on that diesel?" Tran asked.

"Negative, Captain," the chief said. "A lot of noise still in the water right now, though. We might pick her up any second."

"Find her and hold her." Tran's voice was grim. "It'll be payback time soon enough."

"Captain, I'm a little bit worried about this," his XO said, handing him a scribbled damage control report. "Structurally, we're fine, but radio thinks we might have lost the ELF. Do you want to give it a try now?"

Tran studied the message for a moment, working out how that would affect their mission. With no ELF communications, they would have to come shallow and trail an antenna to query the satellite for other messages. Coordinating the attack with the carrier battle group—and eventually there would be an attack, of that he was certain—would be a hell of a lot trickier. And more dangerous. "Give it another half an hour, and let's see if we regain contact on the diesel. I know she can't track us off an ELF transmission, but I don't want her hearing any extra noise in the water right now. None of them."

They would have to come shallow in a while, let the battle group know that their ELF capabilities were damaged. Maybe it was just the receive side—they'd try a transmission over ELF, and see if they could get confirmation by return satellite message.

But what good would that do them, simply to be able to transmit? It was receive capability that was critical to coordinating their attack with the battle group, not the transmit side of the house. And the odds that one capability had survived on the single antenna when the other had not were small.

Still, he would have to find out. He told the XO to draft the casualty report and have it ready to go out in two hours. Already a list of tasks was arranging itself in his mind, prioritizing itself as a checklist. First, locate the submarine. Second, assess the extent of the damage. Third, check the area for other contacts. Fourth, when it was safe to do so, come shallow and transmit the casualty reports of the battle group.

"We've got her back, Captain," the sonarman said. "I have a firing solution."

"Good. Hold contact, weapons tight, and wait for my order." Tran's voice was grim. "We'll teach them just how big a mistake it is to take on an American submarine."

SIXTEEN

Sick Bay
USS Jefferson
1400 local (GMT-10)

Jack Simpson stared at the khaki-clad Navy doctor leaning against the bulkhead. "I'm not willing to agree to that."

The doctor shook his head patiently. "I'm sorry, but it's standard procedure. You and your wife took a pretty nasty spill out of that boat. I'm going to insist that you stay in Sick Bay at least overnight."

Jack glanced over at Adele and could see that she was starting to do a slow burn. Despite their weariness, they'd come through too much, done too much, to be confined to sick bay now.

"If there's nothing wrong with us, then we're not staying here," Adele said firmly. She started stripping off the hospital gown they'd put her in as soon as they'd arrived in sick bay and reached for her own wet clothes. "I'm not injured, I'm not taking up a bed. And that's, that's."

"You don't seem to understand, Mrs. Simpson," the doctor said slowly. "I know you're not on active duty, but you are on board a U.S. warship. And, in my judg-

ment, your failure to agree to a reasonable request is just
further evidence of your mental instability at this point.
Under the circumstances, I have no doubt that the admiral
will support me in this."

"Who's the admiral?" Jack demanded.

The doctor gazed at him thoughtfully. "Admiral
Wayne commands the battle group. Admiral Magruder
has just arrived on board to take charge of the joint staff."

"Tombstone Magruder?" Jack asked. A slow smile
spread across his face. "Tomcat jock?"

"Admiral Magruder is a naval aviator," the doctor said
stiffly, "and I believe his aircraft of choice is the F-14
Tomcat."

Jack's smile broke into a broad grin. "Not so fast with
that hospital gown, honey." He laid a gentle hand on her
shoulder. Then he looked over at the doctor and pointed
at the pile of wet clothes on the deck. "Have someone
take those down to the laundry, do a freshwater rinse on
them, dry them, and get them back up to us. Either that
or route us out the appropriate uniforms from the lucky
bag," he said, referring to a slush fund of clothes normally maintained by the welfare and recreation commit-
tee. "And let Admiral Magruder's chief of staff know
immediately that Commander Jack Simpson and his new
wife are on board and, at his earliest convenience, would
be honored if they could pay their respects in person."

The doctor paled slightly. "You know Admiral Magruder?" he asked, deep suspicion in his voice.

Jack nodded. "That I do. And believe me, if it'll get
me bailed from this joint, I'm not above capitalizing on
it. The admiral and I spent a fair amount of time together
at the flying club—he owns a Pitts Special, I believe."

No, I don't believe at all—I'm damned well certain of
it. Stony and I have gone around too many times just
admiring that baby for me to be mistaken about that.

"Let's get a move on, Doc," Jack said briskly. "I'm not going to want to keep the admiral waiting."

Flight Deck
USS Jefferson
1410 local (GMT-10)

Lobo shot Hot Rock an ugly look full of venom and distaste. "How the hell did I ever let you talk me into this?" she demanded.

Hot Rock shook his head and smiled at her. "You're loving it, and you know it, babe," he said easily. "Hold on, let me settle another one of these around your shoulders." He hefted a twenty-pound tie-down chain, doubled it, then settled it firmly over her neck draping down her front. "Too much?"

"Fuck you, Hot Rock," Lobo said, venom dripping from her voice. "I'll match you tie-down chain for tie-down chain any day of the week."

Hot Rock patted her affectionately on the shoulder. Weighted down with a hundred extra pounds of sheer iron, she probably wouldn't be able to catch him if he had to make a run for it. "There, there, little girl. We're just doing our part to win the war, aren't we?"

He could hear her teeth grinding over the noise on the flight deck. Two F-14s were already taxiing up to the catapult, and the noise was deafening.

He surveyed her slim, muscular form, now clad in a nondescript coverall rather than the Nomex flight suit he usually saw her in. With her hair tucked up under a cranial, goggles over her eyes, and no rank or name insignia anywhere on her coveralls, she was one of a dozen sailors hustling gear belowdecks. A damned fine attractive woman at that, but still just another sailor on the flight deck.

He ran his hands down his front, felt the oily fabric under his fingers. Well, they had to look the part, didn't they? After all, it wasn't like they were going to go flying anytime soon.

After pitching their case all the way up the chain of command, Lobo and Hot Rock had finally given up. The admiral was too pissed at them, too terminally pissed, to ever consider any promises they could make to be on their best behavior in the air from now on as worth anything at all. In fact, the CAG had informed them, they'd be lucky not to face a board of inquiry and have their wings stripped. As it was now, they were both off flight status, at least pending resolution of the current hostilities.

And after all, it wasn't like the battle group really needed them right now. There was to be no anti-air activity over the island, and the *Jefferson*'s flights thus far had been limited to CAP and ASW. There were more than enough pilots—pilots willing to obey orders, Batman pointed out coldly—to fill the required slots. So, until further notice, the admiral had suggested that Hot Rock and Lobo, along with their RIOs, get their sorry little asses out of his stateroom and find some way to make themselves useful.

It hadn't taken them more than three hours of pacing the passageways of the ship to feel utterly useless. All around them, activity continued at a heightened tempo, everybody seemingly hurrying to an operationally important task. Only the four aircrew were walking slowly and looking for something to do.

Finally, after three hours, Hot Rock had come up with this. He'd purloined four sets of dirtied and weathered coveralls from the maintenance chief, presented them to them, and made his pitch.

"Listen, we're not going to be flying," he began bluntly. "I think that should be pretty obvious to all of us. So, the question is do we sit on our hands and be pissed about it or find something to do?" With that, he held up the coveralls.

"Flight deck?" Lobo asked. "Come on, you want me to be a plane captain?" She laughed incredulously.

Hot Rock shook his head. "Nope. We've got qualified plane captains. What we need to do is some of the other stuff that you don't have written quals for. There's no way the handler would let us on his flight deck as a plane captain. We don't have the sign-off card."

"So we wander around incognito?" Lobo said.

"We work incognito," Hot Rock corrected. "You know how much there is to do up there—or maybe you don't," he corrected. "If you don't, it's about time you found out. Believe me, an extra pair of hands shows up to do unskilled labor, there aren't going to be too many questions asked."

"Like what?" Lobo asked.

Hot Rock shrugged. "I don't know. But whatever it is, it beats sitting on our asses down here, doesn't it?" He surveyed the other two faces, then nodded. "I thought so. Come on, let's go find something to do."

As soon as they'd made their way out to the flight deck, they'd noticed a group of sailors near the stern hustling tie-down chains. They'd been on deck earlier to secure the aircraft during the weather but were now just cluttering up deck space. Each sailor carried four tie-down chains, approximately eighty pounds of extra weight. A few of the larger men carried six to eight tie-down chains.

"Where are they taking them?" Lobo asked, as Hot

Rock unceremoniously draped the first tie-down chain around her shoulders.

"Just follow the crowd," he said. "Just follow the crowd."

The crowd, as it turned out, was heading down three ladders to the line shack compartment for an S-3 squadron. No one questioned the appearance of four extra non-rated sailors helping out with the workload, although the leading petty officer did seem faintly surprised at how quickly restowing the tie-down chains went. He stared at Hot Rock for a moment, started to ask something, and then was overcome by another crisis almost immediately.

The four made their way back up to the deck. "Well, what next?" Hot Rock said, looking around the flight deck for more opportunities. "Let's face it, guys, if we ain't flying, we ain't qualified to do shit up here, are we?"

Flag Conference Room
1430 local (GMT-10)

Tombstone stared at the bedraggled figure standing in front of him. He surveyed the wet hair slicked back from the broad, smiling face, the freshly scrubbed though haggard face, and then swept his eyes to the woman standing next to his friend. He took two steps forward and held out his hand. "You must be Jack's wife. Tombstone Magruder—pleased to make your acquaintance."

She took his hand gravely, and he noted how cool it felt. "I've heard a lot about you, Admiral. I'm pleased to make your acquaintance, although I'm sure we both wish the circumstances could be different."

"Of course." Tombstone shook his head, bemused. "If I'd had any idea it was you and Jack on that boat, life would have been a lot simpler."

"The question is, what can we do now, sir?" Jack asked, a sudden shift in his voice indicating this was now a question posed by a junior officer to a very senior one.

Tombstone studied them both for a moment longer, then glanced at the doctor standing next to them. "Status?"

"As I told the Simpsons, I'd like to keep them overnight in Sick Bay. Just to make certain," the doctor started. Jack and Tombstone exchanged a cynical look. "After what they've been through . . ."

"We weren't in the water that long, Admiral," Adele broke in. "We exited the vessel before the impact, and there's certainly no danger of hypothermia in these waters." She left unspoken the other very real threat, that of sharks.

Batman spoke up then. "Admiral, that situation we were discussing—do you suppose . . . ?" He broke off, and shot a significant look at the Simpsons.

"Just so," Tombstone said. "Very well, then—Commander Simpson, I do have one mission that you and your wife might be especially suited for. Things are about to get real busy out here. You can imagine the constraints we're operating under." Briefly, Tombstone sketched in the restrictions on air combat and missile employment. "Now, I notice that civilian traffic has fallen off some, but there's still a number of lookie-loos out in the harbor, trying to figure out what's going on. The Chinese don't seem to doing anything about them. If you're willing, I have a boat that you could take—the same one that brought me in, the *Lucky Star*. Civilian marked and pretty damned fast, for all that she might have a bit of a gimpy engine. But at least she's not a military vessel. Any chance you could cruise over by the Chinese battle group and take a look at what's going on?" He pointed at Lab Rat. "Commander Busby can fit you out with another cell phone so we can stay in contact."

"Of course, sir," Adele said.

Lab Rat held up a cautionary finger. "Admiral, there's every chance that the Chinese took note of the markings and the hull configuration of the vessel that brought you to the carrier. And they were pretty damned intent on shooting it while you were enroute. I'm not so certain it would make an effective spy boat."

"There's that." Tombstone gazed levelly at the Simpsons. "There's some risk, to be sure. And you'd be operating as civilians, not military prisoners of war. But I think that the Chinese are probably a little too busy to keep any permanent records of that engagement, not with the air battle that was going on. If you look out in the harbor, I think you'll see another ten or fifteen boats that could be mistaken for this one. So there's some risk, but I don't think it's that substantial."

"Neither do I," Adele said. Both carefully ignored the fact that *Heaven Can Wait* had been shot out from under the Simpsons. "In truth, Admiral, we welcome any opportunity to get back into battle. And if this is how you think we can most effectively support the battle group, we'd be honored to undertake this mission."

A rare smile split across Tombstone's face. "I kind of figured you'd say that. We've just met, but I've flown with this guy before, and I know how he operates. I figure any woman who could put up with him would have to be twice as ballsy." A slight red flush spread up Tombstone's cheeks as he realized how politically incorrect he'd been. But damn it all to hell, did it really matter? Adele Simpson knew what he meant, knew it was a compliment of the highest order. If some politically correct hack wanted to bitch about an admiral's choice of words under these circumstance, then to hell with him.

"When can we leave?" Adele asked.

The chief of staff spoke up. "Your boat's tied up on the far side of the carrier. I'd like to take about half an hour, get it fully stocked up, let you and Lab Rat work out the coordination and code. That'll give the boson's mate time to run a couple of stripes down it, maybe disguise it just a little bit. So I'd say thirty minutes, no more than an hour."

"We'll be ready," Adele said. She turned to her husband. "Won't we?"

"You'd better believe it."

Forty-five minutes later, the small vessel was ready to go. Under Adele's direction, Jack piloted away from the massive carrier, careful to steer away from the sea chests, the giant suction intake inlets that sucked seawater into the ship for a variety of purposes. Jack appreciated the clean, hard thrum of the engines, the feel of the helm vibrating under his hands. Tombstone—correction, Admiral Magruder—had been right about the boat's qualities. He'd have to keep an eye on the diesel engines, but the mechanics on board the carrier said that they thought they'd corrected the problem.

An hour later, *Jefferson* was merely a dark smudge on the horizon, while the first outlines of the massive Chinese ship were already visible. As he piloted, Jack kept up a steady scan for any aircraft, but the only contacts he could see were F-14s. A few jump jets made routine takeoffs and landings on the Chinese ship, but evinced no curiosity in the Simpson's boat.

"So how do we look like a pleasure craft?" Adele asked. "It's about time we started trying to maintain our cover, don't you think?"

"Break out those fishing rods and the cooler," he directed. A couple of sailors had raided the MWR compartment to provide them with evidence of their reasonable cover story.

Jack backed the boat off to a more than reasonable ten knots, and felt the motion of it change as the swells took it more heavily. He maneuvered around to get the waves on the quarter bow, then set the small boat on autopilot. In the stern, Adele cast out the first line.

"The way the set and drift is running right now, we should start easing up on her," Adele said as she reeled in the line and rebaited her hook. "Let's keep an eye on the rest of the boats, see what they're doing. We'll make like fat, dumb and happy tourists, out for a little fishing and a good look at the invaders. Just look at them— nobody looks like they're taking this too seriously, do they?"

From what Jack could tell, there was very little evidence that most of the boaters took any notice of the invasion at all.

"Something's happening," he said suddenly, staring uneasily at the massive ship. "Something about the stern—hold on, where are those binoculars?"

Adele handed the binoculars with a cautionary, "Watch the angle of the sun, and get down behind the cowling— no point in their seeing us staring at them with binoculars."

"I'll bet most of the boaters are, though," Jack muttered, but still ducking down behind the cowling. He tweaked the binoculars into focus, and stared at the stern of the ship. Something about the angle . . . "A well deck," he said. "Get on the horn, let Lab Rat know—that damned thing is not only an aircraft carrier, it's an amphibious assault ship as well."

"How long have we got?" Adele asked as she punched the speed dial button for Lab Rat's direct line.

"If it's anything like an American ship, it will take them at least thirty minutes to get the well deck flooded and the ships deployed. Maybe less—we don't know what technology they're using. But I'm betting it will take them even longer, since we're dealing with a converted merchant ship of some sort."

He studied the ship and watched her settle in the water while he listened to Adele report their facts to Lab Rat. If the Chinese were sending troops ashore, it was going to be damned difficult to dislodge them once they were in place. With a sinking feeling, he found himself wondering just how long this siege would last.

CVIC
USS **Jefferson**
1442 local (GMT-10)

"You're certain of this?" Lab Rat said, his expression mirroring the doubt in his voice. "An amphibious ship?"

He listened carefully while Adele Simpson ran through the details of what Jack was observing. Finally, he said, "Stay on the line for a moment—I'm going to get the admiral on the other circuit." Still holding the cell phone against one ear, he picked up the white phone and punched in the number for TFCC.

Batman's reaction was even more incredulous than his own, but the wealth of detail in Adele Simpson's report quickly convinced both of them. Batman heard Lab Rat put the call on the speakerphone, then the dark, somber tones of Tombstone Magruder joined in the conversation.

"Tell them to get the hell out of the way," Tombstone said finally. "If we let those troops go ashore, it will be like trying to dig out gophers dislodging them from the island. Whatever else, we've got to stop those transports."

TFCC
1443 local (GMT-10)

Just then, the phone mounted on the table leg, out of sight just to the right of Batman's chair, buzzed. He picked it up, said, "Admiral," and then listened. A look of consternation crossed his face. "I see. Very well, I'll be there immediately."

Batman placed the phone back in its hanger, then turned back to the assembled joint staff. "We have another problem. The stern of the second ship just let down in back. There's a well deck inside, according to the helo pilot." He gazed around the assembled crowd, making sure they understood what he was saying. "They're disgorging small boats. Each one looks to be carrying around a hundred and twenty men. And they're heading for the coast."

Batman turned to Bam-Bam. "Break off one of the S-3's to get as close in as she can and take a look at what's going on. The Simpsons are riding pretty low in the water—there's a chance they've misinterpreted what they've seen." But as he listened to his TAO give the orders, Batman had a sinking feeling that he was not going to like the report coming from his S-3 any better.

Viking 709
1445 local (GMT-10)

Commander "Rabies" Grill put the S-3B Viking into a gentle turn to the right. The airspace immediately above the Chinese aircraft carrier was abuzz with MiGs, but they seemed to take no notice of his surveillance patrol at this distance. The ship was maybe eight miles away, her structure clearly visible, especially through binoculars. His copilot kept up a careful scan, noting the activity on the deck, the configuration of the ship, and the direction and size of its wake.

"What's that mother doing?" Rabies muttered. He hummed a few bars of "Love Me Tender," then said again, "What is that mother doing?"

Without dropping his binoculars, the copilot replied, "Not much. But if you start singing again, I swear I'll pitch these binoculars right through the windscreen." Rabies chuckled quietly. His love of country music was well known among all the S-3B Viking aircrews. In a moment of undeniable malice, the VS-29 operations officer had assigned only those individuals with perfect pitch to Rabies's aircrew. A betting pool had already been started among the rest of the squadron, wagering on which of the other three occupants of the aircraft would be the first to crawl sniveling on his knees to the operations officer. Himself, Rabies had ten bucks on the copilot.

"Can you get around the stern of her again?" the copilot said. He leaned forward slightly in his seat, oblivious to the ejection seat straps holding him in place. "Because I think I see—hell!"

"What is it?" Rabies goosed the S-3B up to top speed of four hundred and twenty knots, and everything in the cockpit started rattling.

The copilot yelped, dropped his glasses momentarily, and shot an angry look at Rabies. "She was designed for this speed twenty years ago. Don't press your luck, asshole."

Rabies refrained from rejoinder.

"Sir, you're going to be out of range of the sonobuoys," the AW in the backseat complained. "I'm already starting to lose contact—damn."

"Well, it's not like you were holding contact on anything, was it?" Rabies replied, a practical note in his voice. "That diesel's gone sinker, and you're not going to see her until it gets dark."

"You never know," the AW muttered darkly. "If she takes a shot at the carrier and we're not on station—"

"Our primary mission is to keep an eye on that bastard conceived-in-hell aircraft carrier," Rabies replied. "And if my beloved copilot wants a closer look at her ass, then that's where we're going."

"Holy shit. I'm not believing this," the copilot said, stark horror in his voice. "Not the carrier, but the ship next to it. It's a fucking amphibian transport."

"What?" demanded Rabies.

"The stern just levered down into a ramp, and seawater's flooding the back of it. You know what that means, don't you."

Rabies nodded glumly. He did indeed. It meant the ship was equipped with a well deck, which meant that she had a covey of nasty little target boats inside of her capable of transporting men and equipment to shore. Easy targets for the most part—the max speed, unless they were hovercraft, was usually well under twenty knots. Not even with a harpoon—he'd get in close and take them with guns.

"Any boats coming out?" Rabies asked.

"Negative. It'll take them a while to flood the well deck if they're anything like our transports," the copilot replied.

Rabies picked up the mike. "Homeplate, this is Dragon Zero Seven," he said. An answer came back from *Jefferson* immediately.

"Roger, *Jefferson*, got a visual on the second big bad boy. My copilot reports that it's an amphibious transport. The well deck's flooded—once they get it stabilized, I suspect we're going to see mama laying some eggs. What do you want me to do about it?"

"Dragon Zero Seven, wait. Out."

Rabies sighed. Typical of the new Navy. If he had his way, he knew what he'd do—make an approach on the boat immediately and start strafing those little bastards as soon as they got spit out the ass end. Waterborne turds, that's what they were—might as well kill 'em at sea before they had a chance to make landfall.

He glanced up at the airspace over the carrier and revised his plan. Might not be such a good idea to wander into the middle of that cluster fuck of fighters while he was armed with torpedoes and harpoons. He doubted if any of the nimble MiGs would stand still long enough for him to take them with guns. Still, he was willing to give it a try if *Jefferson* said so. He'd never had a chance to use the ejection seats in the Viking, and it might be interesting to—

"Dragon Zero Seven, this is Homeplate. Weapons tight—I repeat, weapons tight. Maintain briefed distance and continue observations. We're sending you out some playmates."

There were two sighs of relief from the backseat as it became clear that Rabies would not be allowed to enter the airspace around the Chinese aircraft carrier. Even the copilot looked relieved. Rabies's tendency to shoot first and ask questions later was well-known amongst the community.

Rabies sighed and tapped impatiently on the throttle cluster. "Damn. And I was hoping to be an ace."

TFCC
1450 local (GMT-10)

Batman listened to the report from the translator with a grim expression on his face. "A full division crammed inside those amphibs? He was certain? And a submarine in the area, too?"

The translator nodded. "He was certain, Admiral. Especially about the submarine. He's the equivalent of one of our sonar technicians, and he knows that they've anticipated having to deal with at least one U.S. submarine."

Batman was silent for a moment, then said, "So why's he talking? Does he think we'll torture him?"

"As I understand it, he's planning on asking for political asylum." The translator pursed his lips for a moment, deep in thought. "As there's something more that's motivating him, I'm certain. He kept mentioning a senior pilot by the name of Chan. Chan Li. Evidently this fellow thinks Chan is out to get him."

"Okay by me," Batman answered. "I don't care why he's talking, as long as he's talking." He turned to Bam-Bam. "Get a message to *Centurion*. She's been holding contact intermittently on something, and if we give her an exact classification, it'll help her localize it."

Lab Rat broke in with, "In these waters, ASW is going to be difficult, sir. Especially near the harbor. The water's not bad, but the ocean floor is littered with metal. It's going to be difficult for the airborne assets to depend on their MAD contacts."

They all fell silent for a moment as history hit home. That the remnants of that gallant fleet on the seabed should make their problem now more difficult seemed cruelly ironic.

"The floor's charted," Lab Rat added. "There's no area that's been mineswept more thoroughly. That'll help." He left unspoken the last thought—it would help, but it might not be enough.

SEVENTEEN

Flight Deck
USS Jefferson
1500 local (GMT-10)

After two hours of humping tie-down chains, watching aircraft, and conducting FOD walk-downs, the four aviators had a new appreciation for the complexity and skill required of the enlisted flight deck technicians. They'd all seen the other ratings in action time and time again, ever since their earliest days in flight training, but they'd never actually had to perform the work themselves. They quickly discovered how very little they actually knew about what goes on behind the scenes.

Hot Rock was taking a break from hauling sonobuoys up from the ammunition locker to the flight deck when he ran into Lobo. He slipped behind the island with her and wiped the sweat off his face. "You always see those guys crashed out just inside the passageways with their headphones still on during flex deck operations. Man, I never realized how tired you got doing this stuff. How are you holding up?"

"Fine." Lobo's voice was confident, but Hot Rock noticed how she winced as she settled down onto the non-

skid next to him. "You're right, though. It is hard work.
Just had a chief order me to get out to the LSO platform
and take them some water and some paper cups. You
want to go?" Just then the 1MC went off overhead.

"Launch the Alert Five Tomcats, the Alert Five Hornets, and all backup sections. Stand by for full flex deck
operations. Green deck; green deck."

Hot Rock and Lobo scrambled to their feet and dashed
toward the island. Hot Rock stopped just short of the
hatch, and Lobo crashed into his back. "What the hell
are you doing?" she asked angrily.

"You forget—we're grounded." Lobo could hear the
frustration in his voice. "They've got more than enough
flight crews for all the aircraft—no way we're getting on
the schedule, not even in a full Alpha strike."

"Yeah, but—" Lobo's voice broke off when she could
find no way to reason around the order grounding them.
Their seniority and experience kept them on the flight
schedule most of the time, but this wasn't most of the
time. With more aircraft, they might have had a shot at
it, but there were more than sufficient aircrews to man
up every airframe on board the carrier.

"So we stay up here," Lobo concluded glumly. "That
sucks."

"And out of the way," Hot Rock added. "That sounds
like the LSO platform to me."

Ten minutes later, after finding that there were a lot of
shortcuts out to the LSO platform that they'd never
learned, they stepped out onto the small platform on the
port side of the ship just below the level of the flight
deck. Both pilots immediately moved forward without
thinking to stand next to the officer guiding the aircraft
in.

"Back off," a harsh voice said. "Jesus, what are they
teaching you in boot camp these days? Don't you know

enough to stay out of the way?" an LSO snapped at them.

"What's—" Hot Rock began. A strong hand closed on his collar and jerked him back out of the way. "What the hell?"

"Didn't you hear the lieutenant?" a chief petty officer asked. "Get your ass out of the way—now!"

"What is it?" Lobo asked, as they both backed out of the way.

"Pay attention—this isn't going to be pretty," the chief said, shouting to be heard over the noise of an approaching Tomcat. "Nugget inbound has lost his cool—he's boltered twice and the LSO is trying to talk him in. Getting low on fuel, too, but he's shaking so much right now he can't even take a pass at the tanker. This is going to be ugly."

He pointed down at the cargo netting that dropped from the LSO platform to a spot that was affixed to the hull of the ship. "Anything goes wrong, you jump for that net. There's a hatch down there off to the side—you can make it back into the ship that way."

Hot Rock and Lobo exchanged glances. If a Tomcat pilot was in trouble, then it had to be someone they knew. Neither of them recognized the LSO—it was from one of the other squadrons onboard—but both could now see the Tomcat inbound. The pilot was clearly having problems maintaining altitude and orientation to the deck. The Tomcat wandered around the sky like a wounded goose. Wavering back and forth off center line, sometimes too high, far off and too low.

"Man, oh, man—I'm looking at a ramp strike waiting to happen," Lobo breathed. "Get some altitude, buddy, come on, come on . . ." Her voice trailed off as she realized the chief was staring at them curiously. Four feet in front of them, the LSO was repeating virtually the same words.

They both stared at the incoming Tomcat, silently willing it across the flight deck. As the nose of the aircraft passed over the stern, they both breathed a sigh of relief. At least it wouldn't be a ramp strike, a head-on full speed impact into the stern of the ship. But just when they thought he would make it, snagging the four wire, the stern of the ship jutted abruptly up. It caught the Tomcat just forward of its main landing gear, snapping the struts like matchsticks. The tail-end of the aircraft slammed down, and the aircraft itself commenced a flat spin across the nonskid, headed directly toward them.

"Down!" the chief shouted, and he yanked both of them down to the railing and over it and into the cargo net in one motion.

They were staring in horrified fascination when the chief yanked them down. Behind them, they could hear other feet clanging on the metal deck plates, feel the hot breath of the burning Tomcat, now on fire, hurtling over their head and into the ocean.

As they hit the cargo net, they hit on their backs and rolled over to see the lieutenant flying through mid-air toward them. Just as his forward section cleared the cargo net, the shattered remnant of a landing gear strut snagged his foot. It ripped the flesh open in a thin smear of blood and hung in the air a moment. The impact slammed him hard into the side of the ship, and he crumpled into an ominously still heap in the bottom of the net.

The chief scrambled down after him. Before he even performed first aid, he stripped off the lieutenant's headset and clamped it over his own head. Then, simultaneously making his report to the Air Boss and checking the lieutenant to see if he was still breathing, he briefed the Air Boss.

Hot Rock glanced out and could see two more Tomcats wheeling into position on final approach. He stepped forward, tapped the chief on the shoulder, then started to remove the headset. The chief clamped one beefy fist over Hot Rock's hand. "What the hell you doing, kid?" the chief snarled.

"I'm Lieutenant Commander Stone," he said calmly. "And this is Lieutenant Commander Hanson. We're both F-14 pilots. Both LSO qualified. And I think you could use one of those about now."

The chief stared at them for a moment, disbelieving, then sudden recognition dawned in his eyes. "I know who you are. Didn't recognize you in—Sir, what the hell are you—never mind." He ripped the headphones off, shoved them in Hot Rock's hands, and turned his attention back to the lieutenant. "Air Boss knows what's going on, and Medical is on the way. He said the forward part of the aircraft slid completely off and they're checking the catapult for damage right now. May be a couple of minutes until we can launch, but we've got two birds inbound." He pointed aft. "Think you can get them in?"

"If there's no damage to the wires, yeah," Hot Rock said.

"Keep in mind they're going to be a little shook up." He glanced at the two of them then said, "You know how it is. You see somebody buy it right in front of you getting on the deck, you're going to be kind of shaky coming in. Don't let on that you're a replacement LSO."

"This part I know how to do, Chief." Hot Rock climbed back up the net and stationed himself on the undamaged portion of the LSO perch. Lobo joined him. She put her head up next to his, pulling the earpiece away from his ear slightly so she could listen in.

"Tomcat Two-zero-one, call the ball," Hot Rock said, falling easily into the LSO pattern of coaching a bird onto the deck.

"What the hell is going on down there, LSO?" a panicked pilot's voice asked. "Jesus, is he—"

"Tomcat Two-oh-one, call the ball," Hot Rock repeated, keeping his voice calm and professional. "Keep your mind in the game, mister. You've only got one thing to worry about right now, and that's putting that turkey down on the deck."

"Yeah, but—"

"Tomcat Two-oh-one, call the ball," Hot Rock repeated, letting the repetition cue the pilot's mind back into the familiar pattern of the landing sequence.

"Roger, LSO, Two-oh-one ball." The pilot's voice already sounded calmer as he focused on the immediate problem at hand. "Four thousand pounds on board."

"Roger, Two-oh-one, say needles?" Hot Rock asked, asking the pilot to tell him how his glide slope indicator held the aircraft's position in relation to the ideal glide slope.

"Roger, needles show high and to the right."

"Two-oh-one, LSO, disregard needles, I hold you on course on speed. Keep it coming in, you're headed straight for the three wire."

"We got a green deck?" the pilot asked, the anxiety surging in his voice again.

"Roger, that's a green deck," Hot Rock said. "Green deck, green deck . . . looking good, *Two-oh-one*, a little power, a little power, that's it, watch your attitude, attitude, that's it, that's it . . ." Hot Rock settled easily into the familiar singsong patter of an LSO walking a Tomcat down the invisible slope that linked his last position on final approach to the number three wire on the deck. He could feel Lobo's hot breath on his neck as she listened, heard her subvocalizing the same patter he was putting out over the airwaves to the nervous pilot. "Looking good, looking good—got it!" he shouted as Tomcat *Two-*

oh-one slammed down onto the deck in a controlled crash as it crossed the three wire. "Good trap, *Two-oh-one*."

"What the hell is going on down there?" a new voice demanded on the circuit. "Chief said the LSO was out—Henry, what are you doing?"

"Air Boss, it's Hot Rock and Lobo," the pilot answered, suddenly not at all certain that he was on solid ground. Sure, he knew what he was doing, but he supposed he should have asked the Air Boss's permission first before taking over the LSO duties without even informing him. Still, with a turkey in the air and a nervous pilot, the last thing the Air Boss or the Admiral would have wanted was to put the pilot back in the starboard marshal, particularly not when it looked like they were going to need every airframe they could get airborne within the next hour.

"We happened to be out here, and when the LSO bought it, well . . ."

There was silence for a moment on the circuit, then the Air Boss said, "I hold Two-oh-five inbound next. Be advised, we're still a green deck."

"Roger. Two-oh-five, LSO, call the ball."

For the next half an hour, Lobo and Hot Rock efficiently brought the remaining aircraft back on deck. Just as the last aircraft touched down, the Air Boss said, "As soon as we secure from flight quarters, the admiral wants to see you in his office."

Lobo turned to Hot Rock and grinned. "We're either in big trouble or—"

"Or we're back on the flight schedule," Hot Rock interrupted.

Fifteen minutes later, they were back on the flight schedule and headed for the paraloft to gear up for launch.

EIGHTEEN

Jefferson set a new personal best record for launching the most fighters in the least amount of time. For Bird Dog and Gator, the minutes seemed like hours. Bird Dog kept worrying about his new wingman, Lieutenant Junior Grade Kelly Green, and her backseater, Tits.

Lieutenant Junior Grade Kelly Green—the name had been her parent's doing, and the squadron hadn't looked beyond that for a call sign—was the squadron's newest nugget. As the most inexperienced pilot on the flight schedule, she was paired with Bird Dog, on the theory that he'd be able to teach her the ropes and keep her out of trouble. Gator had loudly expressed the opinion in public that in this particular instance, there was little hope of the latter.

"She'll be okay," Gator said reassuringly over ICS. "So will Tits. I trained him myself, and you've been watching Kelly in action for the last three months."

"Don't remind me." Bird Dog snuck a quick glance aft through the canopy and spotted Kelly immediately in position, two thousand yards aft and two thousand yards above him. The tall lanky brunette—and yes, she did have green eyes to go with her nickname—had been a source of contention between he and Lobo ever since the new pilot had joined the squadron.

But what was he supposed to do? Just pretend she knew everything she was supposed to? If she were going to fly as his wingman, he had to be damned certain he could count on her. Certain enough that he didn't have to look back and check to make sure that she was in position visually, even though his heads-up display fed the information to him automatically.

In the last three months, they'd spent endless hours talking about tactics. She'd started out slightly in awe of him. Evidently word of his combat experience in every theater around the world had already traveled throughout the Tomcat community, and she appeared slightly in awe of him. She'd gotten over her awe a little too easily for his taste, but that's the way women were, weren't they?

And at least she was flying with a guy who had a sense of humor, Tits. Not like Gator, that old sourpuss.

"Okay, just like we practiced," he said over tactical. "Another round of AMRAAMS—I'll take the lead, you take the guy behind him."

"Roger." From the calm, collected tone of voice, no one could have guessed that Kelly was about to take her first live shot.

"Then we close in with the Sidewinders. Remember, these guys have maneuverability on us. We have to exploit our greater power, get them into the vertical game, you remember?" Bird Dog asked.

"I remember," Kelly answered.

"Okay, on my mark—now!" Bird Dog said.

The Tomcat jolted slightly as the heavier missile leapt off of its wing, white smoke gouting off the stern as it traced an unerring path toward the lead aircraft.

Bird Dog's MiG broke right hard, and curved down below the two Tomcats, clearly intending to come up behind and position himself for a tail shot.

"Oh, no, you don't," Bird Dog said softly. "Not if I've got anything to say about it."

He pulled the Tomcat into a hard right-hand turn, ascending and rolling as he did, coaxing the MiG into the vertical game. Once he'd grabbed five thousand feet of altitude, he rolled back into a nose-down position, and found that it worked just as he'd planned—he had a perfect, slightly trailing side shot on the other MiG.

He flipped the weapons selector switch from AM-RAAM to Sidewinder and blasted the lighter IR-seeking missile off the wing. Without waiting to see how it did, he grabbed for altitude again, fully expecting the MiG with being preoccupied with trying to shake the Sidewinder for at least ten seconds.

The heads-up display clobbered immediately with radar returns, indicating that the other aircraft had ejected flares and chaff. He rolled easily out of range of them, coming back into level flight at nineteen thousand feet, and turning back toward his quarry.

The MiG was nose up, screaming through the sky in an almost vertical climb. A few more seconds and its soft underbelly would be directly in his line of fire. Bird Dog goosed the Tomcat with a touch of afterburner, closing the distance. For a brief moment, he considered going to guns, then dismissed the idea. Not a perfect angle for a Sidewinder shot, but it was worth a try. Save the guns for when he really needed them, when they were up close and personal instead of almost at the edge of the guns' maximum range.

"Got 'im, got 'im," a howl came over tactical.

"Good kill, good kill," he heard Tits cry in response. "Nailed him with the first AMRAAM."

"Some guys get all the luck," Bird Dog muttered. "I had to give them the stupid bastard, and now Kelly's going to have to help me out with this one." For indeed, the MiG was proving to have a far more capable pilot than he'd counted on. Everything in the intelligence reports indicated that the Chinese fighter pilots got significantly less training than American ones did, and that their equipment was often poorly maintained. But the bloke in front of him, dancing that MiG through the sky, clearly had not been reading the same intelligence reports.

The MiG shot up past him, sunlight gleaming off the undercarriage, glaring in his eyes, momentarily blinding him. The symbols on his heads-up display were blanked out by the glare.

"Joining on you now, Bird Dog," Kelly's voice said over tactical, a deep tone of satisfaction in her normally sensual alto voice. "On your high six."

"She's got the shot, Bird Dog," Gator pointed out. "By the time we get nose up to nail his tailpipes, she'll be there."

"It's my MiG," Bird Dog insisted. "Mine."

He yanked the Tomcat around again into a hard turn, and felt the gray creeping in at the edges of his vision. Too many G-forces, too many—sure, he'd pulled more before, but it was always a risk. Behind him, he heard a muttered protest from Gator, then silence as the RIO blacked out.

The Tomcat responded beautifully, turning harder and tighter than he'd ever thought possible for her to do. He lost some speed in the maneuver, and drained off even more as he pitched the Tomcat nose high to track the MiG down. He punched the afterburners, felt the surge slam him back into his ejection seat, and again felt his consciousness start to fade. "Not now, dammit. Not now," he muttered, fighting off the darkness. He eased the afterburner back, and felt the gray start to recede. But by then the MiG had already topped out, and was heading back down toward him.

"Fox two, fox two," Kelly howled. "Bird Dog, break right!"

"Fuck you, Kelly," Bird Dog howled. At the same time, he cut the Tomcat to the right as directed. No pilot in his right mind ever ignored a break command from a wingman.

But his forward momentum was just too great. Had she been more experienced, Kelly would have seen it. She would have known that Bird Dog could not get his aircraft out of the line of fire in time.

Bird Dog saw it happen as if in slow motion. The AMRAAM seemed to creep through the air, a long, white cylinder with stubby fins hurtling toward him, yet seeming to creep along at a snail's pace. The MiG was still descending, picking up speed, and was now almost parallel with him. His Tomcat felt sluggish, and was just starting to come right in response to his order as the MiG passed by.

The AMRAAM seemed to gently caress the MiG, and then started disintegrating. Bird Dog howled, aware that they were close, too close, too damned close. He could see the other pilot's face through the canopy, the Chinese's expression masked by the oxygen mask and helmet.

Just as the MiG exploded into flames, his canopy popped off and he and Gator were spit out like watermelon seeds. He felt a moment of sheer, raw fear, hanging suspended in the air, his parachute not yet deployed, the ejection seat separating from its pan with almost painful slowness. He tried to twist his head around to see

Gator, but couldn't stop his motion tumbling through the sky.

The combination of excessive G-forces, ejection, proved to be too much. He felt his gorge rise, hot, foul liquid crowding the back of his throat. Bird Dog puked, then passed out.

Tomcat 208
1515 local (GMT-10)

Kelly watched in horror as the burning MiG airframe reached out tendrils of flame to stroke the Tomcat carcass. Shrapnel peppered the fatally wounded American aircraft, and thin spews of JP8 fuel sparkled in the air for a microsecond before the entire mass exploded into an incandescent fireball.

She stared down at the water below, ignoring the repeated calls from *Jefferson* asking if she saw any chutes.

"I've got 'em!" Tits said. "There, just forward of our nose. Two of 'em. Ain't that the most beautiful thing you've ever seen?"

It was, except for the MiG exploding into flames. In that brief millisecond when it had been her kill and her kill alone before disaster reached out to stroke her lead.

Finally, the incessant queries from *Jefferson* could no longer be denied. As she descended through ten thousand feet, keeping her eyes fixed on the chutes below, she answered their repeated inquiries with, "Tomcat 203 bought it. I have two chutes, repeat, two chutes. I'll be orbiting overhead, awaiting SAR aircraft." She flipped her transponder beacon to indicate the emergency distress code.

"What happened up there?" a new voice asked.

Kelly recognized it immediately as Batman. "I took a shot at a MiG, nailed him, Admiral. But Bird Dog was too close. He punched out just before the fireball got to him."

"Are they okay?" Batman's voice asked.

She shook her head, knowing he couldn't see the gesture. "I have chutes. I'll know more in a little bit."

"How did you manage to get too close?"

"I don't know exactly, sir. I called for a break right and took the shot. Maybe I called too late, maybe he didn't break fast enough. I don't know, sir."

There was a long silence, then Batman said, "How are you for fuel?"

She glanced down at the fuel indicator and grimaced. "Five thousand pounds. Enough for a pass at the boat."

"You want a tank before you take a shot at the deck?" he asked. What he really meant was, was she so shook up that she needed a couple of passes to get on board.

"No, I'm fine."

"Well. Just concentrate on getting on board, now. We'll sort this out later." Batman's voice was grave, but not unkind.

The Air Intercept Controller was on the circuit immediately, giving her a vector around the starboard marshal and into an immediate approach on the carrier. She followed his instructions carefully, precisely, forcing her mind to concentrate on the second most dangerous evolution any carrier pilot undertakes, right after tanking. Tits, unusually quiet behind her, simply murmured a few reassuring, "Looking good, looking good," from time to time.

She rolled in on the deck on a perfect flight path and handily snagged the three wire. She waited, the Tomcat throbbing at full military power, until a yellow shirt stepped in front of her and indicated it was safe to reduce power. Then she eased the tailhook up, dropping the three wire, and taxied carefully across the deck and into her spot. She and Tits ran through the shutdown checklist quickly, and popped the canopy while the plane captain mounted to safe their ejection seats and help them out.

Finally, she swung a leg over the aircraft and started down the boarding ladder, the footholds that popped out from the side of the aircraft. She jumped off the last one, felt a slight jar run through her as she landed heavily on the flight deck. She heard Tits hit the deck behind her.

As she headed for the island, she noticed the hatch pop open and a rangy female figure step out. Short clipped blonde hair framed an iron mask of a face.

Lobo. Shit, I don't need this right now. Everything that's gone on over the last three months, all the crap she's given me, and now I shoot her guy down.

Kelly halted in front of Lobo and regarded her gravely. The older woman stood there, her face unreadable, her arms crossed in front of her. Finally, Lobo spoke. "You saw chutes, right?"

Kelly nodded.

Lobo closed the distance between them and slung one arm around her shoulders. "Well, then, he'll be okay. He's got Gator keeping an eye on him, you know."

Kelly felt the first shiver of weakness go through her, and the carefully maintained fighter jock facade start to crumble. She tried to speak, found her voice was too gravelly, and stopped.

Lobo swung around to face her again. "Do not do this," Lobo said, her voice low and dangerous. "Everything we've fought for—I've fought for—do not lose it now. I swear to God, I'll kill you if you cry."

Cold fury flooded back into Kelly. The tears that had started in her eyes dried and the lump in her throat vanished. She nodded tightly, then said, "Let's go."

Lobo shook her head. "No, not yet. I want you to understand this—shit happens up there, you know? I know, and Bird Dog sure as hell does. We all take our chances, knowing what can happen every time we strap a Tomcat to our ass. But that's naval aviation, and you either learn to live with it or you get out. So that's what you get to decide now, lady. Can you handle it? If you can't, you might as well put those pretty little gold wings on the admiral's desk as soon as you walk into his stateroom. Because if you can't handle it, then you don't have what it takes to be out here. You read me?"

Kelly lifted her chin and glared at the other woman. "I read you. Now, if you'll excuse me—I'm quite certain that there are a number of people I need to talk to." She marched off with Tits trailing close behind her. Tits shot Lobo an oddly grateful look as they entered the skin of the ship.

Lobo shook her head as she watched them go. The younger pilot didn't understand now, but maybe she would someday. And whenever she did, she'd thank Lobo for what she'd just done.

Bird Dog—by God, you make it out of this alive or I'll kill you. Lobo shook her head, remembering her own days as a POW, the torture she'd endured, the rape, the beatings. Yet, she'd made it out, and even back into flight status. And if she had anything to say about it, so would Kelly Green.

Just then, the 1MC announced, "Attention all hands. SAR mission successful—two souls recovered. Alive. Well done."

It was Lobo's turn to fight back tears.

NINETEEN

The small compartment was a cacophony of inbound pilot calls, reports from the Air Boss on deck status, complaints from the handler on the staging of the aircraft, and surveillance reports from the CAP and SAR already airborne.

For Tombstone Magruder, after two and a half decades of naval service, keeping track of the different threads and progress of all phases of the launch sequence was completely automatic. He gave it no more thought than he did breathing, as his mind sifted through the information, evaluated it, and automatically assigned it a priority in his thinking.

But when a little-used speaker directly behind his elevated command chair crackled to life, he lifted his head up sharply. He turned to look at Batman, whose face was grim.

"The SEAL team on the ground," Batman explained. "We've got them patched through the Marine SINC-GAARS gear."

"Go ahead and talk to them," Tombstone said. "They're already used to your voice."

Batman nodded and picked up the mike. He motioned to the TAO to hunt down the SEAL team representative and have him standing by. "This is Homeplate, go ahead."

"Bad news, Admiral. We found the bomb, but we can't get to it right now. It was disguised as a beer truck, and the Chinese airlifted it out with a helicopter. We followed them, but they planted it in Caneohe Bay with the bomb still on board. Can't get down with my current draeger closed system rebreathers, so I'm going to need an assist here."

Batman swore quietly, then keyed the mike and asked, "What do you need from us?"

"Minesweeper for starters, sir. I've got a pretty good idea of where it went down, but I'm going to have to localize it."

"No problem. The USS *Chief* is in the area. Can you guys get out there?"

"Sure can, Admiral. I've got some special gear for us ordered in as well. Just in case we have to make the deepwater dive."

"I suspect you'll have to do that," Batman answered.

"So do I. But what I can't figure, Admiral, is how they're planning on detonating this. I mean, the thing's down in at least a hundred feet of water."

"Transponder on that submarine," Tombstone said. He turned to look at Batman, his face turning pale. "When's the last time we held contact on her?"

"Murdock, Admiral Magruder is suggesting it's sub-marine activated. We've got one in the area, unlocated for the past four hours. Any indication you've seen of her?"

"Negative, Admiral, but we'll keep an eye out. For

now, I think we just need to localize it and worry about the detonation sequencing of it later."

"Roger, the *Chief* is at your disposal." Batman handed off the microphone to the TAO, who reeled off a set of frequencies and time coordinates to enable the SEALs to contact the *Chief* directly.

Navy Red crackled to life just then, and Tombstone immediately recognized the voice. It was his uncle, Admiral Thomas Magruder, the Chief of Naval Operations.

"*Jefferson*, this is CNO. Be advised that we have an ultimatum from the Chinese. To negotiate a settlement on the Hawaii issue or they detonate special weapons at noon tomorrow. Interrogative your status?"

A cold, still silence settled over TFCC. Tombstone glanced back up at the screen, saw the waves of fighters and surface tac aircraft sweeping in on the Chinese invasion and calculated the odds. "This is Vice Admiral Magruder, sir. Any indications that they can detonate it right now?"

"No one's certain, but the intelligence folks seem to think not. I take it you're in contact with Murdock?"

"That's affirmative, sir. He's just updated us on the probable location on the special weapon and we've dispatched the USS *Chief* to assist in recovery operations."

"Good. I suspect it won't be hard to find. The question is how do we defuse it at that depth?"

"We've got other problems here right now, Admiral," Batman chimed in. "I know we've got orders not to provoke the situation over land, but we've got to stop the incoming infantry deployment. Once they're ashore, it's going to be hard as hell to dislodge them."

"Agreed. We've got less than twelve hours, gentlemen. Let's make this work."

As the CNO clicked off, Batman switched over to the

SEAL circuit. "You're current on the deadline requirements?" he asked Murdock.

"We are now, sir." There was a new, grim note in
Murdock's voice. "We'll make it happen, sir."

Viking 701
1535 local (GMT-10)

"Madman, Madman," the TACCO called from the backseat. "Smoke now!"

In the forward righthand seat, the copilot blasted out
a smoke flare. This would mark the spot where the Viking had had its first detection of an underwater metallic
mass. Later passes over the same area would serve to
triangulate the exact location of the suspected target.

Rabies toggled his ICS switch on. "You sure about
that?"

"It's a hard data point," the TACCO said, his voice
excited. "Let's get some sonobuoys in the water, see if
we can locate this bastard."

"I dunno," Rabies muttered. He glanced over at the
copilot. "You know what I'm thinking, don't you?"

The copilot nodded glumly. "It's right below us."

And that, Rabies reflected, was the essential problem
with Madman detections. The Magnetic Anomaly Detec-
tor, or Madman, could locate a large metallic mass a
significant depth under the water, based on the distortions
such a mass would cause in the earth's magnetic field. It
was fairly precise, with the main inaccuracies induced by
the aircraft's motion over the target and local variances
in the earth's magnetic field.

For all its precision, however, it couldn't tell you what
the mass below you was. Shipwrecks, ore deposits, and

underwater pipelines could all lead to false results. Most
of the known ones were well charted, and ASW experts
always double-checked a chart before putting weapons
on target.

"I know what we're over," the TACCO broke in. "Believe me, I've been over her a thousand times, maybe.
This is different."

Rabies and the copilot exchanged a disgusted look.
"Yeah, yeah," Rabies said. Still, he put the S-3 Viking
into a hard righthand turn, glancing down to check the
location of the smoke, and brought the S-3 in low over
it at right angles to his previous course.

"Madman, Madman," the TACCO sang out again. Another smoke flare was punched out of the underbelly of
the potent little torpedo bomber.

"You're sure about this?" Rabies asked. "Because I
gotta tell ya, I've got this gut feeling that tells me we're
about to look awful silly."

"No way." The TACCO's voice was confident. "I've
got a live one. The sonobuoys will confirm it."

"Unless he's lying dog-o on batteries," the AW pointed
out. "We might not get any acoustic signals at all."

"All right, all right," the TACCO said. "I know that.
And believe me, I also know where the *Arizona* memorial
is."

The *Arizona*, sunk during the attack on Pearl Harbor
by a Japanese kamikaze pilot, was one of the most well
explored shipwrecks in this part of the world. Every inch
of her noble carcass had been thoroughly plotted on
charts.

"Whatever this is, it's about fifty feet to the north of
where the *Arizona* should be," the TACCO said. "Come
on, how many times have we briefed this? The best place
for a submarine to hide is right next to a well-known
MAD anomaly on the ocean floor."

"You sure he would get that close?" Rabies asked.

"He could, if he's got a good skipper. And all indications are that this is a smaller submersible. Sure, that would be too close for comfort for any of the big boomers, or even one of the larger attack submarines. But for a little fella like this, no problem. So do I get my sonobuoys or what?"

With a sigh, the copilot punched out the first of a series of barrier and localization sonobuoys. The TACCO recommended positions for them or in front of them on his own tactical display console, and indeed the aircraft could have ejected the sonobuoys completely on its own at the appropriate locations without any human intervention.

"Okay, I'll call it in," the TACCO said, sheer satisfaction in his voice. "I got you, you little bastard. I got you now."

USS Centurion
1537 local (GMT-10)

Petty Officer Pencehaven arched his back and pressed his shoulder blades hard against the plastic chair. Even ergonomically built, even padded in thick plastic and cotton batting, there was no way the chair was anything but a device of torture after a couple of hours. Especially when it was so deadly quiet outside. If he'd had some more contacts to track, had the possibility of a hostile submarine contact on his screen, or anything even remotely resembling something interesting to do instead of listening to the soft hiss of biological noises and water in his earphones, staring at the green waterfall display until his eyes ached, anything at all, the chair wouldn't be quite so uncomfortable.

It wasn't particularly fair, either. Pencehaven glanced up at the clock and swore quietly. Another two hours until Renny Jacobs came down to relieve him. And that asshole was always early, thank God. Sliding his way into Sonar, smirking like somebody was going to give him a gold star for showing up fifteen minutes early. Well, if he wanted to be a suckup like that, let him. Watches were scheduled for a four-hour stretch, and you didn't gain any brownie points by being early every night.

Still, even a random visit from Jacobs would be good for a distraction about now. Oh, sure, there were plenty of possibilities. They all knew that there was a submarine in the area, and they all knew that it would be one that wouldn't look like anything else on the sonar screen. That alone was enough to keep Pencehaven from settling into a complete stupor, the possibility that he might miss first contact on a new class of boat. Still, after the first hour, even that possibility wore thin.

He shifted from side to side, trying to loosen a stiff muscle that ran along his spine. Overdid it in the gym last night, working out on the weight bench. You had to make an effort to stay in shape on board a submarine, and Pencehaven made it a point to be the most buffed out submariner on the boat. Jacobs might have a sharp set of ears on him, there was no doubt about that, but Pencehaven was absolutely certain that he could kick the skinny young man's ass anytime he wanted.

He spent a few minutes musing over the possibilities of beating the crap out of Jacobs just for the hell of it, and then became aware of a faint . . . well, it wasn't exactly a sound, it was too soft for that. It was more like a rub, the sound of silk gliding over rough skin, just the way it had been when he'd last been on liberty—wait, there it was again. He shut his eyes, suddenly oblivious to the ache in his back, the uncomfortable chair, and the possible outcomes of his long-standing feud with Jacobs.

There it was again. *Rub, whish, rub*—what the hell was it? He glanced over to make sure the tape recorder was running, then studied the green waterfall display in front of him. He zoomed in on one particular object, and studied the inverted V's piling up on each other, and tried to extract some signal from the random noise generating spikes there. Sure, the computer was good at it, better than he was most of the time, but there were always times when the computer missed something. Especially when it was an intermittent noise, and one that sounded . . . well, the only way to put it was fuzzy around the edges.

He tapped the screen with his pencil. There. Maybe just—yes, that was it. But the spikes of green signal were barely sticking out of the surrounding noise. He watched, correlating the rising signal amplitude with what he was hearing through his headphones.

Suddenly, irrevocably, he knew for certain that he had it. There was no way to exactly quantify what it was that convinced him that it was so, but he was certain nonetheless. Without hesitating, he toggled his microphone on. "Conn, Sonar, submarine contact, bearing one-three-five, range—well, around five thousand to ten thousand. I need you to maneuver to clarify the bearing for me."

"Sonar, are you certain?" Pencehaven recognized the voice of the commanding officer.

"Yes, sir," he replied confidently. "I'm certain."

"Because the bearing you're indicating along with the range latitude you're giving me correlates very closely to the *Arizona* memorial. You knew that, right?"

Pencehaven swore silently. Yes, now that he thought about it, it did correlate to the *Arizona*. It could be a current washing through a portion of the old wreck. Why didn't they clean it up? There was no sense in leaving rusting metal down on the ocean floor just to clutter up the sonar and navigation picture for the rest of them.

"Yes, sir, I know that. But it . . . it . . ." Suddenly, Pencehaven wasn't exactly sure as to how to explain it. "It sounds weird, sir. Not like anything else we've heard down here."

There was a long pause on the circuit, then, "Okay, we'll slip on over there and take a look. What's the source of the signal?"

"It's mechanical and hydraulic, sir. I'm not exactly certain what. Intermittent. And I can't put a name to the exact equipment." Pencehaven was aware that a note of desperation was creeping into his voice.

Why didn't the skipper believe him? They knew that there was a submarine in the area, one that wasn't in the acoustic library. This was just the sort of thing that you would expect to hear.

"Maybe a bilge pump of some sort, sir," he said, grasping at straws. "All I know is it doesn't belong there."

"Okay. Like I said, we'll get a little closer." Pencehaven could hear the doubt in the commanding officer's voice.

He stared in frustration at the screen, resisting the urge to tap his fingers on the console. Why wouldn't it give up one sharp, clear transient, some electrical signal that he could clearly peg as being foreign. Was that so much to ask? Who the hell could run so silent except for a U.S. submarine? But it wasn't one of theirs, of that he was certain. He knew the acoustic signature of every piece of equipment on every U.S. boat. No, this was something different, his earlier certainty returned.

The question was, how was he going to convince the captain? Acid flooded into his stomach as he realized what the answer had to be. He turned to the junior sonarman sitting next to him. "Send a messenger down to wake up Petty Officer Jacobs. Tell him I need him up here."

TFCC
1540 local (GMT-10)

"That's got to be it, Admiral!" Lab Rat shouted. "By God, we've got him now!"

Batman studied the interlocking areas of probability generated by the S-3 Viking and the submarine. Not a lot to go on, but it was all they had at this point.

"It's only one submarine," Batman said. He pounded on the plotting table with frustration. "And a little one, at that. Why the hell is one submarine driving the whole course of this battle?"

Lieutenant Green spoke up. "Submarines always have, sir. Ever since their widespread use in naval warfare. A recent example, in the battle of the Falklands, the mere rumor of a British Swiftsure class attack submarine was enough to force the Argentineans into some rather desperate ploys. And when the Brits thought that an Argentinean diesel was deployed, they expended darn near half of the world's sonobuoy resources trying to find it. Killed a lot of whales along the way, too."

Batman shook his head in frustration. "I know that. It's just not fair, dammit! I'm sitting here on the most powerful aircraft carrier in the world, and there's a little bit of metal cobbled together in the water, keeping me out of the action." He looked up at the two of them, rage in his eyes. "How certain are you of this?"

Lab Rat fielded the ball. "I won't say it's a certainty, Admiral," he said slowly, tracing the two areas of probability with his finger lightly. "And the position report from the submarine is none too certain. Both of them are holding contact on something that they think—just think, mind you—might be a submarine. The problem for both of them is that their contacts are located in the immediate vicinity of the *Arizona*, which could account for both detections. It could be a submarine—or it could be a lot of jittery aircrew desperate to find a contact."

"Any shot they took, Admiral," Green chimed in, "would probably result in substantial damage to the memorial itself. And if it's not a submarine, all that will do is blast pieces of the *Arizona* all over the seabed floor, thus further complicating the ASW problem." She shook her head, not discouragingly, just figuring the odds. "If we were having a tough time telling known anomalies from submarines before, we'll have an impossible time after that, not to mention the difficulty of doing any minesweeping without a clean chart."

"Goddammit," Batman said. "At some point, you gotta go with your gut. Both that submarine crew and that S-3 crew know about the *Arizona*, and they still think that they're holding a submarine. But you're right about one thing—even if we do kill this one, you'll have a hell of a mine problem after that. So what do we do?"

The three fell silent for a moment, then Green spoke, her voice hesitant. "I have an idea, sir. But I'm not sure how practical it is."

"Flight quarters, flight quarters, all hands to flight quarters," the 1MC blared.

"Spit it out, Lieutenant. I've got an air strike launching in about two minutes, and this aircraft carrier isn't going to have time to worry about one submarine. I want it dead, and I want it dead now."

Green leaned over the chart table, the edge of the table butting up against the hard, flat expanse of her abdomen. She started to talk, slowly and quietly at first, but gaining confidence as she spoke. When she finished, Lab Rat turned to Batman.

"The sub skipper's going to hate you for this," he said.

Batman nodded. "I know. But that old girl down there has been blasted too many times already. She deserves a chance to fight back. This time."

TWENTY

"What you got?" Jacobs asked as he stumbled into the sonar shack. His eyes were still bleary around the edges, his face slack with exhaustion. "The messenger said you needed me."

Pencehaven shook his head. "Need isn't exactly the right word. Oh, hell, it is." He jerked his thumb at the junior sonarman sitting next to him. "Take a hike, Jack." The sonarman slid out of his seat, and Jacobs took his place.

Pencehaven took a deep breath. "We haven't always been on the best of terms, Renny. I know that. But let me show you what you've got. Your ears—your ears are better than mine on something like this. The skipper doesn't believe me because of what happened last time. But I've got something this time; I want you to take a look at it and back me up. They'll listen to you. And somebody's got to listen before this little bitch gets away."

Pencehaven sketched in the last fifteen minutes, then passed his headset over to Jacobs. "Here—I can still hear it."

Jacobs leaned back in his chair and his face assumed that oddly peaceful and serene expression that Pencehaven had come to associate with his nemesis. His eyes were shut, his mouth barely open, his breathing slow and regular. For all appearances, he might have been taking a nap in the sonar shack. Suddenly, Jacobs popped upright in the chair. He reached out for the communications switch, then hesitated. He turned to Pencehaven. "You're right on this, you know. You didn't need me to tell you that."

Pencehaven heaved a sigh of relief. "You heard it?"

"Of course I heard it," Jacobs said dismissively. "You'd have to be deaf not to hear it. And you're right, it's probably a bilge pump of some sort. The one thing we know is it isn't ours. So call the captain, tell him you know you have a contact. It's your contact, you lead the targeting on it. I'll back you up."

"They might take it better coming from you," Pencehaven said.

Jacobs shook his head. "No. The captain will make his decision based on how confident you sound. That was the problem last time—you didn't trust your instincts. But you've nailed it hard and true this time. Now, go for it—do what you're supposed to do." Jacobs's eyes glittered with something that in someone else would be taken for fanaticism.

Pencehaven took a deep breath, his gut suddenly shaky. The safety of the submarine—indeed, the entire battle group—rested on his shoulders, now. He had to do it right, had to make them believe. "Conn, sonar," he began, consciously forcing his voice to sound a little louder, a little surer. "Captain, I have a subsurface contact. Probability high." He reeled off the current range and bearing information, now refined from their own submarine's movement through the water and the angle to

the anomaly. "He's hiding behind the memorial, sir. I'm
sure of it."

"Sure?" the captain came back. "Sure like you were
last time?"

"No, sir. That was a mistake. But this time I'm sure."

"Get Petty Officer Jacobs in there," the skipper said.
"Pencehaven, you have to learn that this isn't a solo
game. We live and die by teamwork."

Pencehaven glanced over at Jacobs, his eyes grateful.
"He's here with me now, sir. And Petty Officer Jacobs
concurs."

"Then why the hell didn't you say so?" the captain
snapped. "Good call, Pencehaven. Your aw shit status is
rescinded effective this moment."

"Thanks, Renny," Pencehaven said awkwardly. "I owe
you one."

Jacobs shook his head. "No. I owe you one. Because
if you hadn't gone with your gut on this one, you would
have ignored the contact. And the next sound I heard
might've been a torpedo heading for my bunk."

"Okay, let's run the targeting problem," Pencehaven
said, and began punching in figures. "Snapshot protocol—
you on it?"

Jacobs's hands were flying over his keyboard.
"Couldn't get rid of me now to save your life," he murmured. Finally, his targeting solution solid, he looked
back up at Pencehaven. "This time, we do it right."

Viking 701
1600 local (GMT-10)

"I have a targeting solution," the TACCO announced
calmly.

Rabies didn't reply as he listened to the voice coming over his headset. Finally, he said, "Aye, aye, Admiral," and flipped the switch back over to internal communications. "Negative on the firing solution," he said.

"What! It's mine!" the TACCO howled.

"No go, buddy. There's a friendly in the area—the submarine's taking the lead on the kill."

"The sub's gonna kill my contact?" the TACCO bitched.

"That's affirmative. We're all on the same team here, remember?"

In the backseat, the complaints subsided to an angry muttering occasionally drifting around the cockpit. Rabies shook his head sadly, commiserating with the TACCO and the AW, but understanding the reasoning. The last thing an American submarine wanted was an S-3 dropping torpedoes into the water it was operating in. Yes, letting the submarine prosecute this contact was a better solution, no doubt about it.

But what exactly had the admiral meant when he said that the submarine had an advantage that the aircraft didn't? And why had he said that the enemy contact was a pushover?

USS Centurion
1602 local (GMT-10)

"Conn, radio. ELF message requesting we come shallow for coordination with battle group."

The captain gripped the arms of his chair. "I don't want to come shallow right now," he said quietly, frustration evident in his voice. "I'm holding contact, damn it."

"Sorry, Skipper. The battle group seems fairly insistent." The radioman's voice was apologetic.

The captain sighed heavily. "You heard the man. Conning officer, make your depth eighty feet. Prepare for communications with the battle group."

As the submarine rose smoothly through the water, the captain thought sour thoughts about the Navy, about surface ships, and about one admiral aviator in particular.

Five minutes later, his worst fears about aviators were confirmed. "You want us to do what?" he almost howled, but then caught himself at the last moment. "I'm not sure I understand, admiral," he said in a voice more suited to the close confines of the submarine. Silence was a reflex with most submariners, and the skipper was no exception. "What you're proposing is . . . shall we say . . . not without its risks?"

"I understand that, Captain." The admiral briefly outlined his concerns about a torpedo attack, then concluded with, "Besides, I think you'd agree it's time the old girl had a chance to fight back. She didn't. Not the first time, not against the attack that put her on the bottom of the ocean, there."

The captain sighed, and considered the physics of the problem. Sure, the bow of the submarine was particularly strengthened with measures designed to prevent her from flooding in the event that she did run into something. But still, Murphy's Law prevailed. If something could go wrong, it would. "She wasn't built as a battering ram, Admiral."

"I'm not asking for a battering ram, Captain, just a gentle shove. We've got an expert up here who thinks that will be all that it will take. A couple of nudges, then you back on out of there at best speed."

Backing out at best speed. Yeah, sure. The captain refrained from pointing out just how unwieldy a submarine going astern was, the difficulties of maneuvering, and just how much noise she herself would kick up. "The southeast corner, you say?" he asked delicately.

"Affirmative. One nudge, the southeast corner."

"Aye-aye, Admiral—we're on it." The captain clicked off the circuit and gazed around the control room with a sense of unreality. Finally, he said, "Okay, you all heard the admiral. Conning officer, take us to the southeast corner of the *Arizona* and prepare for . . . nudging."

TFCC
1603 local (GMT-10)

"Incoming!" General Haynes clamped down on the edge of the table and ducked involuntarily. The two Navy officers on either side of him shot him a surprised look, while the Air Force officer grinned enigmatically.

Sheepishly, the Army officer straightened up. "What is it with you people?" he asked good-naturedly. "You ever get used to that?" *That* was the hard thunder rolling through the compartment, the noise that was as much felt as heard, the bone-jolting sensation that rattled computer screens, shook coffee mugs, and rendered conversation almost impossible.

Batman shrugged. "Around here, we call it the sound of freedom."

The Army officer breathed deeply. "Where I'm from, we call it the sound of artillery," he grumbled quietly, but returned to the task at hand.

Tombstone pointed to a small TV screen located in one corner of the room. "Watch—what you're hearing will make more sense then."

The plat camera showed an overview of the flight

deck, and now the Army officer could see the source of the noise. A Tomcat on the bow catapult was in full military power, trembling on the catapult with the JBDs, or jet blast deflectors, at right angles to the deck behind her. As he watched, he saw a small, blurred figure on the deck to the left of the aircraft whip off a sharp salute, then another figure dropped to the deck and held up one hand.

The Tomcat moved almost imperceptibly at first, but after the first few microseconds, it picked up speed at an astounding rate. It shot down the catapult, trailing steam and fire in its wake, and blasted off the bow of the aircraft carrier. It disappeared from view for a few moments, then he saw it struggling back up into the air. "I thought he was a goner," the Army officer said softly, his voice hushed with awe.

Batman shook his head. "All in a day's work for those fellows," he said. He pointed at Admiral Magruder. "For me and him, too. Years ago."

"Not so long as you'd think," Tombstone shot back.

The plat camera showed two more F-14s already taxi-ing into position, the jet blast deflectors now flat on the deck to avoid impeding their progress, to allow them easy access to the catapult, the flight deck crew in their spe-cially choreographed dance around the waiting aircraft. Seven seconds later, the roar thundered through TFCC again.

"This goes on all day and all night?" the Army officer asked, doubt in his voice.

"The Tomcats are the worst," Tombstone said. "Or the best—depending on how you look at it. The other guys, you can hear them launch, too, but after a while you can tell what's launching by how bad your compartment rat-tles."

"Or whether your computer reboots," Batman put in.

"And in just a few minutes, they'll be within each others' engagement envelopes," Tombstone said, turning away from the plat camera to study the tactical display located at the forward part of the compartment. "It'll be all over but the shouting. Do you think this is going to work?"

Batman said, "It has to. We don't have any other choices."

"Admiral, it's the S-3," the TAO shouted, not even turning around to look at them, his gaze fixed on the screen in front of him. "He's reporting audibles, audibles from his submarine contact—looks like she's going to make a break for it!"

Both Batman and Tombstone swore softly. Then Batman said, "Okay, everyone. You know the game plan. Let's get started."

"What about the submarine?" the Coast Guard officer asked.

"Our sub is on him. And if he misses, we'll have him clear the area and turn the S-3 loose on him. Put a couple more ASW helicopters airborne, then forget about it."

USS Centurion
1610 local (GMT-10)

The sudden barrage of green lines dancing across his screen and the hard thrum of mechanical noise in his headset sent a huge wave of relief flowing through Petty Officer Pencehaven, followed immediately by a rush of adrenaline. If he'd had any doubts at all—and he'd had a few, he admitted to himself—they were now evaporated like the early morning dew.

The acoustic signals tracing across his display, as well

as the churning noise of the propeller completely re-
solved the question of whether or not there was a submarine hiding behind the *Arizona* on the seabed floor. He
turned to glance at Jacobs, a wide smile on his face.
"Guess we got him."

Jacobs shook his head. "Guess *you* got him," he
pointed out. His smile deepened a little bit, until it almost
looked like a snarl. "But we're gonna kill him—together."

"Sonar, Conn. I need that targeting solution now!" the
captain's voice said.

"Updating now, sir. Done," Pencehaven said. "Request
weapons free."

"Weapons free. Fire at will. Flooding tubes three and
five—it's all yours, boys. Good work."

Pencehaven double-checked the solution, his finger
poised over the fire button. Then he glanced over at Jacobs, took the other man's hand, and pressed it firmly
down on the button. "First kill is yours, buddy," he said.
"And thanks."

A low rumble shot through the submarine as the torpedo left its tube. It appeared immediately on his acoustic
display, just after the noise saturated his headset. The
automatic gain control cut in, reducing the noise to a
tolerable level.

"Looking good, looking good," Jacobs chanted softly,
watching the contact on Pencehaven's screen. "You can
run, but you can't hide."

And indeed that was true with the Mark 38 ADCAP
torpedo. It had both acoustic and wake homing capabilities built in, as well as a logic discriminator that kept it
away from its own submarine. Once it caught the first
sniff of a contact, it was virtually impossible to avoid.

Pencehaven and Jacobs watched as the torpedo fell
into a lazy circle, then broke the arc to zero in on the

contact now streaking across their screen as a bright green lozenge. "Recommend we go active, sir," Pencehaven said. There was no longer any advantage in maintaining strictly passive and acoustic contact. The other submarine knew that they were there. With a torpedo, it could reach no other conclusion than that it was not alone in the ocean.

As they watched, bright noise splattered across the screen, overlapping clusters and blobs of brilliant noise. The contact faded out, its acoustic return blanked out by the noise.

"Sir, we need that active," Pencehaven said urgently.

"I hear, I hear—go active," the captain said.

The submarine had evidently detected the torpedo—and who could not, as much noise as she put in the water—and ejected a series of noisemakers. They spun frantically through the water, churning up massive flumes of air bubbles, probably with acoustic generators inside them as well. The entire passive spectrum was clotted with new frequencies, lines that wavered crazily in and out of contact, completely obscuring the other submarine.

They could see that the torpedo was distracted by a noisemaker off to its right. It fell away from its original course, and started to make an approach on the noisemaker. Jacobs made the correction automatically, steering it away from there and back onto its original course.

"How much longer?" Pencehaven asked.

"Another five hundred yards," Jacobs said. Another five hundred yards, and the wire umbilical that still connected the torpedo to the submarine would snap, terminating the submarine's guidance capabilities.

"Man, look at her go. What's she doing, forty knots?"

"Has to be," Jacobs agreed. "Her propulsion has to be—"

"Let's get another shot off, boys," the captain's voice ordered. "No sense in taking any chances."

"Second shot, aye, sir," Pencehaven said promptly. Without even looking, he could tell that Jacobs was readying the second shot now. This one would be his, all his. He waited until Jacobs nodded, then depressed the fire button. Another low rumble swept through the submarine along with the whish of compressed air exploding outward from the tube.

"Shit!" Jacobs and Pencehaven exclaimed simultaneously.

"Inbound, inbound!" Pencehaven shouted. "Torpedo, torpedo in the water, bearing zero-zero-zero relative. Range, ten thousand yards. Snapshot procedures." He had Jacobs toggle off another torpedo immediately down the line of bearing, then held tight to the arms of his chair as the submarine broke into a hard turn to the right. "Noisemakers, decoys," he ordered.

Suddenly, the water around them was as alive with sound as it had been around the enemy contact. The submarine had managed to snap off a torpedo at them, and while the American submarine had sent one immediately down the same line of bearing, their main problem right now was not to guide their torpedo onto the target, but to avoid being a target themselves. Jacob snapped the wire guidance and said a silent prayer that the torpedo would find its mark.

The submarine was now traveling at one hundred and eighty degrees off its base course, establishing a line of bearing. It then cut hard to the right again, then to port, crossing its own wake several times. Finally, the depth tilted down at a steep angle. Pencehaven watched the depth indicator, and noted that they were moving below the thermocline, entering a region of the ocean where sound waves would be bent downward rather than upward. The change in depth across the gradient was intended to obscure the noise of the American submarine from the other torpedo.

"Can't be much of a torpedo," Pencehaven whispered, his voice barely audible. "Look, it's buying the first noisemaker." And indeed, the screen bore out his observations, as Jacobs watched the loud, slow torpedo fired by the minisub take dead aim on the first noisemaker they'd ejected. Thirty seconds later, they both pulled their headsets off long enough to avoid being bombarded by the noise of the explosion. "Wonder how many she carries," Pencehaven said, his voice slightly louder.

"Can't be more than one or two," Jacobs observed. "Not as small as she is."

"Back to the hunt, boys," the captain's voice said over the circuit. "I'm coming shallow—I want two more torpedoes up that bastard's ass."

The thermocline was a tricky bitch, one that worked both for you and against you, Pencehaven reflected. Sure, it obscured your own noise from an enemy submarine, but it also blocked the return of your own active sonar transmissions, although of course they'd gone silent during evasive maneuvers. The best hunting is done when both the submarine and the target are in the same acoustic layer.

As they came shallower, the enemy contact reappeared on their screens. "Got a targeting solution," Jacobs announced.

"Hold fire, hold fire!" the captain shouted. "We're too close to the carrier."

Pencehaven swore silently. The carrier was showing up as a large, green lozenge on his screen, her acoustic signature unmistakable on both the waterfall display and in his earphones. Nothing but a carrier had that peculiar chug, chug, the rhythmic thumps that accompanied flight deck operations, the peculiar hiss and whine of reactor coolant pumps. "No way we can take the shot," he observed.

"The best thing the carrier could do is get out of the way," Jacobs said. He shook his head in frustration. "We've still got two torpedoes in the water, though. Maybe one of them—" As he watched, the submarine contact disappeared from their screen.

Viking 701
1621 local (GMT-10)

Rabies let out a howl of glee. "Okay, boys and girls, time to earn our pay. It's all ours." The *Desron* had just handed off contact prosecution to the two ASW helicopters and the S-3. While their torpedoes were essentially the same type as those held on the submarine, with the helos bracketing the contact and providing a precise location, the targeting solution was improved by a factor of five.

"Who goes first, the helo or us?" the TACCO asked.

"Helo's closer in—not within minimums, though," the copilot pointed out. "I'd say the helo."

Sure enough, moments later, the *Desron*'s TAO said, "Paddywhack Six Zero One, take target with torpedoes."

The TACCO let out a groan of frustration. "It was mine, all mine," he said brokenly. "If only—"

Rabies put the S-3 into a tight turn, putting them nose on to the attacking helo. They watched the torpedo fall off of her hard point, splash noisily into the water, then dive. In the crystal clear waters, they could follow the course of the torpedo down to a considerable depth. Rabies fancied he could even see the outline of the minisub, a darker blotch against the white sand seabed and coral.

But wait, was that . . .

"Homeplate, you've got an inbound torpedo," he said, his voice calm despite the tension twisting his gut into a knot. "Repeat, torpedo inbound!"

"We've got it, Hunter," the TAO snapped.

As he watched, Rabies saw the *Jefferson*'s wake change in its configuration as the aircraft carrier started to turn. It was a standard ASW evasive maneuver, but was probably of no use in these waters. First, the carrier was just too massive, took too long to commence a change in direction. Her turning radius was measured in miles instead of yards. Second, the range was just too close. There was not time for the carrier's wake to even reflect the change of course, much less for it to do any good.

USS Centurion
1630 local (GMT-10)

"With a target that big, she can't miss," Pencehaven said. He stared at the geometry of the attack, sick dread filling his heart. Sure, it wasn't his boat that was going to get nailed, and he was glad about that. But what about the six thousand plus men and women on board that aircraft carrier? And wasn't that the heart of the entire battle plan, having the air power to establish air superiority for the troops who would follow? An idea flickered through his brain, and without thinking, he toggled the communications switch. "Captain, recommend course two-four-zero, speed flank plus," he said firmly. "Sir, if we can get close enough in, we can eject our noisemakers into the path. We've already seen that it's a stupid torpedo—it'll go for it, sir. I'm sure of it."

"The carrier's got her own noisemakers," the captain said.

Pencehaven shook his head. "It'll be too close, sir. Even if they destroy the torpedo, it looks like it's going to be astern of her. The overpressure wave and the explosion itself may damage the carrier's propellers. I know she's got four of them, but if she loses maneuverability . . ." Pencehaven didn't need to finish the sentence. Everybody on board the submarine knew what it would mean to lose a propeller—a dramatic decrease in maneuverability. And if the aircraft carrier couldn't maneuver, she couldn't turn into the wind to launch and recover aircraft. "Recommend we deploy noisemakers for the carrier's protection, sir," Pencehaven concluded.

Men don't rise to be the captains of submarines if they're prone to indecision. The captain's answer came back immediately. "Roger, conning officer, come right, steady course two-four-zero, flank speed. Engineer, give me everything you've got. We'll be noisier than a pig, but let's see what this old tub can do."

I know what this old tub can do, Pencehaven thought. *We're on refresher training, for heck's sake. If ever there's a time that she's got max speed available, it's now.*

Beside him, Jacobs looked sick. "We're going to be back within range, then," he said, "And noisier than a bitch in heat."

"Not a problem, Renny," Pencehaven said with more confidence than he felt. "Like I said, these are stupid torpedoes. They went for the noisemakers once—they'll go for it again. And we both know she's probably only carrying two. After that, she's going to have to cut and run, and then we'll nail her ourselves."

"We haven't been so good at that so far," Jacobs pointed out.

Pencehaven shook his head, waving away the comment. "She's mine, Renny. She's all mine."

Everything inside the submarine was shaking now as the submarine approached max possible speed. The water was coursing over her like a thick fluid, sound echoing through her limber hulls, vortices creating noise as the water flowed over every protuberance in her hull. The submarine was built for silence, but it was almost impossible to run silently at flank speed. The equipment required to maintain the engineering plant, the water over the hull, even the rattle of the periscope in its tube all contributed to the cacophony now pouring into the water.

As they watched, the contact turned back to meet them.

"Okay, bitch. Let's see what you've got," Pencehaven said softly. As they watched, the other submarine accelerated to her own flank speed. No new torpedoes appeared in the water. For a moment, Pencehaven marveled. They'd pegged it that time, hadn't they? Two torpedoes, that was all. And now she was out of weapons, and running for safety. But she wouldn't find it, not anywhere in this sector of water, not as long as USS *Centurion* was there.

"Captain, she's headed back to the *Arizona*," Pencehaven said. "I recommend you let her think we've lost her, then execute the maneuver recommended by the carrier."

"Roger, that's the plan," the captain's voice said, now firmly in control. "Go active, stay in a search mode. As soon as we lose contact. Let her think we're clueless. Then secure on my command, and we'll close the *Arizona*."

TFCC
USS Jefferson
1645 local (GMT-10)

It was the Army officer's turn to look puzzled as the naval officers and Coast Guard officer clustered around the table turned pale. He looked from face to face, searching for a clue, then looked back at the tactical display. "What's that funny symbol?"

Finally, Magruder spoke. "An enemy torpedo. And it's headed straight for us."

"But what's *Centurion* doing?" Green broke in. A frown creased her face, then slowly cleared. She turned to Lab Rat, and nodded solemnly. "Seems that we're not the only ones with some good ideas around here."

They all stared at the screen as the *Centurion* screamed toward them, her speed leader increased to an almost unimaginable length for a submarine. New symbols popped onto the screen, evidence that she was ejecting noisemakers. As they watched, the torpedo symbol turned abruptly left, and headed straight for one. Just as abruptly, the *Centurion* changed course, then disappeared from the screen.

"I'm gonna owe that man a beer," Batman said softly. He turned his attention back to the TAO. "How many more fighters have we got to launch?"

"Six more, sir," the TAO replied. "All standing by and ready to go."

Batman turned to Tombstone. "Just like the old days, isn't it?" he asked softly.

"Not quite," Tombstone said. "We're not in a cockpit."

TWENTY-ONE

USS Centurion
1700 local (GMT-10)

"Conning officer. I want you to listen to me very, very carefully." The captain's voice was calm, betraying no hint of nervousness. "This is just like making an approach on the pier. You just can't see it. We're going to use the same speeds, the same tiny course corrections. And on my signal, let engineering know that I want this boat backing down as hard as she's ever backed in her life."

The conning officer nodded nervously, and glanced at the Chief of the Boat, who was positioned behind the helmsman and the planesman. The chief nodded. "Piece of cake, Captain," the COB said, more for the conning officer's ears than for the captain's. "Done this a hundred times in my sleep."

The captain grunted. "Well, if you were contemplating a nap now, I suggest you put that off for a while." Although the joke was lame, pent-up nervousness in the small compartment sent a wave of quiet chuckles through the crew.

"Okay, men—here we go. All ahead one-third, indicate turns for one knot."

The submarine's movement was not perceptible, but everyone watching the speed indicator saw it creep slowly up. It quivered, barely moved off the zero mark, and held there. "Good job, engineer," the captain said softly, noting how well the engineering personnel were maintaining steam pressure in the main turbine. "A really sweet job."

They crept forward for what seemed like an eternity, and then the captain ordered, "All stop." He glanced around the control room, then said, "Sound the collision alarm." A red light began flashing in the compartment in a distinctive pattern to indicate an impending collision, albeit one that was intentional. "All hands brace for shock," the captain continued, his voice still quiet.

Suddenly, the submarine jolted. Violent movement were not a normal part of the submariner's life, and even the more experienced crew members gasped. A horrible grinding noise rang through the submarine like a hollow bell, and equipment shuddered in its racks. Pencils and papers not secured were flung to the deck. Then one sailor let out a moan of panic.

"Steady, steady," the captain warned. "Remember, we're doing this on purpose."

The noise and shuddering seemed to go on forever, growing louder and deeper as the submarine's hull made contact with the ancient battleship now permanently at rest on the Pacific floor. Finally, there was a perceptible decrease in the motion. Then it ceased just as suddenly as it started.

In sonar, Jacobs and Pencehaven had taken off their headsets to avoid damage to their ears. They listened to the noise of the collision through the overhead speaker, then slapped their headsets back on as soon as the noise ceased. Softer, but clearly discernible, they heard the groan of old metal shifting in its position, of tons and tons of World War II steel moving from where it had been planted so many years before. The *Arizona* might not be breaking up this time, but there was no doubt that their maneuver had had its intended effect.

"I hear her!" Jacobs shouted, his sensitive ears the first to catch the sound of a new noise. "Propellers turning— she's going to try to make a run for it." But even as he spoke, he could tell it was no use. The *Arizona*, once it decided to move, was an inexorable force. And the submarine had sought out a position too close to her side for protection.

TFCC
USS **Jefferson**
1702 Local (GMT-10)

"We got it," a voice howled over the SEAL circuit behind him. Batman turned to stare at it, and a grim smile broke out over his face. He turned to Tombstone.

His former lead nodded, then said, "Weapons free on all Chinese units. I want that ship a blackened, smoking hull in the water, do you hear me?"

"Aye-aye, Admiral," Batman answered, his voice filled with savage glee. "A smoking hull it is." He turned to Bam-Bam with fire in his eyes. "Make it so."

TWENTY-TWO

USS Louis B. Puller
1703 local (GMT-10)

Lieutenant Brett Carter stared up at the speaker as though he could convince himself that the words that were coming over were true. His operations chief was already putting his watchstanders in motion, anticipating the lieutenant's next command.

Finally, Carter picked up the microphone and answered up. "Puller, roger. Out." He turned to the chief, his mouth still slightly open. "You heard."

The chief nodded. "I did indeed."

A new fire seemed to infuse the lieutenant. It had been a long day, longer than any one that he had ever had, fraught with uncertainty and the unexpected challenges of command. It had been his decision to get *Puller* under way at the first warning, his decision to steam straight out from port rather than wait for orders. At the time, he'd experienced gut-wrenching uncertainty alternating with the conviction that he'd screwed up so very badly that Shore Patrol would be waiting for him on the pier when *Puller* steamed back in to port.

But now . . . now this. Vindication, if he'd needed it.

"Firing keys," Carter ordered, and it all went rather swiftly from that point on. The three Chinese vessels were already designated in the system as hostile targets and it was a simple matter to assign two Harpoon anti-ship missiles to each one. The six missiles rippled out of the quad canisters mounted along the sides of the ship with a slight jar.

As Carter watched the symbols materialized on the screen, each on arrowing straight and true toward its intended target, he felt a surge of pride. Challenges, responsibilities, crisis—all in all, he figured it had been the kind of day that he'd joined the Navy expecting. No matter what his next operational tour, it would be years before he would again have command—albeit only temporary—of a warship. And after today, he knew that nothing else he could do would ever equal that experience.

Tomcat 204
1705 local (GMT-10)

"Kelly, my dear, are you ready for this?" Bird Dog said over tactical. He glanced over at his new wingman as he asked it, taking his eyes off his heads-up display briefly. "You're about to get blooded, woman."

After four hours in Sick Bay, complaining at the top of the their voices that they were fine, Bird Dog and Gator had been released to full duty. Sure, they had a few cuts and bruises, but no worse than after any of their previous ejections. Gator insisted that, because of their experience, they were more qualified than the doctors to assess their own physical conditions.

"I'm ready," the calm voice of his new wingman said. "So is Tits."

"Hell of a name for a RIO," Gator cried happily. "You get Tits, I get Gator—now how did that work out?"

"Perhaps if Gator's full name were Theodore Irving Turner, he might be Tits as well," came a deep bass voice from Green's backseat. "It's just like your mother always told you, Bird Dog—don't mess with tits."

Gator suppressed a snort of disgust. His head was buried in the soft plastic cover surrounding his radar scope as he worked the angles and dangles, the relative velocities and kill ratios in his mind. Four MiGs headed out against two Tomcats and two Hornets—well, the odds were in their favor, weren't they? Still, in Gator's ever so humble opinion, Bird Dog had never taken this shit seriously enough. No, not seriously enough by half. And from the sounds of it, neither did Lieutenant Kelly Green or her RIO, Tits.

"Thor, you come in and get that first pair tied up," Bird Dog said a second later. "Me and Kelly are going to go high and come in on the second two. You think you can handle them?"

"Oh, I imagine two Marines are more than enough to take care of a couple of MiGs," a slow Southern drawl came from Hornet 106. "Hellman can pull his share of the load."

"All right, weapons free," Bird Dog said. "We don't know who the hell is in that boat down there, but evidently the Chinese are as interested in him as we are. They want him, they can't have him. That's the rules of the game."

"Are you going to get us in the game or not?" Gator demanded from the backseat. "Or is this little mutual admiration society taking up too much of your time?"

In answer, Bird Dog slammed the Tomcat into afterburner and went into a steep, tail twisting climb. Gator gasped as the G-forces pounded against him, sucking the blood down from his head and toward his feet. "Dammit, asshole," he squeezed out, simultaneous grunting in an M-1 maneuver designed to force blood back up to his brain. He could feel the pressure suit activating around his legs and torso, but Gator was never one to leave the question of whether or not he stayed conscious entirely to automation.

"I thought you were in a hurry to get somewhere," Bird Dog said innocently, but he backed off the throttles and eased off on his rate of ascent. "AMRAAM as soon as we're ready."

"About five seconds, I make it," Gator said, breathing more easily now as the G-forces subsided. "Stand by— now!"

The ATG-71 radar with advanced avionics held solid contact on the incoming bogey. The aircraft shuddered slightly as the AMRAAM dropped off the wing, the advanced avionics automatically retrimming the aircraft.

"Fox One, Fox One," Bird Dog sang out. Fox One was the call assigned to a medium-range missile, such as an AMRAAM or a Sparrow. "Looking good."

"Not good enough," Bird Dog said. He punched the Tomcat into afterburner. "Let's get up close and personal for some knife fighting."

Hornet 106
1706 local (GMT-10)

Bird Dog wasn't the only one flying with an inexperienced pilot on his wing, and for the Hornet pilot, the problem was particularly challenging. At least in the Tomcat, the pilot had a RIO sitting right behind him, ready to double-check plans and provide a sanity check

if the pilot became overwhelmed. Not so in the Hornet—
the pilot took over all the RIO's duties in addition to his
own.

As confident as Thor had sounded over tactical, he had
his own private doubts about his wingman. First Lieutenant "Hellman" Franks was on his nugget cruise, still
learning that there were old pilots, there were bold pilots,
but there were no old, bold pilots.

Not that Thor had anything against showing balls. No,
not at all. After all, they were both Marines weren't they?
And Marine fighter pilots at that.

And it wasn't that Hellman wasn't a damned fine pilot,
either. He was, as Thor had seen all too often on the
bombing range and during workups. He'd sailed through
basic and pipeline training at the top of his class,
achieved near miraculous scores on the bombing range,
and was considered by all to be one hot shit pilot. If he
lived long enough, he'd be looking at fast promotions in
the Corps.

Still, there was an edge to the man that bothered Thor.
Sure, you want to get airborne and get the other guy fast
and hard, but you want to do it clean. You take chances,
but only those you have to. And you remember that
you've got a multimillion-dollar aircraft strapped to your
ass that Uncle Sam would really prefer that you bring
back in one piece.

"Okay, Hellman, just like in refresher training," Thor
said over tactical, switching to the private frequency the
two of them shared. "You know MiGs, and this is no
different than training. Except no mistakes."

"You ever see me make a mistake, Thor?" a Virginia
drawl asked. "Anywhere?"

"You've never been in combat before," Thor said
bluntly. "You suck it in, Marine, and do it the way we
taught you."

"Don't worry about me, old man," Hellman shot back. "I'll keep your ass out of trouble."

Old man—why that little punk better . . . Thor pushed the thoughts aside, saving sorting that out for another time. Compartmentalization, that was the key to survival in the air. You keep focused on your task, don't let your wife, your dog, your wingman, your anything, not even your bladder, distract you from what you've got to do.

"Take high," he said abruptly. "Follow my lead. We take the first one with AMRAAM, the second with Sidewinder."

"Or guns," Hellman added.

"That bastard better be real dead before we get within gun range," Thor said. "Now get your ass high."

Hellman peeled off and put the Hornet in a steep, almost vertical climb. Thor shuddered as he thought of the fuel the light aircraft was sucking down. Another thing you learned early on, flying the Hornet. You had a maneuverability and speed that the Tomcat couldn't touch, but God were they thirsty aircraft. You saved fuel when you could, knowing that it might be longer than you liked between tanking.

"Tally ho," Thor said over tactical, acknowledging to the air traffic controller in CDC onboard Jefferson that he had contact on his incoming bogeys. "Hornet One-zero-six engaging lead flight of MiGs."

MiG Number Eight
1708 local (GMT-10)

Second Lieutenant Tai Huang curled his hand around the stick of his MiG, thankful that the thin cotton glove between his hand and it would absorb the moisture he felt

seeping out of his palms. As section leader and lead for
the forward-most pair of MiGs in this flight, it was his
responsibility to order his disposition of forces, along
with the assistance of the air traffic controllers on board
the Chinese carrier. It was a new way of working, one
that none of the four were completely at ease with yet,
even after countless practice sessions before they'd left
their homeland. But even after two hundred hours of concentrated airborne coordination, he still felt uncomfortable without a ground control intercept, or GCI,
whispering guidance in his right ear over the circuit. Still,
if the GCI could learn his job, then Tai could do it as
well. No matter that the GCI didn't have to concentrate
on dancing a powerful aircraft through the air, evading
missiles, and generally remaining airborne while he
thought out the disposition of forces. It would have been
impossible with earlier MiGs, but the 33 was so advanced
it virtually did his thinking for him. Automatic trim control, heads-up display to prevent him from ever having
to look away from the battle in front of him, and a host
of electronic and weapons avionics that could virtually
fight the battle on their own.

Almost, but not completely. As long as there were men
in the cockpits of the enemy, there would be men in the
cockpit of a MiG.

Just as now. While the MiG avionics was already suggesting that the section of two aircraft behind him be
vectored to meet the oncoming Hornets, Tai knew better.
Huan Tan, the lead in the second flight, was an excellent
pilot and a particular master of the intricate geometries
when a lighter, more maneuverable aircraft such as a
MiG took on a monster like a Tomcat. Tai didn't like
admitting it, but it was one of his responsibilities as a
section commander.

He himself, on the other hand, excelled in quick reflex

actions, the bumblebee dance of equally matched foes in midair, the split-second decisions required when a MiG took on an equally agile Hornet. Yes, the correct thing to do was send Huan Tan after the Tomcats while Tai and his wingman took on the Hornets.

He made his orders clear over the circuits linking the four aircraft, even as he gained altitude and changed course slightly to put himself nose on to the lead Tomcat U.S. Marine or U.S. Navy? Too far away to tell. Not that it mattered anyway. Either way, the Tomcat would die. His wingman, Chan, chattered quietly over tactical to him, keeping him posted on every minute decision he made as he gained altitude and came in to form on Tai. They were fighting in the loose deuce position, the one that had been the favorite of American fighter forces for decades.

"On my mark," Tai said. He wasn't referring to a verbal mark, but to the notation that the avionics system would make in the link between the two aircraft data systems when Tai fired his first missile. Tai toggled the weapons selector switch into the proper mode, waited a split second, then pickled it off.

The missile shot out true and straight, descending quickly, its tail fire a bright phoenix in the sky. Seconds later, he heard his wingman cry out in exultation as he, too, fired his first real weapon in anger.

"Climb, climb," Tai cried, gaining more sky even as he spoke. Altitude was safety, granting the aircraft room to recover from fatal mistakes, forcing the Hornet into a level game.

A harsh warning buzz went off just behind his left ear, and a missile symbol popped into being on his heads up display. An AMRAAM, one of the advanced medium-range missiles that all Hornets carried. Well, soon the

Tomcat pilot would soon be too busy worrying about
Tai's missile to be so rash.

Tai put his aircraft into a hard, spine shattering turn,
then pivoted about and waited at an angle just behind the
Tomcat's side as the other aircraft climbed. Behind him,
he could hear Huan Tan chanting quietly to himself as
he chased after the two Hornets.

They waited for what seemed like minutes, but in reality it must have been only a couple of seconds. Tai
jinked hard, kicking out countermeasures, flares and
chaff, then spinning his MiG away from the burning,
noisy metallic cluster that he hoped would suck the AM-
RAAM in. He turned back to face the Tomcat, and saw
empty sky, even though his heads-up display was chat-
tering away that—

Wait. There he was. How the hell had he managed
that? He stared at the heads-up display, glancing rapidly
between the symbol displayed there and the actual airframe hurtling toward him at over Mach 1 in the sky.
Before he could decide what had caused the discrepancy,
the Tomcat had wheeled in and over him, the aircraft
inverted and then rolling back into level flight to place
himself squarely into the position that Tai had hoped to
occupy on him.

"No, no, no, nononono—" His wingman's voice shattered up the scales, high, frantic and frightened. The
heads-up display told him the reason—an AMRAAM
missile inbound on him as well. There was the metallic
cloud of chaff and flares, but Tai could already see it
would not work.

"Brake hard. Descend, descend," Tai shouted, frantically trying to coach his wingman back into basic sound
defensive flying while simultaneously trying to figure out
how to avoid the Tomcat now on his own ass.

Another AMRAAM? No, there would be no need at

this angle. Better choose the Sidewinder, the potent small missile designed for short-range night fighting. The Sidewinder was infrared guided, and would seek out the bright, hot fire of his tailpipe. No chaff, no flare would be bright enough to distract it from his aircraft exhaust once it saw it. There was only one possibility—they'd tried it so often in practice and—there was the shot. Yes. Wait for it one second, then—

Tai pivoted the aircraft virtually in midair, overriding the automatic trim and anti-stall avionics to throw the MiG into a hard, flat spin. It was one of the most deadly emergencies any pilot could face, particularly in an aircraft such as the MiG. They had spent countless hours in the ready room discussing how to recover from one, had drilled repeatedly in the simulator, and even the most skilled of them had managed to achieve only a fifty percent recovery rate from a flat spin at this speed.

Still, fifty percent was better than the certainty of perishing in a hard white blast of noise and fire. If he could just pull it out, at precisely the right moment, he'd have a chance.

The sky spun dizzily around him, and Tai fought to keep his consciousness from fading away. It was important that he try to maintain some sense of where he was in the air, his orientation to the sun, whether the Tomcat had fired another missile.

Just as he felt his consciousness starting to gray out, he instinctively recognized the correct configuration of sun, Tomcat and MiG.

He snapped down hard, throwing the MiG into a steep descent. An almost deadly maneuver, one that usually resulted in an out-of-control tumble through the sky, ending in an uncontrolled impact with the ground. But it was his only chance.

Would the Tomcat follow him down? No, probably

not. He would go help his wingman take on the remaining MiG, certain that no pilot could recover from the deadly tumble through the air.

But Tai could. He'd thought through the problem too many times, and now he felt instinctively that the right moves were his to make. The shudder slipped through the steel frame of his aircraft and passed without attenuation into his bones. He was no longer a separate entity, he was part of the aircraft, an integral whole with the fuselage and wings now in such odd orientation to the ground and sky. He steepened the descent, and felt the spinning motion of the aircraft lessen as the MiG fought for what it was designed to do, maintain an aerodynamic profile with the wind. A little more, a little more . . . he patted gently on the control surfaces, again overriding the automatic trim controls. The spin started to slow.

Finally, when he felt the nose in the proper orientation with the rest of his direction of movement, he stomped hard on the rudder, brutally countering the remaining spin with his control surfaces. For a moment he felt the MiG shudder, scream protests as G-forces wrenched structural members past any tolerance they were designed to accommodate. Then, as he knew it would, the MiG straightened out.

Altitude. He felt a cold punch in his stomach as he realized how far he'd tumbled trying to regain control of his aircraft. Seven thousand feet, no more. Barely enough time to pull it out.

He jerked back hard, demanding, asking with every atom of his being that the MiG honor this one last request. *Pull up, pull up, and we will kill the ones who did this,* he prayed silently. *Pull up, just pull up.*

The water rushed up at him at a dizzying rate of speed.

Tomcat 204
1709 local (GMT-10)

"Got him," Bird Dog howled over tactical. "You see that, Kelly? Now that's the way it's done." He heard Gator sigh in the backseat, and ignored him.

"I saw. Just one question, Bird Dog," Kelly's voice was cool. "What are you going to do about his playmate that's trying to climb up your ass?"

MiG 6
1710 local (GMT-10)

Chan watched Tai spiral down toward the ocean, and swore quietly. They were short enough on airframes as it was, and there were no replacements within three thousand miles. All the more necessary that he eliminate the Tomcat that had gotten his wingman.

He saw the Tomcat now, just ahead. It was doing wingovers, dancing around its wingman like a bumblebee. How foolish, to lose one's grasp of the tactical scenario over just one kill. It would be the last mistake that this particular American pilot would make.

Chan bore in on the American, fixated on his target. A warning beep on his ESM gear was his first hint that all was not well. He broke off, pivoted off of his former course, and searched for the threat.

Without warning, a Hornet descended on him like a hawk swooping down on its prey. It had been hiding high overhead in a cloud bank, watching the action below, waiting for just such a moment. Was it possible that the Tomcats had intentionally feigned inattention in order to entice him into just this sort of position? No, surely not—

the Americans were not that subtle, and they were known to have an almost fanatical fear of taking casualties. While Chan would have risked Tai in just such a manner, he knew that the Americans would not.

Chan slipped off some altitude, turning hard to his right at the same moment. He felt a deep sense of satisfaction at his final position. He was between the sun and the Hornet, thus complicating the task of using a heat seeker against him. Additionally, he had slipped behind the foolish Tomcat, and was in decent if not superb firing position. He also had the Tomcats between his MiG and the Hornet, and there was no way that the Hornet would be foolish enough to shoot through his shipmates just to kill one MiG.

The missile, when it came, was all the more surprise. He heard the warning tone and had just one second to look around before he saw it, arrowing off the wing of another Hornet also coming down from the clouds. He knew it was a killing shot the moment he saw it, and just before it nestled in to the hot target source of his engine exhaust, Chan jerked down on the ejection seat handle.

MiG 8
1712 local (GMT-10)

Tai was tumbling toward the ocean. Finally, at the last moment, he felt the wings bite into the air, and control returned to him as the heavy vibration shuddered out. The air was flowing smoothly over his laminar surfaces again, keeping the MiG airborne.

How far had he been? He dared not glance at the altitude indicator during the mad plummet from air to sea, knowing that if he watched the numbers unroll as he fought for control of the aircraft that he would never, ever believe he could accomplish it. Yet accomplish it he had. Now, as the aircraft eased into level flight, he glanced at the altitude indicator. Four hundred feet above the hungry surface of the ocean. Merely microseconds at the speed at which he'd been traveling. Adrenaline pounded through every inch of his body as he realized just how close he had come to dying.

No pilot that he knew of could have recovered from the deadly flat spin and tumble. He had no equal, not in this chunk of airspace. And now he would prove to the Tomcat just how right that was.

Hornet 106
1713 local (GMT–10)

Thor spared a few moments to watch that crazy Chinese bastard lose control of his aircraft before he returned his attention back to the other MiG. They'd finish this one off, no big deal now. Two Hornets versus one MiG wasn't even a fair fight.

But nobody ever said aerial combat was supposed to be a fair fight. That wasn't the point—the point was to get there, take care of business, and get home in one piece, hopefully with everybody in the squadron making it back, too.

As he turned his attention back to Hellman and the other MiG, he let out a short, heartfelt, "Shit." While Hellman hadn't been taken in by the MiG's initial maneuver to swoop in from above and take position astern, he had made the fatal mistake of trying to turn inside the MiG's turning radius. It hadn't worked—the two were too evenly matched to do that while fighting on the vertical. The best thing to do was disengage from a yo-yo, pull out and away, and circle back in to get in position.

But how had the MiG bastard beat him back into a tail chase? It didn't matter—it would be thoroughly covered in the squadron debrief, and Hellman would get a chance to make his explanations in before an entire crowd of experienced aviators. Thor was tired of being the one carping on him about his dangerous tactics. Maybe hearing it from the squadron's skipper would beat some sense into the young jarhead's brain. But for now, it was time to bail his wingman out before he took it up the ass.

Hellman and his MiG were caught in a flat loop, chasing each other around in ever tightening spirals. Hellman kept trying to cut inside the radius of the circle to take up position on the MiG, spurting afterburner fire as he recklessly waded through his onboard fuel allowance. Thor swore quietly. Even if he did manage to pull the asshole out of this one, he had less than a fifty-fifty chance of making it back to the tanker in time at the rate he was spending fuel.

They were still five thousand feet above him, so Thor came in on a long, flat turn, gradually ascending, timing his intersection with their loop so that he would fall neatly into position behind the MiG. He almost made it without the MiG noticing, but at the last second, Hellman pulled up hard and tried to barrel roll over and around into position. That's when Hellman evidently noticed his returning wingman for the first time.

"Shit!" Thor pulled the Hornet into a hard right turn, standing the aircraft on its wing and then rolling inverted. He lost sight of Hellman behind the breadth of his canopy, and felt cold, clear dread run through his veins. Bitch of a thing, to put away a MiG and then get nailed by your own wingman. "Where the hell is that little bastard?"

A second later, Hellman screamed past him, still gouting afterburner, his canopy just feet below Thor's own. Thor screamed obscenities at him as he went by, not daring to take his hands off the controls long enough to render a salute with his middle finger. And where the hell was the MiG? There—coming in from on high, Thor desperately out of position, Hellman now having completely lost the tactical picture, while Thor's own, more experienced mind immediately worked out the geometries. He yanked hard, pulling the Hornet into a screaming loop, narrowly missing a mid-air collision with the MiG as he did. Just as he went by, Thor toggled the weapons selector to gun and mailed off a short blast. He saw the tip of the MiG's wing dissolve in a spray of shrapnel. One hit his canopy with a hard, ringing blow, and Thor started swearing again, alternately swearing and praying that it hadn't hit a hydraulics line. Or a control surface line.

He rolled upright as he reached the top of his barrel roll and saw that the MiG had Hellman on the run. Too close for an AMRAAM, and too dangerous an angle on his own wingman to take a chance with a Sidewinder. No, this would have to be up close and personal.

"Hellman—break right, break right. Now!" Thor shouted. Immediately, Hellman's aircraft went into a hard dive toward the surface of the ocean. For the first time since they'd been airborne, Thor shoved his Hornet into afterburner and felt the hard kick of acceleration mold his spine and back into the familiar curves of the Hornet's ejection seat. The force snapped his chin up, and he felt the skin pull back from the corners of his eyes and his mouth. He grunted, panting heavily to keep the oxygen flowing to his brain as he dove down on the offending MiG.

"Circle around and come up behind me," Thor ordered, now gaining on the MiG

"Get behind me, get behind me." He wondered if the hotheaded young Marine would obey. It was just the sort of thing Hellman would hate, being aced out of his own kill.

But there was no room in the air for pride, not of that kind. When you were out of position to make the kill and your wingman had it, you let him take the shot. You spend precious seconds arguing about who gets to nail the bastard, and odds are one of you will make a mistake.

Thor yelped in glee as Hellman's aircraft cleared his Sidewinder field of fire, and he toggled off the missile with a harsh, jubilant cry. He watched it go, angling off his wing and reaching hungrily for the burning exhaust streaming out of the MiG's tailpipe.

The MiG realized its danger too late. Chaff and flares exploded out from it, and Thor heard the warble of his ESM gear that indicated the MiG 33 was equipped with some pretty sophisticated electronic countermeasures as well. But the Sidewinder was a relatively simple missile, designed for only one thing, to seek out the hottest source anywhere around, and bury itself in it.

As he watched, the long, slender missile seemed to slide up the tailpipe itself, with the smooth grace of chambering a round in any weapon. Then, with its short, stubby tail fins still visible, it detonated.

Thor broke high, determined to avoid another shower of shrapnel. Already he could tell that the previous blast had nicked something, maybe just a control surface. The Hornet felt slightly sluggish under his hands, as though she wanted to obey his every order but was simply too tired.

Off to his left, now, an expanding fireball of red and orange filled the sky. It was fiery incandescent in the center, darkening to yellow then red, and finally fringed in black, rolling smoke. He heard the tinkling ping-ping of shrapnel pelting his fuselage, and prayed that none of it would reach the remaining missiles hung under his wings.

"What the hell did you do that for?" Hellman's voice asked angrily. "I would have had him."

"Save it for when we get back to the boat," Thor said curtly. "What's your state?"

"Who gives a shit? I—shit." The bravado seeped out of Hellman's voice as he realized just how low on fuel he was. "Oh, man, I'm really in the shitter, here."

"*Jeff*, this is Hornet 106. We're in bad need of a tanker, like within the next five seconds," Thor announced over tactical. He hated emphasizing the blunder his wingman had made in public—the place to air dirty laundry was in the confines of the ready room—but he had to make sure that the Hornets were given priority for tanking.

"Hornet One-zero-six, One-zero-six, come right, course two-three-zero at seven miles. Texaco standing by."

"Wingman goes first, *Jeff*," Thor said quietly. He switched over to the private frequency he shared with Hellman. "You got that?" He could see by his heads-up display that Hellman was already making the course change and heading for the tanker. "You've got one plug at this, Hellman."

"I've never missed a plug yet," Hellman shot back.

"Not until you had to plug that MiG," Thor observed. "It's time to lose the attitude, buddy. You splash that aircraft with a MiG, you've got a chance of surviving as an aviator. But you splash one because you ran out of fuel, you'd better believe your flying days are over. Lose the attitude and take the plug, you got that?" Thor's voice bore not one ounce of mercy. Not now.

"Yes, sir," came back the short reply.

Thor circled overhead as he watched Hellman slide the Hornet in for a plug on the first tank, and watched as he hungrily sucked down five thousand pounds of JP8 from the KS-3 tanker.

And now for his own trip to the Texaco—106 was lower on av gas than he needed to be to take a pass at the boat.

Pacific Ocean
1900 local (GMT-10)

Chan stared up at the sky as the most brilliant stars made their first tentative appearances of the evening. It would be, he thought, perhaps the last night sky he would ever see, and he felt a slight surge of gratitude that at least the skies were clear.

He didn't need radio contact with his carrier to know just how badly the entire mission had turned out. The oily black plumes of smoke towering the sky, still dark smudges against the sunset, told him everything he needed to know. If there were to be a rescue, it would come from the American forces. Chan knew only how he would have treated a downed American pilot had their situations been reversed, and he was not certain that he even wanted rescue. Not at that price.

A split second later, he was quite certain that he would undergo any sort of insidious torture or mistreatment that the Americans might have in mind. Then it happened again—something hard and rough brushed against his leg, something with massive inertia that almost popped him out of the water in reaction.

A third pass, this one more insistent, and Chan started

screaming to every god he had ever known for deliverance, for mercy, for a fate other than the one that was approaching too quickly.

The shark's fourth pass was far less tentative than the previous three, and lasted quite a bit longer.

TWENTY-THREE

The **Lucky Star**
Six days later
1600 local (GMT-10)

The *Lucky Star*, with the Coast Guard officer command-ing, chugged out to a spot directly over the USS *Arizona*. Tombstone's pickup team, along with Tomboy and Bat-man and the Simpsons, were in a loose formation on the stern. No one had ordered them into ranks, but there was something about the solemnity of the moment that man-ifested itself in quiet, somber voices and stiffened back-bones.

"On station, Admiral," Captain Henry said finally. "Standing by for your orders."

"Maintain bare steerageway to keep us in this area," Tombstone said. "I don't want to anchor. This poor old girl has suffered enough insults to her final resting place, I think."

"Maintain station with bare steerageway, aye, sir," the Coast Guard Officer repeated. In the quiet on the aft deck, the visitors could hear the command repeated first by the officer of the deck and then by both the helmsman and the lee helm.

The *Lucky Star*'s engines throttled down to a dull rumble. They were running so smoothly now that they could barely feel the vibrations on the deck, a marked contrast to the rough sound that she'd made but a week earlier.

Amazing what the Coast Guard can do, Tombstone thought. *I wonder where they pinched the funds from to refurbish this old girl.* But on reflection, he decided that it wasn't so much a matter of throwing money at the vessel's engine spaces. No, he suspected that there hadn't been a Coast Guard sailor within a thousand miles who hadn't begged, insisted, or downright whined to be allowed the honor of working on this boat. Spare parts would have materialized, some, he hoped, contributed by grateful Navy shipmates. There would have been no shortage of manpower, and for a brief moment he smiled at the mental picture of thousands of Coast Guard and Navy snipes thronging the pier, begging to be allowed to help to restore the ship to proper working order.

And *Lucky Star* deserved it. While nothing was certain yet, he'd heard from his uncle that the senators and congressmen from Hawaii had been lobbying to be allowed to designate *Lucky Star* as a permanent honor escort for the USS *Arizona*.

Did ships have souls? Perhaps his surface brethren would be better equipped to say, but Tombstone thought that they might. Oh, perhaps not the incandescent life that a Tomcat had, that quick, sweet responsiveness to your every thought. No, if he had to picture it, a ship would have an older soul, a more gallant one—and perhaps, one that knew better the meaning of "Never say die."

There was a stir of motion on the deck, and an honor guard made its stately way forward, the colors guarded and flying proudly in the wind, one man carrying a simple wreath. The crowd parted before them, allowing them access to the rear railing of the ship. Tombstone caught a whiff of fresh paint smell in the air, and knew that more than the boat's engines had been refurbished.

A single trumpeter stepped forward. He wet his lips, and then the hauntingly mournful tones of Taps floated out over the air. The notes slid gently through the thick sea air, glistened under the hot sun and seemed to sink into the ocean of their own accord. Tombstone hoped that somehow, somewhere, the sailors that had gone down to the sea for the last time onboard the *Arizona* heard them and knew that their shipmates still kept the faith today.

A chaplain stepped forward, and said a brief prayer, accompanied by a trumpet playing the Navy Hymn. How many times had Tombstone heard the words to the hymn, under how many different circumstances? They resonated deep in the soul of every sailor, yet never had they meant more to him than they did at this moment, standing on the deck of this gallant little vessel, surrounded by men and women who'd risen to the occasion just as *Lucky Star* had.

Tombstone barely heard the chaplain's words as he stared down at the clear water, at the final resting place for so many brave men. They'd done their duty back then, and had once again reached out from beyond the grave to answer the call to duty. Somehow he knew that they would have been proud that their ship, the USS *Arizona*, had fought one final fight for her country.

Glossary

0-3 level: The third deck above the main deck. Designations for decks above the main deck (also known as the damage control deck) begin with zero, e.g. 0-3. The zero is pronounced as "oh" in conversation. Decks below the main deck do not have the initial zero, and are numbered down from the main deck, e.g. deck 11 is below deck 3. Deck 0-7 is above deck 0-3.

1MC: The general announcing system on a ship or submarine. Every ship has many different interior communications systems, most of them linking parts of the ship for a specific purpose. Most operate off sound-powered phones. The circuit designators consist of a number followed by two letters that indicate the specific purpose of the circuit. 2AS, for instance, might be an antisubmarine warfare circuit that connects the sonar supervisor, the USW watch officer, and the sailor at the torpedo launched.

C-2 Greyhound: Also known as the COD, Carrier Onboard Delivery. The COD carries cargo and passengers from shore to ship. It is capable of carrier landings. Sometimes assigned directly to the air wing, it also operates in coordination with CVBGs from a sore squadron.

Air Boss: A senior commander or captain assigned to

the aircraft carrier, in charge of flight operations. The "Boss" is assisted by the Mini-Boss in Pri-Fly, located in the tower onboard the carrier. The Air Boss is always in the tower during flight operations, overseeing the launch and recovery cycles, declaring a green deck, and monitoring the safe approach of aircraft to the carrier.

airdale: Slang for an officer or enlisted person in the aviation fields. Includes pilots, NFOs, aviation intelligence officers and maintenance officer and the enlisted technicians who support aviation. The antithesis of an airdale is a "shoe."

Air Wing: Composed of the aircraft squadrons assigned to the battle group. The individual squadron commanding officers report to the air wing commander, who reports to the admiral.

Akula: Late model Russian-built attack nuclear submarine, an SSN. Fast, deadly, and deep diving.

ALR-67: Detects, analyzes and evaluates electromagnetic signals, emits a warning signal if the parameters are compatible with an immediate threat to the aircraft, e.g. seeker head on an anti-air missile. Can also detect an enemy radar in either a search or a targeting mode.

altitude: Is safety. With enough airspace under the wings, a pilot can solve any problem.

AMRAAM: Advanced Medium Range Anti-Air Missile.

angels: Thousands of feet over ground. Angels twenty is 20,000 feet. Cherubs indicates hundreds of feet, e.g. cherubs five = five hundred feet.

ASW: Antisubmarine Warfare, recently renamed Undersea Warfare. For some reason.

avionics: Black boxes and systems that comprise an aircraft's combat systems.

AW: Aviation antisubmarine warfare technician, the enlisted specialist flying in an S-3, P-3 or helo USW aircraft. As this book goes to press, there is discussion of renaming the specialty.

AWACS: An aircraft entirely too good for the Air Force, the Advanced Warning Aviation Control System. Long range command and control and electronic intercept bird with superb capabilities.

AWG-9: Pronounced "awg nine," the primary search and fire control radar on a Tomcat.

backseater: Also known as the GIB, the guy in back. Nonpilot aviator available in several flavors: BN (bombardier/navigator), RIO (radar intercept operator), and TACCO (Tactical Control Officer) among others. Usually wear glasses and are smart.

Bear: Russian maritime patrol aircraft, the equivalent in rough terms of a U.S. P-3. Variants have primary missions in command and control, submarine hunting, and electronic intercepts. Big, slow, good targets.

bitch box: One interior communications system on a ship. So named because it's normally used to bitch at another watch station.

blue on blue: Fratricide. U.S. forces are normally indicated in blue on tactical displays, and this term refers to an attack on a friendly by another friendly.

blue water Navy: Outside the unrefueled range of the airwing. When a carrier enters blue water ops, aircraft must get on board, e.g. land, and cannot divert to land if the pilot gets the shakes.

boomer: Slang for a ballistic missile submarine.

BOQ: Bachelor Officer Quarters—a Motel Six for single officers or those traveling without family. The Air Force also has VOQ, Visiting Officer Quarters.

buster: As fast as you can, i.e. bust yer ass getting here.

CAG: Carrier Air Group Commander, normally a senior Navy Captain aviator. Technically, an obsolete term, since the air wing rather than an air group is now deployed on the carrier. However, everyone thought CAW sounded stupid, so CAG was retained as slang for the carrier air wing commander.

CAP: Combat Air Patrol, a mission executed by fighters to protect the carrier and battle group from enemy air and missiles.

Carrier Battle Group: A combination of ships, airwing, and submarines assigned under the command of a one-star admiral.

Carrier Battle Group 14: The battle group normally embarked on *Jefferson*.

CBG: *See* Carrier Battle Group.

CDC: Combat Direction Center—modernly, replaced CIC, or Combat Information Center, as the heart of a ship. All sensor information is fed into CDC and the battle is coordinated by a Tactical Action Officer on watch there.

CG: Abbreviation for a cruiser.

Chief: The backbone of the Navy. E-7, 8, and 9 enlisted paygrades, known as chief, senior chief, and master chief. The transition from petty officer ranks to the Chief's mess is a major event in a sailor's career. Onboard ship, the chiefs have separate eating and berthing facilities. Chiefs wear khakis, as opposed to dungarees for the less senior enlisted ratings.

Chief of Staff: Not to be confused with a chief, the COS in a battle group staff is normally a senior Navy captain who acts as the admiral's XO and deputy.

CIA: Christians in Action. The civilian agency charged with intelligence operations outside the continental United States.

CIWS: Close In Weapons System, pronounced "see-whiz." Gattling gun with built-in radar that tracks and

fires on inbound missiles. If you have to use it, you're
dead.

COD. *See* C-2 Greyhound.

collar count: Traditional method of determining the
winner of a disagreement. A survey is taken of the op-
ponents' collar devices. The senior person wins. Always.

Commodore: Formerly the junior-most admiral rank,
now used to designate a senior Navy captain in charge
of a bunch of like units. A destroyer commodore commands several destroyers, a sea control commodore the
S-3 squadrons on that coast. Contrast with CAG, who
owns a number of dissimilar units, e.g. a couple of Tomcat squadrons, some Hornets, and some E-2s and helos.

compartment: Navy talk for a room on a ship.

Condition Two: One step down from General Quarters, which is Condition One. Condition Five is tied up
at the pier in a friendly country.

CRAF: Civilian replacement airframe program.

crypto: Short for some variation of cryptological, the
magic set of codes that makes a circuit impossible for
anyone else to understand.

CV, CVN: Abbreviation for an aircraft carrier, conventional and nuclear.

CVIC: Carrier Intelligence Center. Located down the
passageway (the hall) from the flag spaces.

data link, the LINK: The secure circuit that links all
units in a battle group or in an area. Targets and contacts
are transmitted over the LINK to all ships. The data is
processed by the ship designated as Net Control, and
common contacts are correlated. The system also trans-
mits data from each ship and aircraft's weapons systems,
e.g. a missile firing. All services use the LINK.

DDG: Guided missile destroyer.

desk jockey: Nonflyer, one who drives a computer
instead of an aircraft.

DESRON: Destroyer Commander.

DICASS: An active sonobuoy.

dick stepping: Something to be avoided. While anatomically impossible in today's gender-integrated services, in an amazing display of good sense, it has been decided that women do this as well.

Doppler: Acoustic phenomena caused by relative motion between a sound source and a receiver that results in an apparent change in frequency of the sound. The classic example is a train going past and the decrease in pitch of its whistle. When a submarine changes its course or speed in relation to a sonobuoy, the event shows up as a change in the frequency of the sound source.

Double nuts: Zero zero on the tail of an aircraft.

E-2 Hawkeye: Command and control and surveillance aircraft. Turboprop rather than jet, and unarmed. Smaller version of an AWACS, in practical terms, but carrier-based.

ELF: Extremely Low Frequency, a method of communicating with submarines at sea. Signals are transmitted via a miles-long antenna and are the only way of reaching a deep submerged submarine.

Envelope: What you're supposed to fly inside of if you want to take all the fun out of naval aviation.

EWs: Electronic warfare technicians, the enlisted sailors that man the gear that detects, analyzes and displays electromagnetic signals. Highly classified stuff.

F/A-18 Hornets: The inadequate, fuel-hungry intended replacement for the aging but still kick-your-ass potent Tomcat. Flown by Marines and Navy.

Familygram: Short messages from submarine sailors' families to their deployed sailors. Often the only contact with the outside world that a submarine sailor on deployment has.

FF/FFG: Abbreviation for a fast frigate (no, there

aren't slow frigates) and a guided-missile fast frigate.

Flag officer: In the Navy and Coast Guard, an admiral. In the other services, a general.

Flag passageway: The portion of the aircraft carrier which houses the admiral's staff working spaces. Includes the flag mess and the admiral's cabin. Normally separated from the rest of the ship by heavy plastic curtains, and designated by blue tile on the deck instead of white.

Flight quarters: A condition set onboard a ship preparing to launch or recover aircraft. All unnecessary person are required to stay inside the skin of the ship and remain clear of the flight deck area.

Flight suit: The highest form of navy couture. The perfect choice of apparel for any occasion—indeed, the only uniform an aviator ought to be required to own.

FOD: Stands for Foreign Object Damage, but the term is used to indicate any loose gear that could cause damage to an aircraft. During flight operations, aircraft generate a tremendous amount of air flowing across the deck. Loose objects—including people and nuts and bolts— can be sucked into the intake and discharged through the outlet from the jet engine. FOD damages the jet's impellers and doesn't do much for the people sucked in, either. FOD walkdown is conducted at least once a day onboard an aircraft carrier. Everyone not otherwise engaged stands shoulder-to-shoulder on the flight deck and slowly walks from one end of the flight deck to the other, searching for FOD.

Fox: Tactical shorthand for a missile firing. Fox one indicates a heat-seeking missile, Fox two an infrared missile, and Fox three a radar guided missile.

GCI: Ground Control Intercept, a procedure used in the Soviet air forces. Primary control for vectoring the aircraft in on enemy targets and other fighters is vested in a guy on the ground, rather than in the cockpit where it belongs.

GIB: *See* backseater.

GMT: Greenwich Mean Time.

green shirts: *See* Shirts.

Handler: Officer located on the flight deck level responsible for ensuring that aircraft are correctly positioned, "spotted," on the flight deck. Coordinates the movements of aircraft with yellow gear (small tractors that tow aircraft and other related gear) from maintenance areas to catapults and from the flight deck to the hangar bar via the elevators. Speaks frequently with the Air Boss. *See also* bitch box.

HARMS: Anti-radiation missiles that home in on radar sites.

Homeplate: Tactical call sign for *Jefferson*.

Hot: In reference to a sonobuoy, holding enemy contact.

Huffer: Yellow gear located on the flight deck that generates compressed air to start jet engines. Most Navy aircraft do not need a huffer to start engines, but it can be used in emergencies or for maintenance.

Hunter: Call sign for the S-3 squadron embarked on the *Jefferson*.

ICS: Interior Communications System. The private link between a pilot and a RIO, or the telephone system internal to a ship.

Inchopped: Navy talk for a ship entering a defined area of water, e.g. inchopped the Med.

IR: Infrared, a method of missile homing.

isothermal: A layer of water that has a constant temperature with increasing depth. Located below the thermocline, where increase in depth correlates to decrease in temperature. In the isothermal layer, the primary factor affecting the speed of sound in water is the increase in pressure with depth.

JBD: Jet Blast Deflector. Panels that pop up from the flight deck to block the exhaust emitted by aircraft.

USS *Jefferson*: The star nuclear aircraft carrier in the U.S. Navy.

leading petty officer: The senior petty officer in a work center, division, or department, responsible to the leading chief petty officer for the performance of the rest of the group.

LINK: *See* data link.

lofargram: Low Frequency Analyzing and Recording display. Consists of lines arrayed by frequency on the horizontal axis and time on the vertical axis. Displays sound signals in the water in a graphic fashion for analysis by ASW technicians.

long green table: A formal inquiry board. It's better to be judged by six than carried by six.

machinists mate: Enlisted technician that runs and repairs most engineering equipment onboard a ship. Abbreviated as "MM" e.g. MM1 Sailor is a Petty Officer First Class Machinists Mate.

MDI: Mess Decks Intelligence. The heartbeat of the rumor mill onboard a ship and the definitive source for all information.

MEZ: Missile Engagement Zone. Any hostile contacts that make it into the MEZ are engaged only with missiles. Friendly aircraft must stay clear in order to avoid a blue on blue engagement, i.e. fratricide.

MiG: A production line of aircraft manufactured by Mikoyan in Russia. MiG fighters are owned by many nations around the world.

Murphy, law of: The factor most often not considered sufficiently in military planning. If something can go wrong, it will. Naval corollary: shit happens.

national assets: Surveillance and reconnaissance resources of the most sensitive nature, e.g. satellites.

NATOPS: The bible for operating a particular aircraft. *See* Envelope.

NFO: Naval Flight Officer.

nobrainer: Contrary to what copy editors believe, this is one word. Used to signify an evolution or decision that should require absolutely no significant intellectual capabilities beyond that of a paramecium.

Nomex: Fire-resistant fabric used to make "shirts." *See* Shirts.

NSA: National Security Agency. Primarily responsible for evaluating electronic intercepts and sensitive intelligence.

OOD: Officer of the Day, in charge of the safe handling and maneuvering of the ship. Supervises the conning officer and other underway watchstanders. Ashore, the OOD may be responsible for a shore station after normal working hours.

Operations specialist: Formerly radar operator, back in the old days. Enlisted technician who operates combat detection, tracking, and engagement systems, except for sonar. Abbreviated OS.

OTH: Over the horizon, usually used to refer to shooting something you can't see.

P-3's: Shore-based anti-submarine warfare and surface surveillance long-range aircraft. The closest you can get to being in the Air Force while still being in the Navy.

Phoenix: Long-range anti-air missile carried by U.S. fighters.

Pipeline: Navy term used to describe a series of training commands, schools, or necessary education for a particular specialty. The fighter pipeline, for example, includes Basic Flight then fighter training at the RAG (Replacement Air Group), a training squadron.

Punching out: Ejecting from an aircraft.

purple shirts: *See* Shirts.

PXO: Prospective Executive Officer—the officer ordered into a command as the relief for the current XO. In most squadrons, the XO eventually "fleets up" to become the commanding officer of the squadron, an excellent system that maintains continuity within an operational command—and a system the surface Navy does not use.

rack: A bed. A rack-monster is a sailor who sports pillow burns and spends entirely too much time asleep while his or her shipmates are working.

red shirts: *See* Shirts.

RHIP: Rank Hath Its Privileges. *See* collar count.

RIO: Radar Intercept Officer. *See* NFO.

RTB: Return to base.

S-3: Command and control aircraft sold to the Navy as an anti-submarine aircraft. Good at that, too. Within the last several years, redesignated as "sea control" aircraft, with individual squadrons referred to as torpedo-bombers. Ah, the search for a mission goes on. But still a damned fine aircraft.

SAM: Surface to Air missile, e.g. the Standard missile fired by most cruisers. Also indicates a land-based site.

SAR: Sea-Air Rescue.

SCIF: Specially Compartmented Information. Onboard a Carrier, used to designate the highly classified compartment immediately next to TFCC.

Seawolf: Newest version of Navy fast attack submarine.

SERE: Survival, Evasion, Rescue, Escape; required school in pipeline for aviators.

Shirts: Color-coded Nomex pullovers used by flight deck and aviation personnel for rapid identification of a sailor's job. Green: maintenance technicians. Brown:

plane captains. White: safety and medical. Red: ordnance. Purple: fuel. Yellow: flight deck supervisors and handlers.

Shoe: A black shoe, slang for a surface sailor or officer. Modernly, hard to say since the day that brown shoes were authorized for wear by black shoes. No one knows why. Wing envy is the best guess.

Sidewinder: Anti-air missile carried by U.S. fighters.

Sierra: A subsurface contact.

sonobuoys: Acoustic listening devices dropped in the water by ASW or USW aircraft.

Sparrow: Anti-air missile carried by U.S. fighters.

Spetznaz: The Russian version of SEALS, although the term encompasses a number of different specialties.

spooks: Slang for intelligence officers and enlisted sailors working in highly classified areas.

SUBLANT: Administrative command of all Atlantic submarine forces. On the West Coast, SUBPAC.

sweet: When used in reference to a sonobuoy, indicates that the buoy is functioning properly, although not necessarily holding any contacts.

TACCO: Tactical Control Officer: the NFO in an S-3.

Tactical circuit: A term used in these books that encompasses a wide range of actual circuits used onboard a carrier. There are a variety of C&R circuits (coordination and reporting) and occasionally for simplicity's sake and to avoid classified material, I just use the word tactical.

tanked, tanker: Navy aircraft have the ability to refuel from a tanker, either Air Force or Navy, while airborne. One of the most terrifying routine evolutions a pilot performs.

TFCC: Tactical Flag Command Center. A compartment in flag spaces from which the CVBG admiral controls the battle. Located immediately forward of the carrier's CDC.

Tombstone: Nickname given to Magruder.

Top Gun: Advanced fighter training command.

Undersea Warfare Commander: in a CVBG, normally the DESRON embarked on the carrier. Formerly called the ASW commander.

VDL: Video Downlink. Transmission of targeting data from an aircraft to a submarine with OTH capabilities.

VF-95: Fighter squadron assigned to Airwing 14, normally embarked on USS *Jefferson*. The first two letters of a squadron designation reflect the type of aircraft flown. VF = fighters. VFA = Hornets. VS = S-3, etc.

Victor: Aging Russian fast attack submarines, still a potent threat.

VS-29: S-3 squadron assigned to Airwing 14, embarked on USS *Jefferson*.

VX-1: Test pilot squadron that develops envelopes after Pax River evaluates aerodynamic characteristics of new aircraft. *See* Envelope.

White shirt: *See* Shirts.

Wilco: Short for Will Comply. Used only by the aviator in command of the mission.

Winchester: In aviation, it means out of weapons. A Winchester aircraft must normally RTB.

XO: Executive officer, the second in command.

yellow shirt: *See* Shirts.